EXPIRED RETURN

LAST CHANCE FIRE AND RESCUE | BOOK 1

LISA PHILLIPS

sunrise
PUBLISHING

PRAISE FOR EXPIRED RETURN

Thrilling, poignant and perfect! This first book is the perfect ignition to Phillips spin off Last Chance Country Fire and Rescue series. I loved it!

—USA TODAY RITA AWARD-WINNING
BESTSELLING AUTHOR SUSAN MAY WARREN

This book is one that I could not easily put down! Expired Return by Lisa Phillips is a fast-paced, emotion-filled, ride for any thrill seeker of the written word!

—TINA LOWERY, GOODREADS

Lisa Phillips crafted an amazing story. Filled with twists and turns, suspense, tension, and second chance romance, this novel is definitely a page turner. I'm looking forward to reading the rest of the series.

—ALLYSON ANTHONY, GOODREADS

Last Chance Fire and Rescue Book 1, Expired Return, is so good! What a great extension of Lisa Phillips' original Last Chance County series!

—HOADBEAR, GOODREADS

1

Pepper pulled into the police department parking lot. She stared at the building and tried to figure out how long since she'd been inside for a visit.

"Are we going inside there, Auntie?"

Pepper shut off the engine and turned to her niece in the back seat. "Yes, we are. They're all really nice, and I just need to talk to them for a second before we go to the vet's."

Her smile cracked, but she'd been pretending everything was fine since Christmas, so that was nothing new.

Eight-year-old Victory, her niece, jabbed the button to release her seatbelt. "Cool."

Pepper climbed out of the car, chuckling. Victory took her hand as they crossed the parking lot—something they'd been doing since the kid learned to walk.

She'd been putting this off for a week. She had to rip off the bandage, ignore how they would react to her, and ask for help.

Pepper shoved open the front door on that note and immediately pulled up short. The woman behind the reception desk had a white pixie cut, better makeup than Pepper could pull off, and earrings that swung when she turned her head.

Ruby's red lips widened, and the smile lit her eyes. "Hey, gorgeous."

"Hey, Ruby." Pepper blinked. "Where's Kaylee?"

"Girl, she hasn't worked here in months. After the third baby, I don't blame her." Ruby tipped her head back and chuckled. "Kaylee and Stuart bought a cute house in the hills. Enough rooms to fill with a whole football team of kids." She smiled wider, still amused. "I get to squish them all every Sunday in the nursery."

Meanwhile, Pepper's chest felt like she'd been hit with a shot of something that burned all the way to her heart.

Victory shifted and looked up at her.

Pepper's cheeks flamed as she realized she'd been holding on to Victory's hand too tight. "I'm sorry, Ruby. That was rude of me, just because I expected Kaylee."

She loosened her grip on her niece's hand, ignoring why she needed that solidarity. Victory shouldn't have to carry the weight of Pepper's insecurities on top of everything else going on in her life.

She lifted her chin. "I need to file a report, please."

Ruby frowned. "Sure thing, doll."

A uniformed officer in the sea of desks behind the counter got up and headed for their break room.

Ruby pretended that was normal. She pasted on a smile. "I'll find someone you can..."

Aiden Donaldson, now the sergeant, walked out the back hall and saw Pepper. He stopped to frown at her. Not exactly openly hostile, but the woman who'd broken his friend's heart wasn't welcome here.

Ruby waved him over. "Can you take a statement from Ms. Miller, hon—uh, Sarge? She wants to file a report." Before he could say yes or no, Ruby hopped off her stool and motioned to Victory. "This lovely young lady and I will get to know each other."

Victory openly smiled, which didn't happen often. Not exactly surprising, given the people who'd been in and out of her life. The kid had more street smarts at eight years old than Pepper had managed in thirty-eight years.

"Why don't you come around, *Ms. Miller*?" Aiden waved her to the half door.

Pepper and Ruby exchanged spots, during which Pepper didn't meet the other woman's gaze. Why did this feel like *she* was the one who'd done something wrong? Oh, right. In their eyes, she had. She'd broken their brother's heart right before his tragic accident.

Pepper glanced back at Victory.

"She'll be fine. Ruby is great with kids."

That's not just any kid. Maybe everyone who cared for a child thought that about theirs, but it was true with Victory. "I know she is."

"Then have a little trust in us."

Eighteen months, and the police in Last Chance County still hated her.

"Come on. Let's get this done." Donaldson motioned her to a seat, unaware of his brash tone.

She settled into the hard plastic chair on the short side of the desk. The edge had a metal ring fixed to it for securing handcuffs. Great. She'd been given the criminal's chair.

Go figure. How about they *have a little trust?*

Donaldson lifted his brows.

Pepper said, "Aren't you going to ask me a question?"

Thankfully, no one else was around to see this. It was seven thirty in the morning, which was why she'd chosen this time. The police department wasn't exactly on her way to work.

"I figured you knew how this worked." Donaldson slid over a legal pad. "But okay, what did you want to report?"

Pepper held herself very still. "I came here because I need help, not to be browbeaten."

"I apologize." He didn't look apologetic. He looked like he wanted to get this over with as soon as he could.

That was what her actions had accomplished.

She'd turned a perfectly nice family man and good cop into a guy with an attitude who wanted her out of here as fast as possible.

Pepper stared at the desk across from her. "My sister asked me to watch Victory for the holidays. She was supposed to be here four days ago to pick her up, but she never showed. She's not returning my calls. That was the first couple of days, and now it's just going to voicemail. Like her phone ran out of battery or something, and I just—"

"Let me stop you there."

She bit her lip.

"Pepper."

"What?"

His face had blanked. "Can you tell me your sister's legal name?"

Of course he needed that. "Sage Katherine Burns."

Aiden scrawled the name on a notepad. "Is she married...or are you?"

Pepper spoke carefully. "Miller is our family name." In the sense she'd changed it legally to match the foster mom they'd lived with for years. "Sage got married ten years ago but they're divorced now."

He asked her for a few other pertinent details, like Sage's address and date of birth. Her phone number.

"She was supposed to be here."

A muscle in his jaw flexed. "Sorry, I can imagine it's an inconvenience having to care for a child."

That wasn't fair. Wasn't the reason at all, but she reined in her reaction. She knew well the story of his child and the reunion that'd happened between Aiden and Bridget. They had two more children now.

It seemed like everyone in Last Chance County had children. There were kids all over town these days.

All the places she liked to go for peace and quiet were overrun with munchkins that Victory loved to make friends with while everyone ignored Pepper and treated her like the pariah she was.

"I can call social services if you don't feel you can—"

Pepper stood up. "How dare you." She could spit fire at him right now. She'd loved and supported Victory since the day she was born. "You know *nothing* about me."

"What's this?"

Pepper whirled around at that voice. *Heart. Breaking.* She loved that gruff, commanding voice more than anything else in the world.

He wore a look a lot like Aiden's. Blank, which she knew—or hoped—had to do with protecting his heart because he still cared for her. Except he probably hated her.

Donaldson sat back in his chair. "Allen."

Former police officer Allen Frees had both hands on the wheels of his chair. He wore a fire department uniform of slacks and a white shirt. Emblems. A badge. His life of service hadn't ended when he landed in that chair after a building blew up over his head.

As far as she'd been able to tell, it barely slowed him down.

He looked at Aiden, dismissing her completely. "What is this?"

"She's filing a report about her missing sister."

"She's done." Pepper turned to the sergeant. "Thanks anyway."

She would have to find her sister on her own, even if the police department in the town where Sage lived hadn't returned any of her calls.

She sucked in a breath and squared her shoulders. "Have a nice day, gentlemen."

Pepper went the opposite way around the neighboring desk. She got almost to the dividing half door when Allen rolled in front of her.

"Hold up a second." His dark brows drew together.

She couldn't look at his shoulders or his arms. They were even stronger than they'd been when they dated.

The two-year anniversary of their first date was coming up in just a few days. Victory was supposed to be gone, and Pepper had gotten the night off work. She'd planned to watch a tragic movie and eat far too much ice cream so she could go to bed and cry herself to sleep.

So what? Her choices were between her and the Lord. They certainly weren't anyone else's business. But she did *not* need Victory to be a witness to her tragedy.

Allen's voice rumbled over her. "Since when do you have a sister?"

Pepper couldn't get into the fact they'd dated for nearly a year and he had no idea about her family. She had to get to work.

"Sage is ten months younger than me. Everyone thought we were twins, even though I was in the grade ahead of her at school. She's missing, and I was hoping the sergeant—or anyone here—could help me figure out how to find her."

He shifted in the chair. He could stand for a few seconds if needed, and she was thankful for that.

She'd seen him getting in and out of his truck in town, sometimes standing to do it and sometimes hauling himself up and lifting the chair across his lap to put it on the seat behind him. She'd *never* stopped what she was doing and watched him move.

Nor had she been hiking and seen him riding his horse in the mountains and paused to watch him pass by. Definitely *not* stalking him like a crazy woman who couldn't let go.

Allen was six feet—four inches taller than her. He was as

imposing in his chair as he was at full height. The accident had done nothing to diminish the pull she felt toward him.

He started to speak, but a running Tasmanian devil hit the reception counter. "Auntie, can I have a *sucker*? They have the *blue ones*."

"Wow." Pepper grinned at Victory. "The blue ones."

Thank goodness she'd managed to talk Victory into a breakfast not involving sugar.

"Sure, Nugget. We need to leave, though." Pepper looked at her watch. She wasn't late, but they did need to leave for her shift at the veterinarian's office where she worked as a nurse. So that wasn't a lie.

Sergeant Donaldson came over, probably thinking he needed to rescue his friend from her. "Coffee, Allen?"

He nodded but didn't look at his friend. He kept staring at her instead. "Thanks. Got some business for the PD."

Aiden headed for the break room.

Allen said, "I'm sure these guys can help you find your sister."

Tears burned her eyes. Pepper didn't even know which thing she was going to cry over. Maybe all of it. Her whole life. She sniffed. "Thank you. I do need to go now."

"Is your sister similar to you in height and weight? Does she live here?"

Pepper frowned. "She lives in Cheyenne."

"Never mind, then." Allen slid his phone from a little pocket on the side of the chair by his leg. "Though, you could tell me what kind of car she might be driving. Color, or make and model. That kind of thing."

Pepper held her body tight so he didn't see her flinch. "Did something happen?"

"I don't know yet. That's why I'm here."

"My sister drives a brand new white BMW. An SUV."

His expression gave nothing away. Something he did when

he didn't like a situation. "Any chance she could be driving something else?"

Pepper had to admit it. "I have no idea."

Two police officers strolled out of the back hallway into the bullpen, as they called it. Both saw her. Both looked at her with distaste.

One called out, "You good, Frees?"

He glanced at them, then at her. "I've got it covered."

"I have to go." Pepper resituated her purse on her shoulder. "Can you please text me if there's anything I need to know?"

Assuming he hadn't "lost" her number.

He gave her one sharp nod. "I can do that."

She wanted to say more, but what good would that do? Pepper strode to the front door. "Let's hit the road, Nugget."

Victory jumped up from the chair. She held out her hand to Ruby. "It was nice to meet you."

The older woman smiled widely. "You as well, babycakes."

Victory giggled, took Pepper's hand, and they went outside. Pepper shivered with the chill of January air, and her niece looked over. "You should've worn your coat, Auntie."

"I guess so." She needed a change of subject. "Do you think it might snow again?"

"Oooh, I hope so." Victory hopped to the car and pulled the door open. "Let's go see the bunnies. And the puppies. And the snake, even though it's gross. And I hope that old cat is still there."

Pepper climbed into her car. This was the life her choices had given her, the only thing she'd been able to do after her family made their own decisions. If there was a problem, she would solve it.

She would find her sister.

With Victory here, this life certainly wasn't a bad one. Maybe everyone thought their own life was a disaster.

At least she wasn't alone.

2

"Anyway, I might have something for you to look into. So give me a call back." Allen tapped the dash screen and ended the call to Tate, where he'd left the local private investigator a message. Maybe his friend could help Pepper. It certainly wasn't in Allen's purview as the City Hall liaison to the fire department.

He shoved the truck into park and let out a long sigh.

I have to go. And wasn't that the truth? The woman did nothing but try to get away from him.

Instead of letting that go around and around in his mind, Allen shoved the door open. He moved his seat back and dragged the folded wheelchair across his body. He set it down on the ground beside his vehicle.

In the process, he got the thing mostly unfolded. Enough he could sit in it.

Allen shifted his body to the edge of the seat and clasped the tether that hung from the grab handle. He braced his foot and lowered himself hand over hand using the rope knots, so he didn't fall too fast.

He'd learned that one the hard way.

He grabbed the last knot and lowered his butt into the chair. Shifted his foot. The other foot. Shut the door. Clicked his keys.

Done.

He thanked God every chance he got that he'd managed to figure this process out—with some modifications to his truck so it was drivable for him. People had tried to tell him the process was too convoluted or that someone with a disability like his couldn't drive anything but a van—as if—or a tiny car. Barf. Well, they could quite frankly pry this truck from his cold dead hands. Or bury him in it.

His grandpa had driven a pickup all the years he'd helped raise Allen. He'd had a heart attack in the middle of his corn-field the summer before Allen turned twelve. That same pickup was parked in front of his cabin to this day, the bed filled with dirt where his stepmom had planted flowers years ago.

The same cabin he'd been advised to move out of after he found himself confined to a wheelchair 99.7 percent of the time—which he'd worked down to sixty-five, thanks. Just like he'd been told he'd have to give up his truck.

Show me a roadblock. I'll bring a bulldozer and go through it.

He locked up his truck and headed into City Hall, only slightly late for his meeting with the mayor. Thankfully, the security guard on duty knew him and got Allen through the check-in process quickly.

His dad's words still rang in his head, followed by Grandpa's favorite verse.

The one he'd printed out and stuck on his fridge at home came to mind. *All things are lawful, but not all are expedient.*

Since he got out of the hospital, he'd been working on widening the boundaries of what was practical every day. *He* determined what he was capable of—not other people.

His teachers had learned the hard way not to tell him what he couldn't do. Then his drill sergeant. Then Conroy, his former boss—the police chief. Now his physical therapist at the Ridgeman Therapy Center's PT annex was working on getting a clue.

So he couldn't go for a run. So what? He'd never liked foot chases, even when they ended with the suspect in handcuffs.

The mayor's assistant opened the door for him, announcing his arrival. "Coffee?"

Allen smiled, even though one of the firefighters he worked with told him it made him look like a serial killer. "Black, please."

"Of course, Mr. Frees." She gave him a nervous smiled and turned to the mayor. "Sir?"

The new Last Chance County mayor turned from the window. Gregory Harrelson wore a suit and silk tie. Dark hair and a mustache. He looked like that actor whose name Allen could never remember. "Green tea, please, Lyla."

Since their meeting was a standing one every Monday morning, one of the chairs in front of the mayor's desk had been removed. Allen eased into the space and pushed the lever down on his wheels.

Thankfully he'd had enough time before this meeting to touch base with Sergeant Donaldson. Even though Mia Barnes—the chief's wife and a former ATF agent turned cop—was technically still the liaison between City Hall and the Police Department, he liked to keep his old friendships going. Plus he was a firm believer in over-communicating.

Allen twisted his upper body and reached into the backpack hanging behind him for his tablet. He had a copy of the statement Pepper had given to Aiden in his email, even though the sergeant had initially been reluctant to give it to him.

Don't think about her.

Harrelson turned from the window. "Let's get started, shall we?"

Allen tapped the screen of his tablet. "Just after midnight

last night, the department responded to a car fire. It was all pretty standard, except for the victim inside."

The mayor perked up. "Oh?"

Allen had learned the hard way the guy possessed no stomach for gory details. The victim had two gunshot wounds in her chest, sustained before the car was set alight. She'd been burned beyond recognition.

He hadn't even been there, but by the time he got to the firehouse he could tell how bad it was from the weary looks on the firefighter's faces—and the smoke smell they all carried in with them.

Allen said, "The police department's homicide detective was looped in. They're going to work with the medical examiner to identify her."

The vehicle had been a green car and not the white SUV Pepper said her sister drove. It was unlikely, though not impossible, that her sister was the victim. He intended to follow up with her, though.

"And the preparations for the Winter Carnival?" Gregory accepted his tea from Lyla, who put Allen's coffee on the edge of the desk in front of him.

Allen lifted his chin. "Thank you."

Since the Winter Carnival had been the biggest topic of their conversations for the last month, the mayor knew he was on top of it. Considering it was the start of their attempt to turn the tide on local community opinion of the fire department, no one was willing to make a mistake.

"We're all set for a huge demonstration involving a crash scene, where the firefighters will work to pull a victim from a car and demonstrate their skills. Both the rescue squad and the fire engine crew will have tasks to work on. The EMTs will also be on hand to treat 'injuries' sustained by the victims."

The mayor frowned.

"Students from the local high school who are involved in

the HOSA community will play the victims." Allen waited a beat and made sure the mayor was familiar with the future health professionals student organization. "They know how to use makeup to simulate injuries and are well-versed in critical incident response themselves. So no worries there."

"Good."

Allen realized he should have figured out better how to let the mayor know they were using real people in the fake incident scene.

What mattered was that the public who attended the Winter Carnival got to see the firefighters' skills in action when it wasn't a high-stress, real-life situation.

He continued. "Through the day we're going to have firefighters on hand to show people all the parts of their truck and the equipment used. Kids can climb up and get their pictures taken in the driver's seat. The arson investigator is going to bring his dog for a sniffing demonstration. And there will be a friendly pickup basketball game between the fire department and police department. We'll have hot dogs and burgers for the barbecue, and the church ladies have pledged plenty of sides."

They'd see how friendly the basketball game turned out. Allen had overheard a wager happening but ignored the rivalry, since the guys at the firehouse weren't hurting anyone by making it interesting.

Harrelson nodded. "Great."

Savannah, the police detective he'd formerly worked with, had informed him hot dogs and burgers were a "Yankee barbecue" and not what anyone in the South would think of when that word was used. As long as no one got food poisoning, he didn't care what she thought *barbecue* meant.

Allen read down his list. "Face painting. Balloon animals. A firehouse-themed bounce house..." He wasn't sure there was anything else.

"You've thought of everything, it seems."

"Of course. This is important." The town had suffered enough at the hands of the previous fire chief. It was high time for some family fun.

When the new mayor offered him the job, Allen had jumped at the chance to be the liaison between the fire department and City Hall. He could make a real difference in how the community saw the fire crew. Everyone loved the local police department, including their newest officer and his K-9. The fire department? Not so much.

He intended to change things. After all, it was the only thing in his life that *could* change.

Which only made him think of Pepper. Dang it, he needed that woman out of his mind.

Everyone believed she'd dumped him because of the accident. He never got the chance to explain otherwise, even though their relationship ended hours before that building exploded over him and trapped half the officers in the department with him in the basement.

He was grateful no one had died, but his life had been indelibly changed.

Eighteen months later and he had to run into Pepper at the police department. It was almost unfair. Still, the conversation they'd had earlier, though it was brief, was probably the most honest conversation they'd ever had.

She had a sister and a niece he hadn't even known about.

That only solidified his belief it was for the best that they'd broken up. After all, she'd shown him only part of who she was when they dated. He'd been all-in, almost ready to propose.

She'd broken it off with barely an explanation.

Then this morning she'd looked at that kid the way he'd always imagined she would look at theirs one day.

"How about a petting zoo?" The mayor turned to his keyboard and typed. "I'll have Lyla ask the local vet...oh, what's his name?"

"Brett Filks." Allen swallowed. Why didn't this town have a vet Pepper didn't work for? They could've used them for this.

"I'm sure he's got some goats, turtles, or something the kids can pet."

Allen knew Brett had a miniature horse or two. But he wasn't sure about a turtle. "Great."

"I'll have him liaise with you about that."

"Sounds good." The lump in his throat proved hard to swallow against. As long as he didn't have to deal with Pepper.

Regardless of all the grief he'd spoken aloud to his horses where only they could hear, the accident had taught him not to wish for what would never be. Their relationship was over. Pepper didn't want him in her life.

Allen wasn't interested in dead dreams. There was too much life to live.

"I'm hoping the Winter Carnival at the fire department is a great success." Harrelson smiled wide, even though there was no press here. "I'll be there promptly at ten to officially open the festivities."

"Sounds good, sir."

He wondered if Pepper would bring her niece, though there had to be a good reason he didn't often see her around town. They should run into each other more. The fact they didn't, aside from the odd occasion, made him wonder if she'd figured that out on purpose. Like she made a point to avoid him.

The kid at the police department this morning had been adorable and rambunctious. Polite. But her life had nothing to do with him.

No matter if he wished for it to be different, it wasn't like anything would ever change.

As he drove back to the fire department, his phone rang.

Tate calling.

Allen swiped the screen. "Put your private investigator hat on. Pepper needs your help."

3

Victory sat across the room in a rocking chair someone had donated to the vet's office. Her legs crossed on the seat, she held a kitten, attempting to bottle feed it. The lack of success had nothing to do with her efforts.

Pepper didn't have the heart to tell her the sad truth about what would likely happen to the smallest kitten of the litter.

"We can try again later if she isn't hungry now." Pepper locked the computer screen and crossed the room.

Two dogs in neighboring pens had both endured the same surgery this morning. One lifted his head, already alert after coming out of the anesthesia. The other was snoozing, his paws twitching as he dreamed.

She took the kitten from Victory and placed it in the knee-height run, where the mother cat lay. She had been struck by a car and given birth early on the side of the road while she was bleeding. It was a miracle they'd been able to save her and any of the babies. But while Pepper saw recoveries like this on occasion, her work here was often characterized by loss of life.

Pepper preferred to work the front office, ushering in people who cared enough about their pets to bring them to routine appointments—meeting all kinds of animals so clearly loved and provided for.

How would Victory react to an unhappy ending to the tale?

Pepper held out her hand. "Let's go see who is in the waiting area. I think there are a couple of corgis coming in this afternoon."

Victory jumped from the chair and took her hand. "I love all squishy animals. But corgis are the best."

"I think I agree with you on that."

"Are they your favorite?"

"They're my favorite dog," Pepper said. "But my favorite animal of all time is horses."

"Oooh. Yeah." Victory nodded. "I wanna get one of those."

Pepper chuckled.

They'd already eaten their sandwiches in the break room, something Pepper did at the middle of every shift regardless of what time it was. Though she only worked nights on a rotation, that stint was coming up in a couple of weeks.

"Mom hasn't called me back," Victory said, her voice soft.

Pepper said, "Me either."

As much as she enjoyed Victory's company, what was she supposed to do with an elementary-school-age child while working the night shift? Victory should be back to school next week. Sage needed to have collected her days ago.

Worry for her sister's fate kept mixing with irritation. She was suddenly expected to accommodate a child as a full-time part of her life?

Where are you, Sage?

The young intern behind the counter studied at the local community college to become a veterinarian. Colleen would be headed back for her spring semester soon, and each of the vet nurses—Pepper included—would go back on rotation to cover the front desk. Since the business ebbed and flowed with the school holidays, her departure would coincide with a lull in activity.

Victory tugged her hand free. "Hi, Colleen."

The young woman paused her typing and smiled. "Hi, Victory. How are the kittens?"

Her niece rounded the counter and hopped onto the desk beside the computer, where she began chattering. Pepper tuned it out. She straightened a couple of pamphlets on the breakfast-bar-height counter—the lobby desk that Victory leaned back to rest her shoulder blades against.

She needed to redo the girl's french braid.

Her cell phone buzzed in her pocket. They were all meant to leave their cell phones in their lockers. However, Brett—the veterinarian doctor at the practice—knew she was waiting to hear back from her sister.

She pulled it out and looked at the screen, hoping it was Allen more than she wanted to admit.

Instead, it was another call from an unknown number. She'd had enough of them to know it wasn't her sister, and there would only be quiet on the other end of the line. Maybe a slight intake of breath.

She stowed the phone back in her pocket. Everything was fine. It was just that seeing Allen this morning had shaken her, coming on the heels of filing an official police report that her sister had gone missing.

That was all.

She'd just about reached the point where she didn't think about him daily. Or wonder if she might have made the wrong choice in ending things with him. Either way, it was done. There was no going back and doing things differently.

Pepper wasn't the kind of person who could have all the things she wanted. Especially not with a good guy who abided by the law and probably didn't know anything about the kind of life she'd lived. He had been a marine and then a cop. Now he was a civil servant working with the fire department.

It was much better that he never found out who she really was. She'd never be good enough for him. At least this way she wouldn't have to live with his reaction—how he felt about people like her. Or see pity on his face.

A dark-gray van pulled into the parking lot, and Brett climbed out. His wife Katherine got out on the passenger side, and Brett retrieved their five-month-old son from his car seat. Katherine brought over the stroller, and the two of them got the adorably chubby baby strapped in.

Pepper held the door open. "Hey, you two, how was lunch?"

Brett pushed the stroller in. "Great."

Katherine spotted Victory over the counter. "I ate so much I think it's time for a walk in the park. And then maybe a cup of hot chocolate from Bridgewater Café. If anyone is interested in going with me?"

Pepper saw through the plan immediately. Not that she believed her boss had orchestrated his wife occupying Victory because he didn't want her in the office. The two of them loved Victory and even babysat her when Pepper had a doctor's appointment.

Victory adored the baby about as much as Katherine and Brett adored Victory.

She ran across and gave him a slobbery kiss. "Hi, Samuel." She looked up at Katherine. "Does he want to see the kitties?"

"Maybe after hot chocolate." Katherine smiled. "What do you think?"

Victory glanced at Pepper. "Can I?"

"Sure thing, Nugget. As long as you get your jacket."

The girl raced from the lobby down the hallway.

Pepper turned around but saw Katherine immediately raise her hand, palm out. "Don't even. I'm happy to have company that can speak whole sentences and not just say da-da."

Brett laughed. "The kid knows which side his bread is buttered on."

Pepper shook her head. "Whatever that even means."

"Well..." Brett clapped his hands. "I gotta get back to work."

Baby Samuel kicked his legs and slammed his fists on his knees. "Da-da."

Katherine looked at Pepper. "See what I mean?"

She just grinned. Victory reappeared, and Pepper helped button her coat while the family said goodbye.

As soon as they pulled away, an older model SUV pulled into the parking lot. Tate Hudson, the local private investigator, climbed out of the driver's seat.

Brett frowned, then glanced at her. "Sage?"

"I didn't call him. Maybe he heard through the grapevine and thought he might be able to help me." If Allen hadn't wanted to give her the information, he might've sent a neutral third party so he didn't have to text or call her. Or see her face again.

Brett squeezed her shoulder. "I'll talk to him."

Pepper shook her head. "It's fine. It's just a weird day."

Tate pulled the door open.

Brett ignored him for a second. "Did those police officers give you a hard time when you went over there?"

Tate glanced between them. There was barely enough room for the door to shut behind him. "What's this?"

Pepper moved so they weren't blocking the door. "Why don't you tell us what this is?"

She didn't want to answer Brett's question any more than she wanted to give Tate information he didn't need. Not that the guy was nosy or a busybody, but he was here for a reason. She couldn't make assumptions as to what that was. Pepper didn't need her business being talked about all over town.

Tate looked at Brett. "You guys have somewhere quiet that Pepper and I can talk?"

Pepper was about to set her hands on her hips when Brett said, "Break room."

"Lead the way." Tate waved a hand.

Pepper walked like a condemned person down the hallway to the break room, where she got herself a diet soda from the fridge. Tate poured himself a cup of coffee. He stood by the sink, his hips against the counter.

The guy was older, a few years more than Allen. He was also big, like Allen at his full height.

She didn't want to think about the similarities more than that. Whatever this was, they should just get it over with. "What's going on?"

He didn't look like he needed to deliver bad news. It seemed more like he thought he had as much time as he wanted to do this. He took a sip and said, "I can help, you know. Find your sister for you."

"I filed a police report. But I'm guessing you already know that, and that's why you're here."

Before he could speak again, the other nurse who had been out to lunch wandered in, swaying. Analise saw Tate and perked up. "Hey, handsome."

He frowned over his coffee cup.

Analise pulled a water bottle out of the refrigerator and slammed the door, nearly falling over in the process.

"Are you okay?" Pepper didn't like the look of this.

She glanced over at her, glassy-eyed. "None of your business." Analise sauntered out, still swaying.

"My advice?" Tate motioned to the doorway with his mug. "Don't worry about things you don't have to worry about. If you're taking care of a kid, your priorities don't involve getting in the middle of other people's messes. Stick to making sure Victory is safe and has what she needs."

"What do you think I've been doing her whole life?" The truth slipped out before she could call it back.

Tate set the cup down. "I'll find your sister for you."

Pepper shook her head. "I don't have the money to pay for a private investigator, and I'm guessing you don't work for free."

"Don't worry about it." He shrugged, apparently not bothered.

Unfortunately, she *was* going to worry about it. The way she worried about everything.

It was a wonder Allen hadn't seen through the façade. But she'd spent years persuading people that what they saw was what they got with her.

That everything was fine.

Tate laid a business card on the table in front of her. "Email me every piece of information you can think of regarding your sister. I'll start as soon as you send it, and we'll get her found."

He walked out before she could object to any of it.

4

J ust before five o'clock, Allen pushed himself out of his office and headed down the hall. The main area of the firehouse was essentially a square of hallways. If he wanted to, he could wheel himself around and around all day, checking to see what everyone was doing.

A few doors down from his office, in one corner of the square, the fire chief, Devon Francis, leaned back in his chair. Eyes closed. Arms folded on his chest. The guy was seventy-four and had served in a neighboring fire department for decades before he was hired to Last Chance County.

Steven Hilden, the previous fire chief and one of the town's founders, had been outed a couple of years ago as being involved in a trafficking ring—among other things. He'd been killed before he could be brought to justice. Devon Francis was chosen as a safe replacement. A guy who would never make waves, let alone think to do any of the things the previous fire chief had done.

So what if he kept a bottle of whiskey in his desk and often napped after his lunchtime drink? Retirement stood on the man's doorstep.

Lately Allen had begun to notice the void in leadership. Not that Francis had changed his game and started to neglect his duties. He'd never done more than what he absolutely had to.

The firehouse officers, including the currently-on-duty truck lieutenant and the rescue squad lieutenant, were all top-notch. Allen had made sure the right people were hired. Amelia Patterson and Bryce Crawford kept everything running smoothly out with their teams. They'd made this firehouse a solid example of professional firefighting.

When they were out with their teams.

Back in the firehouse was another thing entirely. Which Francis was apparently not concerned about.

They needed a great chief to support them and push them. Not just a guy who did paperwork and took naps in his chair. They needed someone who would go out to fire scenes with them and take this house from good to great. Otherwise, the personnel squabbles they had at Eastside firehouse would bleed into their duties on a call.

Allen turned left at the corner where the front entrance was instead of right, which would take him outside.

The lobby couches were empty, the doors permanently unlocked so they were open to the local community because a firehouse should be a place that welcomed anyone. The common room and kitchen were empty, but a huge pot of what smelled like Italian meat sauce bubbled on the stove. Allen's stomach rumbled.

The next corner would take him back to his office after the gym and the lieutenants' offices. Straight took him to the entrance of the engine bay and the bunk room doors. Beyond the engine bay, the doors led to the ambulance garage, a straight line from here to there.

The whole place was so huge it had been dizzying coming from the tiny police department. But then again, the previous fire chief—who should have ended up in jail for life for all things he'd done—had funneled all kinds of illegally obtained funds into building the flashiest firehouse he could.

He'd also used it as the base for his illegal dealings.

Thankfully none of the current firefighters or EMTs had been around when that was happening. Allen had gotten to know all of them in the last year-plus of working here. They were good men and women, solid people who cared about their jobs.

He opened the door to the engine bay and was met with a rush of shouts and whoops.

The garage doors had been rolled up, bringing in the January chill. Both the rescue squad truck and the fire engine, with its ladder on top, had been parked out on the drive.

Both teams of firefighters raced back and forth in a relay, hauling what looked like ten-gallon buckets in each hand. The other three team members, including the lieutenants of each truck, were the ones washing the fire trucks while the fourth man ran to the hose and back to refill their buckets.

The huge digital clock on the wall counted down, each second a chime that rang through the engine bay.

They had less than six seconds.

The two runners sped up. One slipped. The bucket went flying and caught the other man in the back of his knee. Both of them went down. With all their turnout gear on, Allen had to read the back of the jacket just above the hem. He caught *Owens* on the back of Jayson's jacket as one man tackled the other.

The timer counted down the last few seconds, and a deafening alarm blared. Different than the alarm that sounded a callout, but no less loud.

"You tripped me on purpose."

They rolled and Allen saw *Foster*. Zack yelled, "No, I didn't!"

Allen winced. The lieutenants threw their sponges in the nearest bucket.

Crawford, the rescue squad lieutenant, called out, "Benning, get them to break it up!"

It didn't look like Charlie tried that hard. Not when Zack turned and jumped on Eddie, and then it was a dog pile of men and gloves flying. Rescue versus Truck by the look of it.

Allen rolled over to the garden hose and turned the nozzle to jet. He aimed for their necks but managed to spray at least one of them in the eye, even if it wasn't entirely on purpose. "Oops."

They quit pummeling each other and looked at him, still tangled in a pile on the floor.

"Get up. The game is over." He tossed the hose on the ground. "Clean this place up."

As he headed for the doors to go back inside, the fire engine lieutenant, Amelia Patterson, spotted him by the doors. She met him with that determined stride. The rescue squad lieutenant, Bryce Crawford, did the same, though it was more like a satisfied strut.

They'd been on callouts when Allen returned from meeting with the mayor that morning. After they returned, he'd been on the phone for a while, and they'd been running training out here. With a chief who didn't care much about what they were up to, each team was accustomed to getting on with their jobs.

And they did them well. Until a brawl erupted, and it became clear they might be able to fight fires and save people, but they couldn't get along.

Amelia, blonde and five foot ten, was the kind of woman some guys might mistake for being a pushover. She would educate them quickly though. She was a tough leader, and the guys respected her for it. Most of the time, anyway.

One day whatever she hid below the surface would spill out. Allen wasn't sure what would happen then, but he prayed the fallout wouldn't be catastrophic.

Bryce Crawford was the kind of guy public relations wanted

to put on a firefighter calendar. They wanted his identical twin right there beside him, but Logan was currently off fighting bushfires in Victoria, Australia, so Allen had managed to get the PR department to shelve the whole calendar idea—at least for now.

The two lieutenants glanced at each other.

"What is it?" Allen had worked hard to be approachable over the last year.

Back before the accident, when he'd been a police officer, some people got the idea that he was the one to be sent in when a suspect was being difficult. It wasn't untrue, but he didn't need those skills here. He'd also become a believer lying in that hospital bed. For the first time in his life, faith became real.

Amelia cleared her throat and shifted from foot to foot in an uncharacteristic display of nervousness. "We just...we heard Pepper was at the police department when you were there. Everything okay?" She made a face like the words tasted sour on her tongue and glanced at Bryce. She muttered, "Next time, you ask."

Bryce didn't look sorry.

Allen sighed. "Because the two of you suddenly decided to care about my personal life?" He'd never brought that with him to work before.

"Of course we do." Bryce shrugged.

Allen cut him off before he got going. "Everything is fine. Pepper is just looking for her sister."

Which was why he'd called Tate to have the private investigator look into it. There was only so much the police could do. Allen was still waiting on identification of the woman from the car yesterday.

Amelia frowned. "Is this about that kid she has with her?"

Bryce flinched. His last girlfriend had two children who'd caused chaos when they visited the firehouse, and she'd dropped hints daily about him marrying her so he could be their father. Sure, that would have been noble, but Bryce had done the right thing by not getting in any deeper with her. The latest news around the firehouse was she got engaged less than two weeks after Bryce broke it off with her.

"Let's focus on making the Winter Carnival a success, okay?" He didn't need them getting in his business just because they were high achievers who had to constantly look for something to fix.

Allen wasn't anyone's pet project.

Bryce turned to Amelia and motioned with his head toward the two teams cleaning up from their training exercise.

She made a face but didn't argue with his request to scram. She strode back to her people. "Let's go, guys! I want the water mopped up before the engine bay floor turns into a sheet of ice."

Someone groaned.

When he turned back, Bryce eased against the door frame. "I was thinking—"

The alarm sounded. A deafening chime that would wake even the heaviest of sleepers.

From the speaker on the wall came the crackly voice of the dispatcher. "Rescue 5. Truck 14. Ambulance 21. Residential collapse, multiple victims trapped."

En masse, the entire group raced to their engines. The men's bunk room door flew open hard enough to hit the wall, and the two EMTs skidded across the bay to the garage at the end of the building where their ambulance was parked.

Seconds later their vehicles swung onto the street, lights and sirens going.

Allen wheeled around the engine bay. He tossed the last of the buckets, mops, and sponges to the side so they could pull in when they returned.

Back in the kitchen, he turned off the red sauce so it didn't burn. He cooked a couple of servings of spaghetti—just in case his occasional visitor showed up.

It only happened when the trucks were gone. The older man didn't like a crowded firehouse.

The shuffle of boots on the tile floor brought the edge of a smile to Allen's mouth. He got two paper bowls, because he couldn't reach the ceramic ones in the cupboard above the toaster, and dished out two servings of food. Bottles of water. Plastic forks. It meant more than one trip to the table with the stuff on his lap and the need to push himself.

His guest stood by the door until everything was laid out. Then he made his way over, a slight limp in his stride from an old injury to his hip. Allen guessed the older man had shrapnel in him.

His coat was ragged, as was the cap on his head. But without either one, he would suffer in the January chill outside. He wore multiple layers under the coat and probably more than one pair of pants to keep out the cold.

Allen had followed him one night to try and figure out where he slept. But he'd lost the guy between two streets.

"I saw her this morning." Allen twisted spaghetti around his fork and took a bite.

The older man did the same, the gray stubble on his jaw shifting as he chewed, his gaze on the meal.

"It hurt more than I thought it would. Seeing her upset." He twisted the cap off the man's drink for him. "Of course, I want to help her. Which would be a complete disaster since she wants nothing to do with me."

The homeless man tipped his head to the side, just a fraction.

"It's been eighteen months. I should probably be over her by now, right?" Allen blew out a breath and took another bite.

If anyone came back from their callout, the older man would get up and leave immediately without a word. He wouldn't take the rest of the bowl with him. Allen prayed they weren't interrupted. It was the only way he could ensure the guy ate a good meal.

He continued. "Maybe I'll never be over her."

Seeing the older man always made Allen think about what his own later years would look like. So many scenarios in his life could've ended with him on the streets. He wanted to get the older man to the Ridgeman Therapy Center so that he could talk it out. Get some kind of help.

Allen's cousin Natalie worked there as a counselor, so it wasn't like it would be a stranger the older man dealt with. She'd discussed it with Allen a bunch of times. He wanted to get the guy in his truck and drive him up there, but she kept stressing the need to let him make his own choices about where he went. Wait for the guy to ask for help.

Allen sighed and continued eating. If he even suggested it, the older man just got up and left without finishing. So he kept his mouth shut and chewed.

Fifteen minutes later, the homeless man pushed his chair back. He took his bowl and fork and tossed them in the trashcan with the empty water bottle.

On the way out, he lifted two fingers and touched his temple in a salute.

Allen watched him go. "Have a good night."

5

Pepper sat in her hallway across from the bathroom, back to the wall. In front of her, Victory splashed around in the bathtub while Pepper read from the Bible app on her phone. It was the only time she'd figured out to fit it in, even if she wasn't sure it was working.

They'd had dinner, made a game out of folding laundry—that for some reason involved karate—and watched a couple of episodes of Victory's favorite cartoon.

She could hardly remember her evenings before her niece came to stay for the holidays. Now she wondered what she would do when Victory went home with Sage.

She wanted Victory home with her mother, where she should be.

Pepper also loved having her here.

This whole situation gave her whiplash, her emotions swinging back and forth.

Did she want Victory back with Sage, or did she just want to wrap the girl up and protect her from her mama's instability? The fact that keeping her would be a lot like kidnapping shut down those thoughts pretty quickly. Regardless of how she felt about her sister's choices, and the fact that Pepper's house was more stable—and drama free—might be a consideration. If this were a court battle.

Pepper let out a sigh and tried to focus on the words.

Hear my prayer, O God; give ear to the words of my mouth.

Tears filled her eyes, but she wasn't going to cry in front of Victory. She wanted to be able to pray like that, but the girl saw enough fake tears from her mother. She wouldn't know what to do with Pepper's sudden rush of sadness—grief at the fact God seemed to never hear her.

Victory started singing a chorus she'd learned in children's church, loudly and off key. Which oddly sounded like when Pepper tried to sing. Laughter bubbled up, along with the sense of irony that she grieved so much right now, and yet Victory seemed more settled than she'd ever been in her life.

Pepper blew out a long breath and looked up where the wall met the ceiling.

Sage would come back. Victory would go home with her, and Pepper's sister would continue the volatile divorce and custody battle with Elijah. Sorry. *Doctor Burns.*

Pepper had been expected to call him that, even at the dinner table on Thanksgiving.

Victory turned all the way around. A tsunami sloshed over the side of the bath onto the towel Pepper had laid around the bathmat where the linoleum on the floor had started to peel away from the caulking.

"Doing okay, Nugget?"

"Aye, Captain!"

Before Pepper could ask what game Victory was playing, her phone rang. The number that flashed on the screen wasn't listed in her contacts.

Victory called out, "Potential spam?"

Pepper smiled. Her phone didn't say that on the screen, but she said, "Probably."

She didn't answer the phone, just laid it face down and discovered a cobweb dangling from the hallway light fixture. She didn't want to answer it in front of Victory, whether it was spam or a heavy breather.

Victory released the plug, and the bath began to gurgle as it drained. Pepper stood up, easing the door almost closed as Victory grabbed her towel. The kid whipped the towel from the rail with the force of one of those people who took a tablecloth from a loaded table without toppling over any cups or dishes.

"I need to clean up the kitchen," Pepper said. "Come find me when you're dressed, yeah?"

"'Kay."

She headed down the hall, a smile tugging at her lips. Her curtains were open in the living room, though the slatted blinds meant no one outside would be able to see in. She liked the cozy feeling of having them closed.

Pepper tugged one side of the drapes to the middle and her gaze landed on someone outside, across the street. She parted the slatted blind with one finger, enough to see a man standing under Mrs. Basuto's oak tree.

Whatever his reason for being there, watching Pepper's little yellow house, she didn't think he would be if he knew the mother of the police lieutenant kept a shotgun in her closet.

Move along, buddy.

It didn't take long to add their dinner dishes to the washer. When she was done, she wiped the counters. She placed her phone on the breakfast bar. When she lifted it to clean the surface, she turned it to see the screen.

No more calls or texts.

Maybe she should send Allen a message to ask if the police had any news for her. Or find out if Tate did, since it had been hours since she'd emailed him all their information so he could start looking for Sage. Allen had been pretty cryptic, but she gathered there was someone unidentified, involved in an accident, and they needed to ascertain if it was her sister or not. She sincerely prayed her sister wasn't lying in the morgue, waiting to be identified.

That thought sparked more tears.

As much tension as there was between her and Sage, the last thing she wanted was for Victory to go through burying her mother. After which her father would no doubt demand full custody, and Pepper would end up in family court fighting for the legal right to give Victory what she needed rather than what *Dr. Burns* felt like giving her when he remembered she existed.

Pepper pushed away her better judgment and called Allen. He could pick up or not. That was up to him.

"Frees."

The words caught on her tongue.

"Pepper?"

"Yeah." She had to clear her throat. "It's me."

"I know that. I have caller ID."

That meant he hadn't deleted her from his contacts when they broke up. Although, he'd been in the hospital dealing with a life-changing condition, so that might have had something to do with it. Not that he secretly wanted to keep her number saved.

Allen said, "Did you need something?"

Pepper had to get ahold of herself, or this would get even more awkward. "Just that you didn't follow up with me about the car that might be my sister's."

"Right."

She held a breath.

"The medical examiner hasn't ID'd her yet."

Pepper sucked in a breath.

"You don't know if it's your sister. Given it was a different car, it's unlikely." The warmth of his voice helped.

"It could be her. Until I hear either way..."

"I know."

A tear fell. She swiped it away. "Thanks for picking up."

She wouldn't be calling again. This wasn't healthy. God didn't want her to live in this state of grief for what would never be—could never be. The kind of person she was didn't live happily ever after. Not with a good man strong enough to overcome adversity—or so it seemed.

"No problem."

She couldn't help it. "How are Breezy and Candy?"

He chuckled. "As ornery as ever. Candy tried to take a bite out of my sleeve, but the forecast for tonight is snow, so no riding tomorrow."

She chuckled but had to brush away another tear. His horses were seen by the vet where she worked. Since their breakup, Brett made the trip across town and up into the hills where Allen's cabin was nestled strictly solo.

She loved that cabin where he lived. The one Allen's father had built years ago.

Heavy fists pounded on her door.

Pepper sucked in a breath and spun around. She nearly dropped her phone but caught the device before it slipped from her fingers and smashed on the bare tile.

"Pepper?" Allen sounded worried.

She lifted the phone to her ear while the fists hammered on the door. "I'm—"

"Answer the door, Pepper! I know you're in there!"

"Who is that?"

Pepper gripped the phone. She knew the voice on the other side of her front door. "Victory's father."

"Answer this door right now—" Burns called her a foul name.

"Don't do that." Allen's voice cut through the chaos and fear in her mind. "I'm sending a police car to your house, okay? Don't answer the door. Let the officers deal with it. Okay?"

Pepper couldn't speak.

"You need to confirm you heard me, Pepper. Or I'm driving over myself, and I'll deal with it."

"I heard you."

He went silent for a long second. "Fine."

She wanted to ask what that meant but sensed movement behind her. Victory stood in the hall in her pajamas and bare feet, her face pale. "Is that Daddy?"

Pepper expected tears in Victory's eyes. Instead, all she saw was hardness. A world-weary soul looking for rest and not managing to find it anywhere. Not even here with her aunt, where she'd begun to believe she was safe.

Pepper strode over and hugged the girl to her front. "We don't need to open the door."

"He'll break it in." Victory's body jerked and she choked back a sob.

It was like looking in the mirror at herself the same age.

I'm scared. He'll get in.

Pepper sucked in a breath and pushed the memories of her own father from her mind. She held on tightly to Victory. "You and I are safe in here."

"Go hide in the bedroom." Allen's voice sounded beside her ear. "In the closet if you can."

"Oh, okay."

Elijah Burns continued to bang on the door. One of her neighbors yelled at him. He replied with a barrage of words loud enough that everyone on the street would hear. They'd all know she wasn't the kind of person who lived in a nice house like this on a normally quiet street. She would have to go back to the type of run-down single-wide where she'd grown up on off-brand canned tomato soup and too much cheap cereal. She couldn't stand the sugary stuff now.

"The police will be there in a minute or two."

Pepper took Victory's hand and pulled her to the bedroom.

They sat in the small space between her bed and the bathroom. Pepper realized she was huddled together on the floor with Sage's daughter the way she had been with Sage.

I'm scared.

Victory squeezed her middle, her head tucked against Pepper's neck.

Allen said, "You still with me?"

I need you. She couldn't say those words. "You don't need to stay on the line." She cleared her throat. "If the police are coming."

"Everything will be okay." His voice sounded warm and so strong beside her ear. "You're safe where you are."

Pepper wanted to put him on speaker so he could reassure Victory the same way.

Allen said, "He'll be gone soon."

"Really, you can let me go."

"That's what you want?"

No. "I don't want to keep you. You probably had a long day."

"You have no idea what kind of day I had."

Pepper bit her lip. The yelling at the other end of her house had stopped. That meant the police were outside, dealing with her sister's ex.

She let out a long breath. She had to get control of herself so she could settle Victory and go talk to them.

She forced out the words, "Have a nice night."

"Pep—"

She hung up.

6

"And so, we thank you all for coming today." Mayor Gregory Harrelson started to wind down his Winter Carnival speech for about the third time. "After an amazing number of entries, the winner of the contest to guess the number of candies in the jar is Amy Brant!"

The crowd applauded.

Harrelson said, "Enjoy yourselves, and remember to—"

Allen figured he would say *vote for me in the upcoming election.*

"—save me some of that cake."

The gathered attendees broke into chuckles and a smattering of applause.

Allen pushed through the crowd to where four grills in a row kicked out smoke and the scent of grilling beef that was about to burn. "Smells good."

Zack, the youngest firefighter at Eastside firehouse, grinned. "Just like my grandma used to make."

"Don't tell me she liked char." Given the look of the food, the kid's grandma burned dinner regularly. But then again, he knew next to nothing about Zack.

Word around the firehouse was that Zack had regularly hung out here since elementary school. More than once, the firefighters had found him sleeping over on the roof, making the firehouse a second home for him. That had slacked off for a while when the issues with former fire chief Hilden came to a head. Now the kid was back and a member of the team.

He probably knew more about this firehouse than anyone that worked here.

Allen said, "I'll take mine just lightly charred."

"Copy that." Zack saluted him with the spatula.

Allen made his way around the crowd and checked in with everyone instead of doing what he wanted. Which was to wheel straight to Lieutenant Basuto, his former sergeant at the police department, and demand answers about what had happened after Pepper hung up on him last night.

It was a form of punishment to make himself wait. It was also about the self-discipline that had him doing hundreds of pull-ups every day, so he had the upper body strength to lift the rest of him around wherever he needed to go. He also did leg exercises so the unused muscles were kept in shape. He worked on walking, hoping to build the stamina to be on crutches someday.

He'd always been fit, but the strength it took to live the life he did now far surpassed what he had needed to be a marine or a cop. And all he did was sit in a chair all day.

By the time he reached Basuto, the guy had a paper cup in one hand and the other held onto the hand of his very pregnant wife.

Allen had been invited to the coed baby shower for their twins but only sent a gift through the mail. He didn't need everything he wanted but would never have right in front of his face, regardless of the fact he was completely happy for his friends.

"Seems like a good turnout." Basuto sipped his coffee and

nodded toward the engine bay, where the bounce house had been set up.

"You know that's not what I want to talk about. But yeah, thanks." Allen looked around. "I'm glad it's going well so far. The firefighters put in a lot of hard work."

"Mmm. Shame they're going to be beaten later on the basketball court." Basuto had on his sweats and T-shirt under a sweater with LCCPD on it.

"I didn't realize you'd be on the team."

"And miss the chance to go head-to-head with FD?" Basuto shook his head. "Just promise me Amelia isn't playing. She fights dirty."

His wife snorted.

Allen said, "Why does that not surprise me?"

"I'm guessing you wanna talk about the callout to Pepper's house last night."

"Who was banging on her door?" Allen wanted the man's full legal name to pass on to Tate, the local PI.

"The officers got his information."

Allen frowned. "They didn't arrest him?"

He could still hear the fear in Pepper's voice in his mind

Basuto said, "He agreed to leave the premises willingly, and when they talked to her, she didn't want to press charges. She explained she's watching her niece until her sister shows up. He has no parental rights. If the dad comes back, she's going to call right away, and he will get arrested."

His wife twisted under his arm so that she faced him. "You didn't tell me there's a kid involved."

Basuto said, "He didn't get in the house. She didn't even see the guy."

"But he scared her, right?"

"Whether he did or not, Mama Bear needs to stand down."

"I'm not going to find him and pick a fight," she said. "I could just keep an eye on him."

"Depends if you want to be on bed rest again."

She groaned. Before she could say anything, someone tapped the microphone the mayor had been using. Allen assumed they would've turned it off or muted the sound equipment since no one needed to use it.

He gripped the handles on his wheels and turned his chair. Fire Chief Francis stood at the microphone.

"Hello? Is this on?" Someone yelled to him that it was, so the chief continued. "Given we're all gathered here, I'd like to make an announcement." He smiled. "I'll be retiring in a month. But since I've got so much vacation time saved up, this will be my last official shift. It's been a pleasure serving the local community."

Allen murmured, "What is he doing?"

Chief Francis lifted his paper cup, and Allen wondered what he'd poured in there. "Thanks, everyone."

Someone started clapping. No one else joined in, so it wasn't long before it petered out and everyone returned to what they'd been doing.

Allen eased back from Basuto and his wife. "Excuse me."

The police lieutenant chuckled behind his cup and muttered something about damage control.

The guy wasn't wrong. But before Allen could get to the chief, Bryce stepped in front of him, blocking his view of the mayor walking over to the chief. Allen used to be able to see over most people's shoulders. Now he had a great view of everyone's belt buckle.

"Boss—"

Allen cut him off. "Before you ask, I had no idea that was going to happen." Now the lieutenants were out a chief, which wouldn't sit well with the brass. They would want someone new hired soon.

"That's not what this is." Bryce paused. "You know my brother fights wildfires, right? Well, he has this friend who works with him. A guy he's known for ages, the senior guy on the team. He's from Last Chance County, and it turns out he's looking to come home for the summer season at least. Maybe permanently."

Allen nodded, looking around Bryce so he could get a read on the conversation between the mayor and the fire chief.

Former fire chief.

Allen said, "That's great. It'll be good to have your whole family in town again." The twins had a sister who worked as an EMT at the other firehouse across town.

Allen wondered if he could get her transferred to Eastside firehouse so she could work with her brothers. He'd have to find out if she was interested in that.

"That's not why I'm telling you," Bryce said. "Logan's friend, Macon James? You should interview him as the new chief." Bryce pulled his cell phone from the pocket of his turnout gear. "I'll forward you his résumé."

Allen frowned. "The mayor gave me the final sign-off on all hiring. There's no way I'll let them bring in a guy who will only make life difficult for you. The new chief, whenever that happens, is going to be someone who's a good fit for this house."

Bryce needed to not worry. Too bad these firefighters were born problem solvers. They'd had entire meetings where they scribbled all over the whiteboard in the conference room with dry erase markers, brainstorming possible candidates for the chief's eventual replacement.

They also thought he didn't know about that because they'd done it in the middle of a shift at two in the morning and immediately erased all the evidence. Except the shadow of their writing remained on the boards.

"Logan said Macon is a solid guy and a great firefighter."

And there were so many other exemplary candidates locally. "I'll take a look at him."

Bryce lifted a hand. "That's all I'm asking."

"Great." He maneuvered around Bryce and spotted the mayor, alone now. A glance around didn't give him any idea where the chief had gone. He pushed his way to Harrelson. "Did he leave?"

"Probably clearing his things from his desk right now." The mayor snorted and forked a piece of cake into his mouth.

A line had formed at the hot apple cider station. Allen had to admit it smelled as good as the burgers. Since he had to watch for cold in the limbs he could only partially feel, he should probably get something hot to drink in a minute. It was that or have to wrap his legs in a blanket. Still, the temperature was supposed to reach a balmy fifty-five this afternoon.

After the snowfall yesterday, the truck firefighters had shoveled the fresh powder to the side of the drive and formed a row of snowmen and women dressed suspiciously like the local city council members.

He spotted a couple of kids throwing snowballs at the chairwoman.

At the end of the drive, Pepper and Victory approached the firehouse, holding hands. Wrapped up in coats, scarves, and hats, they looked like mother and daughter in a way that made his heart ache in his chest.

Allen needed to focus. "Francis is really done?"

"Your guess is as good as mine. This is the first time he's made it official." The mayor shrugged. "Maybe he's in there taking a nap, and he'll wake up and go back to work unaware that he just quit his job."

"Maybe you could put the paperwork through while he's asleep."

The mayor grinned. "You have someone else in mind for the job?"

"The right candidate is out there. And I know what I'm

looking for." His gaze drifted, falling on Pepper and Victory again. The girl ran off toward the bounce house.

Pepper looked around, saw him watching her, and flushed red. He had to wonder if that was interest he saw in her eyes. It wasn't worth lying to himself and pretending she hated him and he hated her. But if she'd wanted a relationship with him, she wouldn't have broken it off.

Harrelson said, "Just so long as they don't turn into a murdering psychopath like the fire chief before Francis."

"I am planning to set the bar a little higher than that."

"Good." The mayor nodded. "Because murder is terrible for PR." He leaned down a little.

Allen sat stiffly. The guy didn't mean to make him feel small on purpose.

"You know what's good for PR?" Harrelson asked.

Allen lifted his brows.

The mayor said, "Cake."

"I believe you."

He wandered off, probably to get himself another piece.

Never in a million years would Allen have figured he'd end up in this job or any of the situations that defined his life right now.

Every time something changed, he figured out how to settle into it and make the most of his circumstances. The hardest had been when Pepper left him. Not just because being paralyzed had come right on the heels of that. He dealt with both at the same time, but had to say the broken heart honestly hurt worse. There was no medicine for that pain.

He rotated his chair around to face the firehouse, feeling the irritating urge to stretch his legs. Which was pretty much impossible unless he had two horizontal bars to hold himself upright.

Allen blew out a breath that puffed white in front of him. He felt his knees and shins under the double layer of clothing.

He needed to get inside where it wasn't so cold.

Pepper stood at the open engine bay doors. She glanced around, a frown on her face.

"Is everything okay?"

"Do you see Victory anywhere?"

The bounce house, a fire truck design with a kind of obstacle course all the way down the center, had so much cover that he didn't know how anyone tracked their children through it. Most of the parents stood around drinking cider or coffee, chatting with each other, not at all worried about where their children were every second of playtime.

"I'm sure she's—"

Pepper whirled around, her hands fisted by her sides. "She's supposed to wave at me every time she goes through. It's been too long. Where is she?"

7

P epper wound between two groups of people and headed down the side of the bounce house, which stretched almost the entire length of the engine bay.

She was glad they'd set it up inside. Not just because of the weather but because it also felt to her like things were contained. Victory was probably here somewhere. Safe and sound. She had likely forgotten to wave at Pepper the last time, distracted by someone or something else.

Except all the instincts she had screamed the opposite. All those internal alerts honed through her childhood to tell her when to panic.

She checked the line of children waiting to get on the bounce house. One of the firefighters stood at the beginning of the assault course, timing the kids so they didn't bump into each other along the way. Making them wait a few seconds before the next one went.

No Victory. She moved around the other side of the bounce house and looked through a couple of windows. One of Victory's friends from church collided with another boy halfway down.

"Have you seen Victory?" Her voice came out breathy, but she tried to tamp down the panic so the kids wouldn't get scared.

"No," one said. "I didn't see her."

Pepper continued along, back to where Allen waited at the end of the bounce house. "Did she come out?"

He shook his head. "I haven't seen her."

"Okay, I'm officially freaking out now." He started to speak, but she cut him off before he could. "Have you ever known me to panic unnecessarily?"

He stared at her. "You don't want me to answer that."

Pepper shook her head. "Why not?"

"Because at this point, I'm wondering if I knew you at all."

She opened her mouth to argue but quickly realized he was probably right. She'd never shown him the real her. But was that the point right now?

If she lost Victory today, then she lost everything good she had left in her life. "Can we please just find her?"

Allen nodded.

She didn't want to think about what it meant, knowing he believed her. That she didn't have to be alone in this.

Like being on the phone with him when Victory's dad had been pounding on the door last night. Hearing his voice in her ear, soft and comforting. The memory of having him that close hurt as much as it had helped at that moment.

Given the frown on his face right now, it didn't seem like he wanted to offer that to her today. Because she'd hung up on him?

Allen had never been petty. Probably it wasn't just because she cut him off rather than admitted she needed him—which was probably the worst part of all of this. Or it would be if Victory was safe and sound.

One of the dads turned around. "Are you looking for Victory?"

Pepper nodded. "Have you seen her?"

The guy waved at the double doors that led from the engine bay into the firehouse itself. "She went in there with a guy."

Pepper gasped. Allen rolled forward in his wheelchair. "Describe him." The authority in his tone stopped her from racing into the firehouse for a split second. Then she realized it didn't matter what the guy looked like.

Pepper raced into the firehouse and slammed into a guy in a paramedic's uniform. "Sorry."

"I would ask where the fire is, but since we're in a firehouse I'm guessing it's not here."

"I'm looking for a missing child."

His humor dissipated and the professional look she'd seen on the faces of cops before dropped over his expression. "In here?"

Before she could answer, the doors opened behind her. She spun to see Allen roll in.

"Dark-blue jeans. Black jacket, dark hair. Possibly Hispanic. The kid has on dark-green pants and a red coat. She has dark hair the same color as Pepper's."

"Split up," the paramedic ordered. "Left and right, meet in the middle?"

"Copy that." Allen pushed his wheelchair down the hallway to the right. The paramedic headed toward the front door.

If someone had taken Victory, they would go for the exit, not the side hall that looped around.

Pepper raced after the paramedic. When he opened a side door and looked inside, she ran for the front door at the end of the hall. Past the common room buzzing with civilians and a couple of firefighters telling stories. An older woman sat at reception, but Pepper didn't pause long enough to talk to her.

She pushed out the doors into the cold January air and skidded to a stop on the salt sprinkled on the front entryway outside. "Victory!"

A green low-slung four-door car sat idling close to the front door. As soon as she stepped toward it, the engine revved and the car pulled out. The driver turned the car in a circle on the street. Pepper ran to the end of the front walk and slipped off the curb. The driver glanced at her, a dark-haired Hispanic man she'd never met. No one in the back seat.

He didn't have Victory.

She ran back to the firehouse. Could her niece still be inside? Maybe she'd run and was now hiding, scared like last night.

Pepper slammed both hands on the reception desk. The woman behind it raised her brows. "Do you have cameras on the front door?"

"Depends who's asking."

"There's a missing child." Pepper gasped. "A car just drove away outside, and I need to see if she was put in it."

Victory would have to be in the trunk, because Pepper hadn't seen her in the car—a thought that made her shudder. Trapped in the dark. No room to move.

She gripped the counter hard enough that her fingers hurt. "I need to find her."

The woman lifted a radio on the desk. "I'll get a police officer here to help."

Her expression said she wasn't sure Pepper told the truth. Or maybe she thought Pepper was unhinged.

"I need to find Allen. See if he found her yet."

Pepper wasn't the kind of person to name drop in order to get access she wouldn't have otherwise. However, everyone who worked here knew Allen Frees. Former police officer, currently the City Hall liaison to the fire department.

That made the reception lady sit up straighter in her chair. "Good idea."

She started speaking into the radio, a bunch of numbers

and words that didn't make any sense to Pepper because she didn't speak dispatcher.

Pepper checked the common room and kitchen. Fear rose and fell in her like the tide, threatening to drown her. *Lord, don't let her be gone.* Not just because she was supposed to be watching Victory for Sage, but also because her niece meant everything.

A way to have a little of what she wanted.

Pepper got to provide a safe place for Victory to be a kid. She didn't have much of that in the rest of her life.

Tears gathered. People around her asked what was wrong as Pepper rushed through each room and tried not to shove them out of the way too much.

She was aware that more than one person followed her and glanced back over her shoulder. Firefighters. "I'm looking for my niece."

The blonde, taller than Pepper, nodded. "We'll help."

She followed the hall around, looking for Allen. She needed to know if he'd found Victory yet. At the next corner she found the paramedic and Allen both huddled together. Watching and waiting.

"Did you find her?"

Allen glanced over and put a finger to his lips. "The intruder is trying to open the window in Amelia's office."

Behind her, the blonde firefighter snorted. "Good luck. It's been stuck for months."

The paramedic by Allen said, "Probably saw someone by the front door and panicked. Tried to find a different way out."

And now they were just standing here watching?

Pepper rushed forward and reached for the door handle. Allen stalled her with an arm across her abdomen. Then she saw the gun in his other hand.

He spoke quietly. "You open the door. I go first." He used a voice that indicated to her this was nonnegotiable.

The paramedic made a noise in the back of his throat.

"Let's go." Allen nodded.

Pepper twisted the handle and pushed the door open. The room was barely big enough for the desk that stretched wall-to-wall on the left side of the rectangular office, partially behind the door. On the other side was a twin bed with enough space to walk down the side.

Victory was on the bed. She'd backed up enough to be scrunched in the corner on the pillow, terror on her face.

The man spun from the window and raised a gun.

"Put that down right now." Allen had the same tone he'd used a moment ago but pointed his gun at the man trying to kidnap Victory.

Pepper squeezed into the room behind Allen. Tried to figure out how she could get between his wheelchair and the door frame so she could go to Victory.

Allen continued. "You failed. You didn't manage to get her out of here, so now it's over. Let her go before this gets any worse for you."

The guy made a face. He didn't like it, but he knew Allen was right.

Pepper looked over her niece to see if the child had been hurt. She had no visible injuries. The mental and emotional scars were ones Pepper knew well. Enough she had to push Allen's chair a little bit forward so she could squeeze through and rush over to her niece.

The gunman shifted, but she didn't look to see. So what if he shot her? Pepper was going to keep Victory safe, no matter if it cost her life. The child's safety was worth the expense of everything else Pepper had to give.

Allen yelled, "Don't do it."

Pepper braced, expecting to be shot, but it didn't come. She gathered Victory into her arms and got her on the floor, covering her niece with her body. It wouldn't save them both, but she had to do something. She winced in case the worst was about to happen. *Don't look.*

She heard a rush of boots and people. Movement and the rustle of clothing. Someone grunted. Something heavy and metal hit the floor beside her head. Pepper just held Victory closer while the child started to cry.

The child was her priority and nothing else. Pepper didn't have anything to do with gunmen or kidnappers. She helped heal animals. She took care of her family.

That was it, even if it cost her everything. Like it had already cost her the relationship she wanted and the respect of a police department who thought she'd dumped Allen for the worst reason.

Because of Sage's choices, Pepper had to keep Victory safe. Even if that meant it was all she did.

A warm hand touched her shoulder. She shifted and looked up at him then. The concern in his eyes.

Pepper shuddered.

Allen's gaze shifted to her niece. "He's gone. You don't have to worry about him. Okay, Victory?"

The child nodded, curling to sit up on the floor.

Pepper managed to say, "She's probably in shock."

Allen frowned at her. She didn't know what that was about, but it didn't matter.

Pepper sat up. "I'm going to take her home."

He touched her shoulder again. "Can you guys do me a favor? I need you to talk to the police, Pepper. Make a statement. Can you wait in my office until I'm done, and then I'll drive you both home?"

"I can take care of Victory myself."

Allen nodded. "I know you can, but I'd like to drive you if that's okay. Make sure you get home safely."

Pepper couldn't say no to the look in his eyes. "Fine. We'll wait for you."

He held out his hand when she stood. Why he thought she needed his help steadying herself when she was perfectly fine, she didn't know. Maybe he thought she was the one in shock.

Pepper swiped away the moisture on her cheeks and held on to Victory's hand. Her niece glanced up at her.

She could do this.

"Come on." Pepper tried to smile. "Let's go wait in Allen's office. Maybe someone will bring us apple cider."

8

Since Trace, one of the Eastside firehouse paramedics, had the suspect covered, Allen leaned aside far enough to watch Pepper and Victory walk down the hallway. His door was only two down from Amelia's, at the corner. He saw them head slowly toward it. One of the cops who'd been outside just a moment ago held the door for them.

They moved inside. Still, Allen's heart squeezed in his chest—the lingering adrenaline from realizing this guy was trying to kidnap Victory. Seeing the fear on Pepper's face.

The suspect must have taken a wrong turn and missed the front doors. Trace and Allen had found him halfway down the south hall, where he'd waved that gun around and dragged Victory into Amelia's office.

Bryce shifted, covering the door, his back to the room. Blocking whoever wanted to enter. "Hold up."

It was Lieutenant Basuto attempting to gain entry to this tiny office already filled with five people.

The cop ordered, "Hand the guy over."

Trace shifted, but it wasn't about the suspect. He also didn't want the cop in here.

Allen was ready to argue for a moment of the suspect's time. Before he could, Bryce slammed the door in the police lieutenant's face, turned the lock, and whirled around. He planted his feet and folded his arms across his chest, looking every bit the rescue squad team leader he was.

To Allen's right, Amelia—whose office this was—crouched to reach under the bed. She pulled out the suspect's weapon and tucked it in the waistband of her turnout pants. Then she folded her arms as well.

The only person between Allen and the suspect was Trace. According to his personnel file, the paramedic had been a cop before he took this job. That made him a different kind of brother to Allen than the others were. But still, this was going to be a team effort.

Trace kicked the rolling chair from under the desk and pointed to it. "Sit down."

The suspect slumped into it, bringing him eye-to-eye with Allen. They should have grabbed some handcuffs from one of the cops in the hallway, because the guy was unsecured.

Allen studied him. He matched the description that dad had given. Allen wanted to find that guy and tell him how much help he'd been. Instead, he drew around him everything he'd been as a cop before an operation cost him the use of his legs. Like a comforting coat, worn in through years of use.

He'd missed this.

"What you choose to do in the next few minutes will determine the course of probably the next decade of your life." Allen pegged the guy as having a couple of strikes against him. Maybe even out on parole.

This wasn't a junkie doing what he needed for a score. This was a guy who made money any way he could and who'd served at least a few years because of it.

He continued. "Do you even know her name, the child you just terrorized?"

The man's dark gaze darted around. "You aren't going to read me my rights?" He had to have seen the cops in the hallway. "I want my lawyer."

Allen shook his head. "You can't demand a lawyer from us. We aren't cops. But we are going to ask you questions, and you're going to answer."

The guy smirked.

"You have no leverage here," Allen said. "We have multiple witnesses who will testify that you attempted to kidnap a child from this fire station. How do you think that will go for you when you're in front of a judge? A group of upstanding members of the community versus you." He tipped his head to the side. "Couple of assault charges. Breaking and entering. Maybe even armed robbery, am I right?"

The guy flinched, just a slight flex of the skin around his eyes.

Trace said, "Tell us who the kid is to you."

Amelia and Bryce stood without moving while what sounded like multiple cops gathered in the hall outside the door. At least they weren't banging on the glass. The suspect could probably see them out the window, but none of the fire department employees in this room were about to hand him over before they got answers.

The suspect blew out a breath. "I didn't get paid enough to keep my mouth shut."

"So you were hired." Allen figured the transaction originated from the girl's father, the same one who'd been banging on Pepper's door last night. If he was still a cop, he'd show the suspect a photo of Victory's dad so he could properly give an ID. "You were just supposed to grab her from the crowd today?"

The guy gave a half shrug.

"And then what?"

"Drop her off at an address."

"Did the guy tell you his name?"

The suspect shook his head. "I didn't know him."

Trace continued asking questions. Allen tuned out the conversation while his mind swam with worry over Pepper and Victory. Wanting to be there in his office right now. Were they okay?

Victory's dad should have hired someone more qualified rather than handing over cash to the first person he could find who was willing to kidnap a child for money. Then again, the fact he'd been unsuccessful in his attempt was a good thing.

Victory was safe.

She'd stay that way if Allen had anything to do with it.

The little girl had even seemed to blink her way out of the shock pretty quickly. Something he'd seen other victims do before. Since everyone dealt with trauma differently, it was hard to say what that meant. But he was glad she could bounce back. Kids were a lot more resilient than people gave them credit for.

On the other hand, Pepper had shown him several key markers of being in shock. She'd seemed worse off than Victory to him, likely out of fear and worry for her niece. There was no way he'd let her drive home—especially not with Victory in the car. Considering the attempts Victory's dad had made in order to see his child, there was no way Allen would leave them unprotected.

As much as he felt like part of the team in here with the others, doing the job he'd been forced to leave behind, he also wanted to be down the hall. With Pepper.

Here, he was respected. He had the skills it would take to get what they needed from this guy before they handed him over to the police—at which point he would lawyer up and no one would get any information from him. Allen knew what he was doing in this situation.

With Pepper, he was out of his depth. He had no idea where he stood.

His physical condition meant he'd likely be a hindrance—or no help at all—if they needed ongoing protection. Did she want him to try? He'd have to put aside the hurt she'd dished out with their breakup. And how everyone felt about her because he hadn't ever cleared up that misunderstanding. But saving a life was always worth it.

"That's up to the district attorney," Trace said.

The suspect lifted his chin. He was becoming belligerent. They weren't going to get much more information from him. "Then hand me over. I'll take my chances."

Allen frowned. "You should be more concerned about spending the rest of your life in prison rather than protecting this guy's privacy."

As far as he could figure, this was just a custody battle. Mom was absent, and Dad intended to play dirty to get the kid. Meanwhile, Pepper was caught in the middle, trying to do the right thing by a child.

She was still the same woman he'd dated. However, the depth he saw in her now was something he couldn't help but respect. She'd walked into the line of fire just to put herself between Victory and harm's way. He'd always hoped it was the kind of person she was—that she would be that person for their children one day.

Seeing it in action today—the risk—terrified him more than he wanted to admit.

Allen didn't want her to believe she was anything but safe. He wanted her to have the peace he'd tried to give her when they were together but never quite seemed to manage. Because there had been so much more going on below the surface.

Behind walls she had never taken down to let him in.

Now that he had a better glimpse of who she was, he had to admit—if only to himself—that she intrigued him more than she ever had before.

The question was, would she accept his help?

Their suspect bristled in his chair, reacting to the idea of being scared of anyone. Or so Allen figured. "Did you ever see his face?"

He shook his head. "It was all over text."

Trace had a phone in his hand. The suspect's cell? They would hand it over to the police along with the kidnapper to be admitted into evidence. The cops would follow up on leads gathered from the device. His call history, message history, and anything else.

The fact he would have no part of that investigation still caused a pang in his chest. How could it not? He'd been a cop for years. He'd loved that life. The way he loved questioning this guy right now.

The cops in the hall right now knew that. It was probably the only reason they weren't breaking the door in and hauling the suspect away.

Trace said, "How'd you get paid?"

"I got the money on that cash app."

"So how did you know it wasn't a scam?" Allen asked. "It could've been an undercover cop duping you into incriminating yourself."

He'd done it a number of times. The chief even had Allen call a guy in prison, telling him he'd heard the guy wanted to take a hit out on the person who testified against him. As an undercover officer, he'd pretended to be the type of guy who'd take money to end a life. A couple of phone calls later, they'd had enough evidence to press charges, and the guy got even more years added to his sentence.

Their witness had never even known she was potentially in danger.

Now Pepper and Victory were being targeted. He wasn't going to leave their future to chance. He would stand with them. The way Pepper had, putting herself in the path of a bullet. He would do that for them so they were both safe.

Whether he was a cop or not.

The suspect sniffed. "I run my business how I want."

Allen shifted in his chair. "Not anymore."

Bryce held the door for him. Allen ignored everyone and pushed out of the room, realizing it might be better this way. He wasn't confined to the same rules as a cop on duty.

Allen could do whatever it took.

"Hey." An officer stood halfway down the hall. His name-plate said *Ramble.*

Allen lifted his chin in reply to the uniformed cop and opened the door to his office.

Pepper sat on the chair in the corner, the one he only used to lay his coat on, her gaze unfocused while she clutched her purse on her lap. There was no other seating. Why hadn't he thought of that when he'd sent them in here?

Across the office, Victory dangled from a set of parallel bars he'd brought in for when he needed to stretch. The kid lowered herself until her arms were straight and she dangled from the bars, then let go to fall four inches.

Victory lay with her back flat on the mat underneath her. "Hi."

Allen smiled. "How do you ladies feel about ice cream?"

9

Two steps from her front door, Pepper stumbled. "What..."

Under her feet, wedged up against the front step, she now had a wood ramp going up to her door. She spun to where Allen pushed his wheelchair behind her, Victory asleep on his lap. Chocolate on her face.

The ice cream had been a good idea to distract the girl from what had happened, but Pepper couldn't get the incident out of her mind.

His hands stalled the wheels. "You had a ramp put in?"

"This wasn't here earlier." Pepper shuddered at the idea that someone had been to her house. "I need one of those doorbell cameras."

"Yes, you do." A guarded expression fell over his features. "Let's get inside."

She whirled around and let them in, placing her key on the entry table in the bowl she'd bought from a local artist.

Allen used the ramp to get inside, pushing himself easily into her house. If it wasn't for that, he wouldn't have been able to get in without both of them to get him over the step.

"It was put there for you."

Allen shut the door behind him. "My guess? Someone at the firehouse who is accustomed to overstepping swung by while we were getting ice cream."

"You didn't ask them to?"

He shook his head. Victory stirred on his lap.

Pepper stepped forward. "Let me get her in bed."

It was late, and the adrenaline and everything else today meant she was passed out. Pepper hadn't picked up Victory in years except in an exuberant hug. With the girl asleep, she had to grit her teeth and lift that deadweight to get Victory to the guest room.

Pepper slid the covers out from under her and took off Victory's shoes. She tucked her niece into bed and sat, brushing hair from her face. She let her fingers linger on the girl's cheek. "You're safe. I'm going to make sure you stay that way."

She wanted to promise that nothing would happen to her, but that might turn out to be untrue.

She could tell Victory that everything would be all right. That had never been the case in Pepper's life, though she managed to make a life anyway.

How did she break it to the girl that this was what people like them had to deal with? She didn't want that for Victory. She wanted her to be happy, the way she'd seemed to be, living here the past few weeks.

It was enough to make her want to try praying again. She wasn't like the people she saw walking into church on Sunday wearing their nice clothes. Bringing each other covered dishes. Eating at the diner after services, bowing their heads to thank God for their food.

It had made her wonder if that was the reason God felt so different. She went to church. She made time to read her Bible. So why didn't God work in her life to fix things the way he did with other Christians?

Pepper sniffed. "Help me keep her safe."

"Amen."

She whirled around and nearly fell off the bed. "Why are you eavesdropping?" She whispered the question to Allen while she eased the door closed without waking Victory. In her experience, even a tornado wouldn't wake the girl when she slept.

"Sorry. You were a minute, so I wanted to know if you were okay and if I should make coffee or something."

Pepper sighed. "I think I need—"

"Tea," he finished. "I already boiled your kettle."

He pushed his way to the open kitchen, dining, and living room. Thankfully there was enough room between the breakfast counter and the fridge he could get into the little square kitchen.

Since he was evidently planning on making the drinks, Pepper sat on a stool. He took two mugs from the mug tree on her counter, and she watched him the whole time. It was a total creeper thing to do, but she'd had an awful day and he was here. In her house. All strong and capable, two things she still loved about him.

How often had she been here alone, wishing she'd never let him go?

But the reason she'd broken off their relationship hadn't changed. So why would things be different now? As a matter of fact, since her family issues were more obvious than they'd ever been, those same reasons were arguably stronger.

"Can you carry the mugs?"

She jerked from her thoughts and saw his expression. He knew she'd been staring. Her cheeks flamed, so she tucked her chin and let her hair fall over her cheeks. "Living room?"

"Yeah, that sounds good."

She set the mugs on the coffee table. He stopped his chair by the couch and locked the wheels. Out of the corner of her eye, while she pretended she wasn't still watching, she saw Allen lay a hand on the edge of the coffee table. The other hand went to the arm of the couch. He braced his legs and moved his hips from the chair to the sofa. For a second in the middle, he put weight on his feet.

"You can stand a bit?"

He sank into the couch and let out a long breath. "Oh, that feels good."

"My couch?"

He chuckled.

She'd never thought it was anything special. "I got it for free. It was on the side of the road, and Brett was available to bring his truck. He and his other friend hauled it in for me."

"So it was already broken in."

She frowned. "I had it steam cleaned, if you're worried. They looked at the frame. It didn't have any broken springs. But I did have to patch the underside of one of the cushions." She glanced over and saw he'd closed his eyes. "You didn't answer my question."

"I don't have irreversible, complete paralysis. I have partial paralysis, and we're teaching my legs to remember what walking means." He leaned forward and grabbed his mug. "Right now, unassisted? I've got about six point five seconds of balance and then kablamo."

"Excuse me?"

"I can stretch my legs with the parallel bars in my office. I'm working on getting them stronger." He took a sip. "It's a process. I hope to stand for longer than I can right now eventually. But sometimes it's like...why wish for something that might never happen?"

The look on his face made her wonder if he was talking about more than just his injury. *I'm sorry* sat on the tip of her tongue long enough that she nearly said it. Pepper handed him his drink.

"Thanks." He took a sip. "Maybe it's just the long day and everything. Normally I'm a bit more upbeat."

"Well, I appreciate you distracting Victory. I'll need to talk to her about what happened, but she should get good sleep first."

"You're the one who protected her."

Pepper bit her lip. "Not well enough."

Story of her life, never measuring up.

"If you want me to help, I need you to tell me everything about her parents and all of what's going on."

Pepper winced. *If.* "Of course I want you..."

She swallowed the rest of the words because he might want her to refuse so he could leave and not feel bad about himself. Then she realized what she'd said.

"Uh...I didn't mean..."

He let out a little noise.

"Now you're laughing at me." She slumped back onto the couch and pulled her knees up. "But I already know I'm pathetic, so it's no surprise."

He tugged her arm so she had to turn to him. "You're the least pathetic person I've ever met."

"I doubt that's true." She pressed her lips together. "Besides, everyone who knows you hates me."

"I inspire loyalty."

She frowned.

"Am I wrong?"

"No."

He grinned. "I tried to be a loner for a long time. Live a quiet life in my cabin. Work a shift and go home to my horses. What's that saying? Introverts only have friends because an extrovert claimed them."

Laughter bubbled up in her chest. "I think you got claimed by the whole police department. Now it's the fire department too. I thought all the cops in town would egg my house when they found out we broke up."

Only because she knew they'd never do anything serious, like target her with citations. They were professionals. They were also deeply loyal to the people they cared about.

A label she'd been stripped of since she'd made the right decision—and the worst decision—and broken them up.

He chuckled around his mug.

Pepper sighed. "This is weird."

"And it's also not, at the same time."

She had to agree with that.

"It only took a near-kidnapping to get you to talk to me."

Pepper concentrated on her tea. She did *not* want to start crying in front of him. What a disaster that would be when she was supposed to be this strong, independent woman. She had a theory that all strong, independent women might secretly be as messed up as she was, and seriously, that was the only thing that kept her going most days.

"I wish I could pace the room right now."

It was more likely he'd walk out the door and not come back. The way he got in and out of that truck was a feat of ingenuity. But she knew he loved the thing—almost as much as Pepper loved his horses.

"Do you hate it?" She motioned to the chair.

"It's strange having feelings for an inanimate object. But sometimes, yeah. Or I hate that my legs don't work." He pushed out a long breath. "The motivation or the contentment comes and goes like waves. Most of the time I deal, but I figure I'm allowed to feel sorry for myself if I want to. It's my business."

"What happened wasn't your fault." He'd been trapped along with several other police officers. People who cared, who had stuck by him.

"I know it wasn't. Still, I get antsy. Sitting in that thing all day feels claustrophobic sometimes, and today was a long day."

A look came over his face, a spark of life. "Sometimes I leave the chair on my porch—which I can drive right up to if I want to—and I get in my truck, and I drive. Hit a drive-through. Take off for hours through the mountains. Pretend I'm like I used to be."

"I don't want to be anything like I was." And that was the core of it, wasn't it?

"Tell me."

If she did, it would mean being weak. Cracking who she was wide open and admitting she needed him more than he needed her.

He shifted on the seat. Itching to move again? "Or don't tell me."

She laid a hand on his arm and squeezed, then let go. "Sage is a disaster. Her life is a shambles. Victory misses more school than she attends, and they either have no money or Sage is flashing cash and going on vacation."

"Like leaving your niece with you this time." When she nodded, he said, "And the dad?"

"He was fired from the hospital for malpractice and went straight to rehab." Pepper held herself still until she knew how he would react to that. He'd been a cop. Maybe he didn't want people like Elijah Burns anywhere near his life.

"I assume there's more to that story."

"I try to stay as far away from him as possible." She shuddered.

He studied her. "Who they are doesn't reflect on you."

"They are who I am."

"I think you believe that, but I'm not sure I do."

"That's because I never let you see." Her cheeks burned. Sage and Elijah. That wasn't even the whole of it.

"But you could let me see, if you were willing to allow it."

"I have to focus on ensuring Victory survives this with her heart and sanity intact."

That was her only priority right now. Not resurrecting something she'd killed. The impossible wasn't true for her. It never had been. Pepper didn't have the power to make her dreams come true.

Allen said, "Maybe you could figure out how to do the same for yourself."

"I wish I knew how."

He started to speak, but someone banged on the door out front. Whoever it was pounded both hands from the sound of it.

Pepper choked back a gasp.

Before she could say anything, he returned to his chair. Allen reached into the backpack behind him and pulled out a gun.

"You stay here." He turned the chair around. "I'll get the door."

10

Allen rolled his chair over and positioned it so he could get the door open and cover Pepper at the same time. Just in case what was on the other side posed a threat to her. Given the way she'd reacted, he wasn't going to leave her to face whoever it was alone.

He had his gun, but even without it he was still the kind of man who stepped in—chair or not.

He also had his phone within reach just in case he needed to call his former colleagues and get some police backup.

He twisted the handle and swung the door past his chair, the gun out of sight for now. "Do you mind?"

The implication being this man was disturbing them. Which, considering Victory was asleep in her bed, was completely true.

However, it didn't turn the tables as he'd hoped.

The man on the other side of the doorstep shoved his way in, pushing Allen's chair back just a couple of inches. Caucasian. Maybe five-ten. Early fifties, maybe.

Allen spun to follow. "You do not have permission to enter this residence."

Pepper stood from the couch and backed away a couple of steps as the man closed in.

Allen moved near enough to grab the guy's arm so he didn't think he could put his hands on her. "Don't even think about it." He yanked the guy back a couple of steps.

He brushed off Allen with a wave of his arm and moved aside. Yeah, he shouldn't consider Allen inconsequential just because he was in the chair.

Allen held the gun, loose and ready. "Who are you?"

Nice clothes, but dirty and unkempt as though he'd been in the upmarket threads for a few days. His hair probably needed cutting a few weeks ago. Dark stubble covered his jaw. His coloring was the same as Victory's, in a way Allen didn't like the look of.

If it were up to him, Victory wouldn't have anything to do with this man. But then, people didn't get the chance to pick their parents.

Pepper swallowed, her gaze on the man. "Allen..."

If she was about to ask him to leave instead of this guy, she could forget it.

"Never mind, I can guess who this is," Allen said. "And I can have the police here in a couple of minutes to arrest him for attempted kidnapping."

The man whirled to face him. "You think I would send someone else to take my child? She must have been scared out of her mind."

Behind him, Pepper frowned.

"So you play the rescuer when you're the kidnapper?" That didn't sound much better than a hired man attempting to kidnap Victory from the Winter Carnival.

The guy scrubbed his fingers through his hair, giving Allen a full view under the hem of his shirt. No gun there in his belt.

He also didn't seem concerned by the fact Allen visibly held his.

"That's why I came here." The man lowered his arms, pleading with Pepper. "Please tell me she's okay."

Pepper folded her arms. She stood straight, holding herself together. Determined to appear confident. "I can't do that because I don't know if she is. But she's physically unharmed, and she's sleeping. Given everything she's been through in her life, this might be a small drop in the bucket. But she was feeling safe, and today caught her off guard."

The guy pushed out a shuddering breath.

Allen said, "I'm going to need your name."

He thumbed in Allen's direction and asked Pepper, "Who is this guy?"

"My guest." She lifted her chin. "As opposed to the person who barged in here demanding attention." She looked at Allen. "This is *Doctor* Elijah Burns. Victory's father." Something shifted in her expression. "*Elijah*, this is Allen Frees."

"Okay." Burns shrugged.

Allen pulled his phone out and used his thumb to enter the name in a text that would go to Lieutenant Donaldson at the police department. He didn't like bugging family guys after hours, but Aiden could pass the info to whoever was on call. Or if he was on duty tonight, he'd look up Burns right now.

Allen stowed his phone. "Mr. Burns—"

"It's *Doctor* Burns."

Pepper bit her lip.

"We're not in your office. We're in a private residence." Allen wasn't going to argue much, but he wasn't showing respect to a guy who'd shoved his way in. "Speaking of, why don't you tell us how you knew about what happened with Victory today? Who might have reason to try and kidnap her if it wasn't you?"

The would-be kidnapper had been paid—they assumed by this man.

Burns's expression shifted. "You think I'm gonna tell you?"

Allen lifted his gun in case Burns got the idea of being combative. "Yes, I do."

It wasn't a threat like pointing the weapon at him would have been, but Burns understood. Which meant he'd been threatened enough to know how the process worked.

"Talk."

Burns's jaw shifted. "It wasn't me."

"Good," Allen said. "I'm glad to hear that, but why is she even in danger? She's not part of anything, and yet someone paid a guy to try and kidnap her. It doesn't make sense. Unless you know who might see Victory as leverage." He figured this guy got in over his head and owed someone money. "They threaten you?"

Burns shot him a hard look. "You know nothing about me."

"So enlighten me."

Pepper hadn't. They'd dated for months, and she never even told him she had a sister or a niece. She'd gone on vacation once, for a couple of weeks. He'd just figured she needed quiet space, and he'd worked a bunch of double shifts while she was incommunicado.

Was she a part of whatever this was?

Given her nervousness right now, he wasn't sure. She could just not like that she was being found out. Or she was genuinely scared of this guy. Scared for Victory.

He didn't like doubting her, but she had lied to him. She hadn't trusted him enough to let him into her life.

Because he'd been a cop? He was the same guy now, just without the badge.

"I just want to see her." Burns turned back to Pepper. "With my own eyes, so I know she's okay."

"It's up to a judge if you're allowed to see Victory. Not me."

Not her sister?

Was Burns aware Sage was currently AWOL? "Have you tried calling Victory's mother and asking her?"

"She's been gone for *days*." Burns frowned. "If I could ask her, I would. But Victory is here, so why would I need to talk to Sage?"

That answered that question. "Do you know where she is? Pepper has been trying to contact her."

Burns didn't seem to care. He looked at Pepper. "Your guess is as good as mine."

Allen didn't buy that he had no idea what was going on. "What guess would that be? Because from where I'm sitting, she might've been kidnapped like someone tried to do with Victory today."

Burns snorted.

Allen said, "Could she be behind the attempt? Sage might want Victory with her and believes that's the only way to get her back."

Pepper gasped. "Why would she do that?"

Allen shrugged. "Could be a lot of reasons. Any ideas, Burns?"

"Like I'm supposed to know?" Victory's father made a face.

Pepper squared her shoulders. "Maybe you should get a clue, Elijah. I've already filed a report that Sage is missing. What will you do when the police ask if you've seen her? Are you going to lie to them the way you lie to everyone? Manipulate people into thinking you're such an upstanding chief of surgery while on the side you're cheating. Making drugs. Getting in with dangerous people. Dragging everyone down with you."

Allen sighed outwardly. Inside, he wanted to clap.

Pepper had just given him a giant slice of the information he needed on what was happening here. He pinned Burns with a stare like he'd known all that and blamed the guy for this upset. "Who tried to take your daughter?"

"You don't wanna know."

"Try me."

Burns didn't. Instead, his expression shifted to one that meant the conversation was over.

Allen had seen it with suspects enough to know they were done talking. The doctor wasn't going to give them any information unless he thought it would gain him something, and Allen had nothing to make a deal with. He certainly wasn't bargaining for Victory's time. Not until Pepper told him a whole lot more about this situation.

"If you're not gonna let me see her, I'm out of here." He huffed over to the door and lifted Victory's coat from the wall, but not enough to unhook it. Burns put the material to his face. "I just miss her, you know?"

"Elijah." Pepper sighed.

Allen wheeled over and opened the door for him. "Good to meet you."

Burns dropped the coat back, like he'd come to his senses. "Whatever." He swept out the door and stomped to a silver BMW parked with one tire bumped up on the curb.

Allen watched him because he needed to see the guy pull away. He wasn't going to risk Burns doubling back to attempt the same crime that had almost been committed earlier. A desperate father would absolutely try and break through her bedroom window and carry her out.

Victory might even be pleased to see him.

Except Allen got the feeling this was a whole lot more complicated than the two of them and their love for each other. A lot of domestic situations were. And as with those, he needed all the information. It still wouldn't be his call to make. That was down to the family court, as Pepper had said.

Meanwhile, she spent every day keeping Victory safe, providing the girl with a stable environment where she could be loved and happy.

The engine hesitated but turned over. The guy needed to

take it to a mechanic, considering the smoke that chugged out the back as he drove away.

Allen shut the door.

Pepper had let him in the last couple of days. He might be frustrated with the lack of information, but she had offered up a considerable amount. Not because she couldn't handle what was happening. Rather, it seemed like she wanted him to know.

Was she willing to trust him the way she hadn't before?

The question was why.

"I need to check on Victory and make sure she didn't wake up."

Allen nodded, watching her go but trying not to be weird about it. She held herself together in a way he was proud of—if she was only a victim in this.

While she was out of the room, he requested regular patrol car drive-bys of her house tonight.

He carried a lot of weight with the police department, having been one of them for years. He didn't like it, but it was what it was. He didn't ask favors too much, making the cops in town indebted to him.

They didn't need to carry guilt.

But the fact was, if Allen called and said Victory should be taken from Pepper for her safety, they would report it to Child Protective Services without hesitation.

Allen pulled up his contacts and found the familiar number. He sent his cousin Natalie a text.

If anyone could help them, it was her.

11

It had already been a long day by the time Pepper turned onto the lane that led up to Allen's cabin. Victory had fallen asleep in the back after spending most of the afternoon designing adoption posters for the cats using a program on the vet's computer. Her boss hadn't minded at all that she'd totally taken over his office.

Brett was wonderful like that. Like another wonderful guy she knew. One who stood with her and supported her. Looked at her with those blue eyes of his.

She pulled over just before his cabin so her car didn't block the lane.

Pepper just needed a minute. Not only to think about how Last Chance County seemed to have a disproportionate number of good men living in town. Sure, there were some bad seeds. They had crime just like everywhere. But wherever she looked there was a good person trying to do good in the world.

Most of them were familiar faces from the church she'd attended when she first moved to town years ago. People who lived lives of integrity and service to others as an outpouring of their beliefs.

The same way she'd tried to do. Until lately.

She was so busy working and taking care of Victory she barely had the energy to pay attention in church. Besides, it wasn't like going had changed her. She couldn't get rid of the stain of her past no matter how hard she tried to live "clean" instead.

Strong fingers tapped the window.

She glanced over, unsurprised Allen had managed to get to her car without her noticing.

He pulled up the handle and eased her door open. The wheelchair he sat in tonight had thicker tires with more pronounced tread. Two handles stretched up from the sides at a forty-five. When he moved the chair back, he pumped the two handles.

"Like it?"

Pepper twisted in her seat and set her feet on the ground but didn't get up. "It goes on the dirt?"

He nodded and grinned. "All-terrain."

"So you can go anywhere?"

"Within reason."

She stared at him. "Is there anything you can't overcome?"

He stared right back. "It might seem that way most of the time, but there were some dark days. Not right away, but it settled in. I had to beat back the despair and frustration on more than one occasion—usually with a heavy bag in the gym. There are still some nights I don't sleep."

Pepper knew sleepless nights like an old friend.

"I like that you think that about me, though."

Before she could respond, Victory cried out from the back seat. "Mama, don't go!"

Pepper spun back around and leaned over the center console. She stretched her arm into the back and squeezed Victory's knee. Then held her hand. "Hey, wake up, Nugget."

The girl blinked, her gaze cloudy with sleep. "Mama?"

"Just me, Nugget."

The back door opened. "Hey, Victory." Allen leaned in and set his forearms on the seat next to her, hands out. "Want to go see my horses?"

Pepper nearly rolled her eyes but caught herself. What eight-year-old didn't want to see horses?

Victory scrambled out of the seat, realized she was buckled in, and jabbed the button to release her seatbelt. "Let's go!"

Allen chuckled. Victory bounced out of the car. He pumped the handles on his chair and led her across the dirt and grass between the cabin and his barn. Both horses stood in the pasture beside the barn.

Pepper tried to muster the energy to go with them. She managed to stand but realized her purse was in the footwell on the passenger side. She retrieved her keys and decided she didn't even care about her phone.

Everything she cared about was right here.

She strolled after them. Halfway across the front yard of Allen's eight-acre spread, another car crested the lane and rolled in front of the house. A huge black SUV that probably had three rows. Pepper froze. FBI? Oh, never mind. She knew that vehicle.

The SUV came close enough she saw the two people in the front seats. Tate Hudson, the local private investigator, and his wife, LCC PD Detective Savannah Wilcox. She'd tried changing her name to Hudson at work, but the cops all still just called her "Wilcox," so eventually she'd given up.

The doors opened. Their kids poured out of the back and ran over to the pasture. Savannah watched them, a wide smile on her face—even though she also looked tired. Pepper knew how that felt but had no idea how Savannah survived four kids between Victory's age and fourteen.

Originally they'd adopted the younger three after their mother went to jail for armed robbery. The oldest was a half sibling. They'd also been given custody of him a few months after the younger ones came to live with them, when his mother was picked up for solicitation. The father had been murdered several years ago, and the kids lived together for years.

Now Tate and Savannah had all four kids for good.

"Don't run, Marcus! Be careful, Clara!" Savannah jogged after the kids, catching up enough to tickle one and race another on their way to the fence. Victory spotted the youngest—her friend from Sunday school—and they hugged each other.

"Figured she might want a friend, and Savannah will stay with the kids while we talk."

Pepper spun to find Tate watching her. The PI was older than Allen, late into his forties.

"When Allen is out of town visiting his brother, he has us come over and take care of his horses every day. The kids all know how to put them up for the night."

Pepper swallowed enough that she could speak. "Thanks."

Tate glanced over her shoulder. "I'll head in and make the coffee."

Allen eased up behind her. "Everything okay?"

She nodded. "Tate showed up the other day at work. I gave him information on Sage, but he hasn't told me if he found anything."

"Let's go see." He motioned with his head, and she walked beside him to the house, where he used a ramp up the porch steps to navigate to the front door. The steps were wide enough for six people to walk side to side. Pepper stayed close to the ramp so she could be near him.

The front door stood open. Inside, by his boots, were a pair of forearm crutches.

Pepper twisted around. Before she could ask, he said, "Goals."

"That's great." He'd told her about PT, and she'd seen the bars in his office.

Allen shrugged. "Right now they're more effort than they're worth, and it's pretty exhausting." He shot her a half smile. "Come summer, who knows?"

Pepper peeked outside once more to ensure the kids were all right. Victory rode on the oldest boy's shoulders while the others helped lead the horses into the barn.

"They'll brush them, feed and water them. Give them too many apples, and come out smelling like the barn."

"I shouldn't hover."

"I'm not going to tell you how to take care of her." Allen shrugged one shoulder. "I don't know how to raise kids. She's good with the Hudson kids, right?" When Pepper nodded, he said, "I wanted my cousin Natalie to come over. She works at Dean's place—the Ridgeman Therapy Center."

"Right." He'd talked about his cousin before. She'd lived with his family while her father was hospitalized.

Allen nodded. "She moved here a few weeks ago after she got out of the Army—was a counselor in the military. Now she helps Dean work with trauma victims and vets with PTSD. But she's settling in still, and she has clients tonight."

"It's great she's close by."

"Yes, it is. I can find out what's going on." Allen maneuvered his chair down the hall to the thick cherrywood table.

It had no chairs until Tate unstacked two from against the wall and set one beside Allen for her.

"Thank you."

He put coffee in front of her and sat opposite them.

"This seems serious." Pepper glanced between the men. "Did something happen?"

Allen's expression blanked. Something she'd never liked on him. "Elijah Burns?"

"Ah." Pepper fingered the handle of her mug.

"We dug into his background." Tate pulled out a notepad and flicked to a page of scribbled notes. "He's Victory's father?"

Pepper nodded. "My sister met him on a cruise."

Tate wrote that down.

"Is it relevant?"

He shrugged. "We don't know what is and isn't at this point."

"That's why we're here." Allen rubbed his hand between her shoulder blades for a second. "To run down what we do know. Like, Elijah doesn't know where Sage is, right? What he does know is who might want Victory for leverage against him. Maybe they already have Sage."

Or she was behind all this.

Pepper winced. They had no idea about Sage. She clenched her stomach and forced the words out. "Two days after Victory was born, Sage left her with me and went to Mexico for a month to stay at a wellness retreat."

Tate frowned.

She didn't want to see the look on Allen's face.

"Okay." Tate made another notation.

"If I told you all of it, we'd be here for a week."

Allen said, "I'd rather be in Mexico." He rubbed her back again. "We can take Victory. Go hang out on the beach."

She twisted to look at him then, unable to believe he would consider that after how she'd ended their relationship.

Allen said, "Tate gets it."

The PI snorted. "Yes, I do."

"Maybe one of you should explain, because I don't." He actually wanted to go on vacation right now, like they were a *family*? She felt like she was losing her mind. Nothing that was happening right now made any sense.

He did the back rub thing again. He should just leave his hand there. It felt nice.

Tate flipped a page. "I have a friend who got me access to

Sage's phone records. I have her texts and call history, but it will take time to go through it and find out if there's anything there that can tell us where she is right now. Or what she's been up to recently." He paused. "Savannah is going to help me tonight."

"Let me know if you need extra eyes," Allen said.

Tate nodded. "Will do." He looked at Pepper. "What we know is that Sage is active. Wherever she is, she's alive and well."

"It couldn't be someone else using her phone?" Something in her wanted this to be the answer. Even as it scared her. "I don't like thinking she's behind this."

"We can probably rule out her being too hurt to communicate. Or that she's been kidnapped. The last few messages don't corroborate either of those."

This was unbelievable. "So she's off living the high life and I'm stuck here with Victory?"

"You don't want me?"

Pepper jerked around to the doorway. Victory stood with the Hudson kids, Savannah behind them.

The little girl's lip quivered.

"Nugget, that's not what I meant."

The oldest boy put his hand on Victory's shoulder, a stern look on his face directed at Pepper.

She tried to explain. "I'm just upset Mommy isn't here."

"I don't want Mommy here!" Victory whirled around and disappeared down the hall.

Pepper's eyes filled with tears.

"Kids—"

She shook her head at whatever Tate was about to say and pushed her chair back. Nothing could make her feel better. Not when she'd broken a little girl's heart.

The way she seemed to break everyone's.

12

Allen twisted the lid on his hot cup and secured it closed.

"That's too much garlic salt." Eddie, a member of the FD's rescue squad, peered over Zack's shoulder in the firehouse kitchen.

The youngest and newest member of Truck 14 shrugged his shoulder closest to Eddie. "Then don't eat any."

Allen glanced over his shoulder at where they stood together by the stove. Arguing like they seemed to always do. "Maybe you guys should take this to the engine bay and do some training."

"After breakfast." Eddie pulled down the parsley. "Add this in."

Zack shook his head. "Give me the cotija cheese first."

Eddie headed for the huge fridge where third shift kept their supplies. "And the bacon bits."

"You want bacon?" Zack said. "Then crack your own eggs. It's not going in mine."

Across the common room, Ridge lifted his coffee cup. "Hear, hear. And I want salsa on mine."

Eddie made a face. "Salsa? That doesn't go with bacon and barbecue sauce."

Zack's jaw flexed, but he said nothing. Though, it wasn't from attempting to de-escalate this situation. Probably more like formulating a response while he whipped eggs in the bowl.

The speaker, mounted high on the wall, crackled to life with the sound of the alarm. Everyone in the room froze.

"Ambulance 21, possible overdose." The dispatcher read off the address.

Trace and Izan weren't in here, so no one got up. Wherever they were in the house—since dispatch knew their location—they'd jump up and respond.

Everyone else went back to what they were doing—watching TV, trying to cook breakfast, or meddling in someone else's cooking.

Allen leaned the hot cup of coffee against his hip and wheeled out of the tense kitchen. He would rather pick his battles than micromanage guys who were supposed to be adults.

Out in the hall, he watched Trace and Izan sprint through the engine bay to their bus. Seconds later, Ambulance 21 headed out from the garage on the other side of the building.

Allen rotated the chair around and saw the police chief—his former boss—walk in the front door.

"Hey." Conroy lifted two fingers. The guy looked exhausted enough that Allen almost chuckled.

"Coffee?"

Conroy shook his head. "I've already had too much."

Allen tipped his head to the side. "There's such a thing as too much?"

Conroy grinned. He glanced at the receptionist, already behind her desk even though she didn't start for the day until eight. "Good morning, Meredith."

"Good morning, Chief."

Allen wheeled the rest of the way over to them.

Meredith's eyes crinkled along permanent lines. "I have some files for you from headquarters, sir."

As often as Allen had told her not to call him sir, she still did. He wasn't officially part of the fire hierarchy, just a liaison between City Hall and their department. However, the fact it denoted respect wasn't something he took for granted.

"Thank you, Meredith. I'll be back to pick them up after I speak with Conroy."

"Very well." She went back to her computer.

Conroy followed him down the hall to his office and headed for the window, settling on the edge of the window ledge like he needed to take a load off. "Is it really true?"

"Is what true?" Allen set the coffee cup on his desk.

"This firehouse has an elevator."

Allen didn't think that was why Conroy had come to see him. "They used to have cookouts on the roof all the time. And ignore the alarm while they were up there, although that was probably for the best considering they used to haul coolers of beer up there and drink on shift."

Maybe not for the best exactly, considering every time the alarm went off meant someone's life was potentially in danger. However, responding while intoxicated created a whole different set of issues.

Thankfully, everyone who now worked for the fire department was either new, or they'd been a black sheep in the department under the old leadership. Anyone the former chief considered a bad egg was someone Allen had purposely made sure the department held onto.

Conroy winced. "I heard about everything that's happening with Pepper." He took a breath. "Are you sure you want to fall back into that and get involved?"

How the police chief had heard about it didn't matter.

"Especially after what she did." Conroy motioned to Allen's wheelchair.

The chief knew she had nothing to do with the incident that had paralyzed Allen. However, there was something Allen did need to clear up.

"This has gone on way too long." He scrubbed his hands down his face. "Chalk it up to me being hurt and then *getting hurt*." He wasn't making any sense. "I should have told everyone. Then it was too late. Now it's even later. She didn't break up with me because I got hurt. She broke up with me earlier that day. *Before* the explosion."

Conroy frowned as though that was the craziest thing he'd ever heard. "Why would she do that?"

"Good question." One Allen was beginning to figure out. Though he was nowhere near having an answer.

Conroy said, "Don't let her get her hooks in you again. She's already burned you once."

"I'll admit it didn't feel too good when she dumped me. But a lot has changed for us in the last couple of years." He, for one, was a lot different than he'd been. How could he not have been changed?

Conroy frowned.

"That's not really why you came here, is it?"

Conroy might be his former boss and his friend, but just like with anyone who might care about Allen, they weren't the ones who had to live his life. Conroy didn't know Pepper. No one did.

Allen was getting the picture. He hadn't even scratched the surface while they were dating. The story she'd told about her sister dropping off Victory days after she was born. Saddling Pepper with a newborn for a month? It was almost unbelievable.

What had happened last night with Victory had wrecked her.

After the kids and Savannah had calmed her niece down and got her to talk to Pepper, everyone had gone home. He'd waited until Victory was likely in bed, then called to see if she and Pepper were okay. If Pepper had managed to settle Victory into resting and the little girl wasn't too heartbroken over the misunderstanding. He'd left a message, and she hadn't called back. Neither had she replied to any of his texts this morning.

In the middle of the night, when he couldn't sleep, he'd called the police department dispatcher directly. A uniformed officer had confirmed all was well at Pepper's house.

The fact that he'd used police resources for his own agenda could be why Conroy was here.

Then again, Allen was pretty sure the police chief wouldn't blame him for giving an officer something to do in the middle of the night—especially when there was a possibility Pepper and Victory could have been targeted again.

No one would fault him for trying to prevent a crime or intervening and potentially saving a life.

Conroy pulled his phone from the inside of his suit jacket. "Can I get copies of all your paramedic reports from the last few weeks? Every incident they responded to where the report lists an overdose."

Allen nodded. "It does seem like there's been an epidemic recently."

Conroy said, "For the time being, what do you think about having a uniformed officer respond along with the EMTs? That way we may be able to get a lead and find out who the dealer is. Too many people are dying."

"You think there's a bad batch of something out there?" Allen didn't have to clean up the mess people made when they broke the law with no regard for the effect it had on other people.

Conroy said, "I think there's a dealer in town who bought a

supply of something cut with whatever is causing people to react. We've had three deaths so far."

"Not good news for whoever sold it to them if they're ruining the business." It might sound callous, but criminals didn't often consider the people they hurt. Only their bottom line.

"We've had an uptick in violent crime as well. I think whoever bought it is out for blood. They want the person that sold it to them *and* their money back."

Allen winced. "That's not good for anyone. Least of all people caught in the middle when these guys get into a war."

"I'll coordinate with the dispatcher if you'll sign off on having a cop at every paramedic callout listed as an overdose."

Allen said, "Good idea."

One had gone out not too long ago, but more personnel on scene from now on would help the police find whoever was behind this. The victims and whoever might be with them could potentially tell the police who'd sold them the drugs.

"Okay." Conroy tapped his phone against his leg and stood. "I'll get—"

Out in the hall, something crashed.

Conroy hauled the door open and strode out, Allen right behind him.

He didn't like not knowing what they were walking into. Conroy would see. At least it got him out of his friend trying again to convince him that Pepper was bad news. Sometimes it seemed like married people just plain forgot what it was like to be single.

A plate of food flew out of the kitchen and hit the wall. Scrambled egg and shards of plate fell to the floor.

From the kitchen, someone yelled, "Dude! That was Bryce's breakfast you just tossed."

"Then keep your nose out of my eggs!"

Conroy stopped at the doorway to the common room, blocking the view.

Allen patted his arm until he got out of the way, then wheeled around him. "Somebody tell me what's going on in here."

Eddie and Zack stood nose-to-nose, both of their faces pinched in frustration. Mickey, the firefighter Allen knew least, sat on the couch drinking coffee, his attention on the TV as though nothing happening behind him was more interesting than his show.

Ridge stood behind Zack. Jayce, one of the rescue squad firefighters, was right by Eddie. The four of them were in a standoff.

Two had ketchup on their clothes, and someone had sprayed mustard on the wall.

"Talk," Allen ordered. "Or I call in Amelia and Bryce from the gym, and you guys will be doing drills the rest of the morn—"

The speaker on the wall erupted. "Rescue 5. Truck 14. Multiple car collision, possible victim trapped."

The ketchup bottle hit the floor. Mickey set his coffee down, the program forgotten. All of them jogged from the room wearing almost identical determined expressions. Although, Allen did see Ridge give Zack a brotherly slap on the back of the head.

Conroy turned to him. "And here I thought *my* job involved babysitting. These guys are on another level."

Allen blew out a long breath. "If you saw them at a scene, you'd hardly know they can't even make breakfast without an issue. They're great firefighters."

"But when they're not fighting fires, they turn back into elementary kids left unattended?"

"Something like that."

Conroy chuckled. He patted Allen on the shoulder on his way past. "Good luck with that."

Allen stared at the doors to the engine bay and watched them pull out, lights and sirens going.

When a civilian was in trouble? All that conflict went out the window and they were about saving people.

Allen wheeled back over to Meredith. "You had something for me?"

She handed him a stack of files. "Headquarters sent over these for your consideration on the next chief."

Great. "Anyone in there you think would be good?"

She blinked.

"Don't tell me you didn't take a peek." Allen grinned.

"Well..."

"And?" Allen honestly wanted her input. He had no idea what to do with this firehouse. After years of being led by a corrupt chief, then being left to their own devices by the interim, they were in a unique spot.

Allen knew they saw him as a leader. However, since he wasn't a sworn-in firefighter, he couldn't take the position. They needed someone who could go out to scenes with them and get them all working together.

Meredith said, "Whoever you hire as the next chief? I doubt you'll find him in this pile."

"Agreed." Allen nodded. "They don't need status quo. And I don't know how it works in other firehouses, but this one is special. They need a chief they can respect. One who will turn this house into a family, not the dysfunctional mess they are right now."

Meredith said, "I'll put that in as my prayer request at Bible study tonight."

"I appreciate that," Allen said. "I'll do the same on Saturday morning at the first responders' prayer breakfast."

He figured he should do the same over his relationship with

Pepper. Then again, there were currently other things that needed his attention before the issue of what may or may not still be there between them.

His dad had used to say, when tasks piled up and things got overwhelming, *One thing at a time.*

One step at a time.

13

Pepper had worked half a shift to cover for the vet tech who hadn't shown up. The one who had apparently been fired, but the lack of gossip in their office meant no one had let Pepper know. Plus, there had been some things happening in her personal life.

The sun had dropped below the mountains, still casting the evening sky in an orange glow with hints of pink as she drove home. Beautiful enough, though the night at Allen's yesterday had been far more spectacular. In the middle of nowhere at his cabin. Up above the town, though not far from amenities.

What are you, a realtor?

Pepper let her breath out in a *pfft* sound. She might have dreamed of living there with him one day, but that wasn't an option now.

No matter how much time they spent together, nothing could erase how he would feel about her when he learned where she'd come from. Who she was.

Her phone buzzed in the cupholder. At the next red light, she checked the screen and saw a text from Tate.

TATE

She's doing fine. It's still up to you if she
sleeps over or not.

Before "the incident" last night—that was how Pepper had
decided to think about it—Victory had already talked to the
Hudsons about spending today at their house while Pepper was
at work. Victory had agreed to go home with her—even if technically she'd had no choice because Pepper was still her
guardian—because they kept this standing play date.

She pulled into a space at the grocery store and sent a text
back.

PEPPER

If she's happy, it's okay with me.

Pepper sighed. *Dinner for one.*

That was nothing new, and she'd been waiting for a night
alone with Victory being taken care of. Now it was actually
happening, she wasn't sure she liked the prospect.

She didn't need all the bad-for-her things she would buy in
the store. Pepper shored up her resolve and pulled out of the
space so she could head home, where she had plenty of food
that would be perfectly fine for just her.

She'd eaten buttered toast and baked beans so many times
as a kid. Sage hated the meal now, but for Pepper there was
something reassuring about the taste—and the carbs. Nearly
everyone she knew spent their free evenings at Backdraft Bar
and Grill. When she'd been dating Allen, they'd hung out there
a lot.

The thought of him made her want to call and see if he was
doing something this evening.

She tapped her index finger on the steering wheel. Maybe
he wanted to come over for dinner. He'd called and texted

today, but by the time she saw the missed notifications, they had been elbow-deep in a litter of German shepherds.

Pepper parked in her drive and got her backpack. *Just call him.* She headed up the front walk, juggling her cell phone as she retrieved her keys from the front pocket.

The door stood open.

Pepper eased it all the way until it hit the door stopper on the wall. She might've forgotten to shut it in the rush of getting Victory out the door earlier. Had she? She wasn't usually that lax with security, but things were far from normal right now.

She dropped her backpack in the hall.

Two arms banded around her from behind. Her phone and keys clattered to the floor. One hand snaked up to cover her mouth. She gasped the second the hand found her lips, but didn't get any air in.

Her feet left the floor.

The guy holding her shifted and the door slammed. "Cut it out."

She bit his hand.

He cried out, jostled her, and got his hand away from her mouth.

Pepper sucked in a breath.

He swung her to the side and knocked her head against the wall. Pepper cried out but didn't lose consciousness. *Lord, help me.*

She hadn't talked much to Him lately, but God knew she needed help now. He knew what would happen next.

If she was going to live through this.

The man carried her in front of him through her house, all the way to the kitchen. Another guy joined them. Her assailant tossed her on the floor by the pantry door.

Pepper scooted until her back hit the pantry door, as far away from the two men as she could get. "What do you want?"

Her head hurt like someone had "rung her bell." Her mom had used the expression to describe what their dad had done to her on a regular basis.

The two men wore jeans and boots. One had a sweater under his jacket, the other just a T-shirt. Dark hair and eyes that had seen things she didn't want to know about.

One sneered. "I should've tossed you harder."

The other didn't react to his friend's comment. "Burns came to see you last night. What'd he give you?"

Pepper touched her forehead. This was about *Elijah*? Never mind, of course it was. "Tell me where my sister is, and I'll tell you."

He squinted. "You might think you're smart. That's because you don't know us. But you'll learn real quick we don't bargain."

"What did he give you?"

Pepper swallowed. She silently thanked God Victory wasn't here. Relief flooded her with the thought, and she doubled down on her gratitude. Peace settled in because it didn't matter what happened to her if her niece was safe.

She forced a breath out slowly and tried to stay calm so she didn't panic. "He didn't give me anything."

One of the men huffed. "I'll keep looking."

He trailed away.

"I'm telling the truth."

The other man leaned against the end of the counter like he had all the time in the world. "We'll see."

"I'm not part of this." *Neither is Victory.* She wanted to tell him that but held her tongue. There was a tiny chance he didn't know Sage and Elijah had a daughter.

His eyebrows lifted, but he said nothing. His answer wasn't about to change. The guy moved away from her, turned, and watched down the hall. "Anything?"

Her phone lay in the hall where she'd dropped it. Pepper

didn't want to know what they'd do when they realized she didn't have squat to give them and knew nothing about Elijah or Sage and what they got up to.

Though she could imagine plenty.

She couldn't call someone for help. Couldn't get out of the house. What could she do?

Pepper looked around for a way to get someone's attention outside. She had smoke alarms. Her neighbors on both sides were families. They might hear and come looking to see if she was all right.

The towel hung on the oven door handle.

She could ignite it with the flame burner on the stove. Would he put it out before Pepper could draw someone's attention?

The man wandered away down the hall, not far enough to give her a clear shot at the front door.

She had another idea, but it was far more desperate. She could wind up killing herself like the old lady two trailers down from them the summer she turned eleven. The whole trailer had exploded.

She looked again at the man and watched while he stretched his arms above his head. The jacket lifted to reveal a handgun tucked in the back of his waistband.

Pepper shuddered.

She reached up and turned on one of the stove burners, coughing loudly the second the clicking noise told her it ignited.

Matches sat in the drawer beside the oven along with one of those igniters Allen used on his grill.

Was she really going to do this?

Pepper slid the drawer open, but he turned around for a second, just a glance. She froze. He didn't notice the lit burner. If he saw what she was doing, he would thwart her—smother any flames.

He took a couple of steps down the hall, then stopped.

Pepper levered herself up to her feet. The jar of bacon grease she kept beside the stove for cooking was almost full. She unscrewed the lid and set the end over the burner, keeping her fingers away from the flames. It didn't lie perfectly on its side. It would have to do though.

She needed help.

Towels. Paper towels. She loaded them around the jar, hoping something would light. She turned the other burners so they let out gas but didn't catch fire right away.

When she was done, Pepper squared her shoulders and headed after him. This had to be good or he would suspect— before he smelled bacon cooking. Before the grease ignited and she destroyed half her kitchen. *Lord, I don't want anyone to get hurt.*

He spun around.

Pepper made sure her body covered the stovetop and prayed he didn't see. She even shoved at him. "You can't go through my things. It's not right!"

He grabbed her arm and dragged her down the hall.

Thank You. "I don't know anything."

"Whatever he told you, whatever he gave you, you tell me now or this gets ugly."

It was definitely about to get ugly. "Just get out of my house!" she screamed. "Get out! Get out!"

He cuffed her across the face with the back of his hand.

Pepper's body spun. She cried out, letting all the pain escape her lips as loud as she could manage. She slammed the wall and started to crumble.

He hauled her up and pressed his body against hers. The faint smell of bacon drifted down the hall, but he didn't notice. He pulled the gun from his waistband and pressed it against the underside of her chin. "What did he give you?"

Pepper sucked in a breath. Her face throbbed. "He didn't give me anything."

"Where is he?"

The second man stepped into view behind him. She had no leverage, and she couldn't prevent anything they wanted to do. Unless the fire got them to leave—or drew attention from a neighbor.

She gasped. "I have no idea."

The man behind him muttered, "She's lying."

His hold gave her no room to move. His fingers pinched her arm so hard tears gathered in her eyes. "You're watching his kid. Of course you know where to find him."

Smoke drifted down the hall, laced with bacon. The grease had reached the smoking point. She could only pray the flame ignited what was in the jar.

He squeezed her arm harder, hauled her away from the wall, and dragged her to the bedroom.

"I don't know where he is." She spoke through gritted teeth while the tears fell down her cheeks. She couldn't give up. Not now.

"I guess we'll find out."

Pepper recoiled. "I don't know where he is. Or Sage. I have no idea."

The guy behind chuckled. Pepper had no clue what was amusing.

A whoosh erupted in the kitchen, then an explosion. The smoke alarm started, the one above the dining table. A second later, the one by the front door began to chime.

Her ears rang. Flames flickered in the hall to her left.

He pressed the gun deeper into the underside of her jaw. "You know where he is."

She tried to shake her head, but there was no room to move, her inhale nothing but a gasp. "I don't."

"We gotta go, Jack." The guy behind patted his shoulder. "We'll get burned alive if we stay."

Both of them eyed the smoke in the hall.

He pulled the gun from her throat. His arm swung down, and he slammed it into her head.

Pain exploded.

And then nothing.

14

A llen slammed the car door and grabbed his wheels. He pushed to the spot where Truck 14 had parked in front of Pepper's house. It had been minutes since dispatch called out a residential fire at her address.

He swallowed down bile and surveyed the chaos around him.

Flames licked up from the kitchen side of the house. Her car sat in the driveway, which meant both Pepper and Victory were somewhere inside.

Amelia stood at the front of the truck, hands on her hips. The three members of her team raced to gather equipment. She clapped her hands. "Let's go."

He rolled up beside her. "What information do we have so far?"

Amelia tugged the radio off her belt. "None." She tossed it to him, so Allen had to let go of his wheels and catch it. "You're the scene commander." She gave him a knowing look. "Stay here."

Allen clenched his teeth together. It wouldn't matter if he objected. Amelia jogged away to help Mickey with the hose.

Zack and Ridge ran to the house carrying Halligans. They would need them if the front door was locked.

"Foster," Amelia called out. "Get me a sitrep on the back of the house. We might need foam."

Ridge raced for the side gate.

Zack broke the front door lock with his tool and stood to the side for a second. Smoke and flames billowed out at the sudden rush of oxygen. He ducked his head and went in.

Allen squeezed the button on the radio. "This is your scene commander. I want a report as soon as you get a visual inside. There are likely two people in there. An adult female, and a female, eight years old."

"Copy that," Zack replied.

"I'm going in as well." Amelia jogged to the front door, leaving Mickey to spray water on the front of the house.

The guy struggled—it was usually a two-man job. But with rescue squad at the elementary school extracting a kid from the fencing, they wouldn't get additional personnel unless they requested it from another firehouse across town.

No one would get here fast enough to help save Pepper and Victory.

It was up to them.

Sirens whirled down the street to his right. He peered down the fire truck at the gathered crowd. Ambulance 21 eased between the people, made its way around him, and parked at an angle so they could load a patient and exit the other direction in a rush for the hospital.

The radio crackled, and Zack's voice came on. "Fire encompassing the kitchen and dining area. Looks like grease on the stove."

Amelia followed him with, "Searching for the residents now."

"Copy that." Allen's stomach flipped, the way it had hearing her address over the intercom at the firehouse.

He'd been trying to pray, but the words got stuck before they could form. Thankfully, God knew what he needed. He knew what Pepper and Victory could use right now.

Trace and Izan climbed out of their ambulance. Izan grabbed a duffel and slung it over his shoulder. Trace pulled the back doors open and grabbed the rail at the foot of the gurney. He pulled it all the way out until the legs extended on the ground.

Whatever happened, they were ready.

Allen stared at the open front door. "Ridge should've called in about the condition of the back of the house by now."

Izan glanced over. "What's that?"

Allen lifted the radio. "Foster, we need that report."

He knew nothing about commanding a fire scene except what was true for any situation like this. Whether it was a squad of marines on a mission or a group of cops rousting a suspect from his hiding place, the key was keeping everyone up to speed and organized.

Ridge didn't respond.

Mickey attacked the fire through the front windows. They needed foam in the kitchen if it was a grease fire inside.

"That looks nasty." Trace frowned at the house.

The smoke had changed color. Allen's radio crackled.

"Stephens—"

Amelia didn't get a chance to finish. An explosion rocked the house. The front windows blew out with a flare of the flames inside. Smoke billowed out the roof vents.

Everyone ducked.

Mickey jumped back to his feet and grabbed the hose. He resituated the spray on the front windows.

Allen grabbed the radio. "Report!"

"Coming out." Amelia appeared at the door seconds after her response. She dragged Zack by his armpits, hauling the kid out double-time.

He wasn't moving.

Trace and Izan ran to her and helped get Zack to the gurney. They lifted him and laid him on top. Everyone hissed.

Zack's eyes flew open, and he sat up, blood running down his face. His eyes were glassy and unfocused. "I have to save her."

"Easy, Stephens." Trace shoved him back down and looked at Izan. "Hurry up."

Zack fought his hold. "I have to! She's still in there."

"Got it." Izan straightened from his duffel and turned, a needle in one hand.

Zack kicked his legs.

"Easy, bud." Trace crooned to him while Izan administered the shot. A second later, Zack stilled.

Amelia locked eyes with Allen. "Find Ridge! I'm going back in." She ran for the house.

Allen got on the radio to respond to her. "Find Pepper and Victory." Then he said, "Foster, come in."

Mickey glanced over, wrestling to keep the hose aimed at the windows. "You want me to find him?"

Allen couldn't worry about a guy who should be able to care for himself. Especially when he'd been unresponsive before the explosion. He got on the radio. "What happened in there?"

Amelia's voice came back breathy. "Mason jar exploded from the oppressive heat. His face shield took the brunt of it, but he still got cut." She paused. "Looking in the first bedroom now."

Allen set the radio on his lap and pushed his chair to the end of the gurney. "What have we got?"

Trace frowned down at Zack while Izan pulled handful after handful of gauze out of his bag. "A million and a half surface abrasions that are all bleeding like..." He bit off a word. "Shoot. This one is bad."

Izan nodded. "I see it." He pressed down with the gauze.

"He gonna be okay?" Allen knew they couldn't tell yet. But he still needed to hear the words.

"Call for another ambulance. He's going in, so if they pull anyone else out you'll need another bus." Izan lifted the duffel and slung it over his shoulder. "Let's go."

Trace nodded. They pushed the gurney toward the ambulance.

Allen changed the channel on the radio. "Central, I'm requesting another ambulance for possible additional victims." He gave the address.

The dispatcher said, "Sending Ambulance 33 to your location. ETA six minutes."

"Copy that. In addition, I need personnel. Rescue squad, or a couple of uniform cops. I've got a missing man." Ridge's failure to answer the radio calls might have nothing to do with the fire.

"Copy, requesting now."

Allen switched the channel back. "Update, Patterson."

She responded a second later. "First bedroom clear."

The ambulance pulled out, lights and sirens going. Mickey watched them depart rather than keeping his attention on the hose so his aim stayed true.

Allen tapped the radio on his leg. It took him a second before he realized his phone was ringing. The display on his watch said it was Tate. He could answer it and talk on his watch but reaching back for his phone in his backpack gave him something to do.

"I'm busy."

"I know," Tate said. "Pepper's house is on fire."

No time to ask how Tate knew that. "We haven't found them yet. Truck 14 is inside."

"Victory is here."

"With Pepper? But her car's on the drive at her house." Were they both at Tate's?

"No," Tate said. "Just Victory. She's having a sleepover. I don't know where Pepper is, but her niece is safe here."

"Got it." Allen hung up on his friend and lifted the radio. "There's only one victim, Patterson. The kid isn't in there. You're just looking for Pepper."

"Copy that. Looking."

Allen took in long breaths. Mickey watched the fire, doing his job putting out the flames. Allen wanted to rush in, but with his chair that would be beyond foolish. He'd never hated the thing quite as much as he did right then. Wanting to be the man he was before the accident took the use of his legs. He felt like deadweight, unable to operate as he had for most of his life.

But this was how it would be for him.

He'd never liked whiners and didn't plan on becoming the kind of person who wallowed about how things weren't fair. He needed to trust the people around him for help.

They were the firefighters.

He wasn't.

Ambulance 33 headed down the street toward him. As they pulled up, the two EMTs pushed the doors open and jumped out.

The driver, Welch, was older, slender enough Allen worried how he carried heavy patients. His partner was the younger sister of rescue squad's lieutenant, Bryce Crawford, and his twin brother Logan, off in Australia and no use to his train of thought.

Andi strode right to him. "Just Truck 14?"

Of course, she knew all about Eastside firehouse even though she worked out of the west side.

Allen said, "Foster went to the backyard and is AWOL. Ambo 21 took Stephens to the hospital with injuries. Lieutenant

Patterson is inside looking for the victim." He motioned to the fourth firefighter on their truck.

Andi glanced around. "We'll go around back and—"

"Found her!" The radio crackled.

Allen's heart practically stopped beating. He didn't breathe. Welch frowned at his partner, but no one said anything.

"Unconscious," Amelia said. "I'm headed out now. Tell Mickey to watch his spray."

"Copy that." He relayed the order.

Two cops strode over from a patrol car. "Need help?"

Neither were officers he'd worked with at the LCC PD. The woman spoke first. "Tazwell. This is Ramble." She thumbed at her partner. "You need us?"

Allen nodded. "We have a firefighter who headed around the back of the house. He's unaccounted for and won't respond to the radio. Ridge Foster. He's in full gear."

"On it." Tazwell nodded. The two of them circled behind Mickey and headed for the side path to the backyard.

Amelia crested the front door.

He let the EMTs go ahead of him with their backboard, even though it was the last thing he wanted to do because everything in him screamed to be the one to save her. Doing that was their job. *Is she even alive?*

Amelia laid her down. Pepper was covered in ash and grime. Her hair splayed out around her head, dirty and sticky with the blood by her temple.

"Looks like she was knocked out." Welch knelt, and his knees popped.

"Any burns?"

The EMTs ignored his question.

Amelia said, "She was by the bed in her room. The flames hadn't reached it yet." She stood out of her crouch. "I need to get this fire put out."

Allen nodded.

She stared at him for a long second, the compassion there the most emotion he'd seen from her yet. All contained in her eyes.

Then she turned away.

"Let's get her in the ambulance." Welch motioned Andi to the other end of the backboard.

They moved past him, carrying her. Allen said, "I'll meet you at the hospital."

Andi glanced back. "She's stable. She's just knocked out, and she'll have inhaled a lot of smoke."

"Thank you."

She gave him a small smile.

Across the front yard, the two officers carried Ridge between them, one under each arm. Ridge's head lolled.

"Hey, Crawford!" Tazwell called out.

Andi turned.

"Got room for one more?"

Welch started to object. Andi waved them over. "We'll squeeze him in."

Ridge had the same wound on his forehead, and he was unconscious like Pepper.

Allen didn't like this. He turned his chair to surveil the crowd.

The assailants could be close by.

15

The first thing Pepper became aware of sounded like someone screaming. She blinked. Lights flashed overhead and sent shards of pain into her eyes. Breath escaped her lips in a hiss, and she tried to sit up. The hospital.

Everything flooded back.

The two men. The fire. Pain exploded in her skull.

But she'd survived.

"Whoa. Easy." An older guy's hand landed on her right shoulder. "Lie back down, ma'am."

Pepper slumped back to the gurney. Every part of her body itched with grit and dirt, and she smelled like a bonfire. "Who's screaming?" Her throat had been scraped raw by the fire she'd set.

The woman EMT walked in front of her—was that Bryce's sister, Andi?—pushing another gurney with a couple of nurses. On top was a guy in turnout gear.

The EMT pushing her said, "Looks like one of the other firefighters."

They wheeled past a bay in the ER where another firefighter in turnout pants and a soaked T-shirt shoved a male nurse away from him. Tiny cuts dripped blood all over his face.

"Zack." Pepper gasped.

Then who was on the bed rolling in front of her?

Argh. Thinking hurt too much. She couldn't remember. Her head pounded harder than the worst migraine, and her voice sounded like she'd sucked on a smokestack for an hour.

Two firefighters were injured.

"Hang on." She patted the EMT's arm. He frowned, but the nurse on her other side slowed the gurney.

As she watched, a brunette slowly eased up to the injured firefighter in the bay. "Stephens, look at me."

Zack's glassy gaze settled nowhere. There was so much blood on his face.

The woman lifted his hands in hers. Her voice was authoritative and gentle at the same time. "Look at me. Breathe."

"Come on." The male EMT shoved them on.

"Who was that?"

The nurse beside her said, "That's Kelsey, one of the counselors at Dean's therapy center. She comes here to visit patients who've been admitted. She specializes in family counseling at the Ridgeman Center."

"What about the firefighter there?" Pepper pointed in front of her and tried again to sit up. The memory of that gun flared in her mind—a weapon pressed to the underside of her chin.

She lifted her fingers to it and found the sore spot. A bruise.

The male EMT beside her had *Welch* on his name badge. "Foster seems to have been hit over the head like you were. Though no one knows how or why."

Two EMTs. Two firefighters who were hurt.

Ridge had been in the ambulance with her, taken care of by Andi. She smiled at Pepper now. "Don't worry. The doctors will care for you, and the police will get your statement."

Andi and the hospital staff slowed. They turned Ridge's gurney into a bay. Pepper was wheeled one bay farther down.

At the end of the hall, she spotted Izan and Trace over by the vending machines. Trace pulled back his foot and kicked the bottom of the machine. Izan eased up beside him like he was trying to talk some sense into his partner. Trying to get him not to break the vending machine out of frustration.

They'd done their jobs. They'd brought Zack here.

Pepper's bed rotated. Her head swam. It was up to the doctors, nurses, and that counselor, Kelsey. She seemed lovely. Pepper's head hit the pillow, and everything around her was swallowed up in darkness.

The next thing she knew, everything had stilled. No more spinning.

Her stomach didn't feel good, and she had a mask on. Cold, clean air drifted into her nose. She had to open her eyes carefully just in case her stomach presented a genuine threat.

Allen sat beside the bed.

She pushed the mask aside. "Hey." The word was barely audible, more like a breathy exhale. Throat still hurt.

He glanced up from his phone. "You're awake."

That smile of his. Pepper's eyes burned with tears.

Allen covered her hand with his. "Hey, it's okay. But put that oxygen mask back on, yeah?" He squeezed her hand and started to pull away. "I should tell the doctor you're awake."

She held his hand as tight as she could and tried to speak. All that came out was a croak.

"Here." He retrieved a cup of water from the table beside her.

Pepper's left hand had a heart rate monitor on her index finger and there was an IV inside her elbow. She left that where it was and used her free hand to steady his. She sipped from the straw.

"Thanks. That's better." She didn't want to let go of him.

The tears remained unshed. Pepper bit her lip.

"I do need to get the doctor."

"I'm sorry."

"None of this is your fault." He shook his head. "But I'm only guessing because I need you to tell me what happened. When you feel up to it, there's an officer outside who will take your statement." A frown creased his brow. "I'm assuming this wasn't a regular accidental house fire. Amelia said the way it started indicates it was deliberate."

Pepper nodded. "I had to. They—" Her voice broke, and she had to cough, even though it felt like she'd swallowed shards of glass.

"Put the mask back on. You need the clean air."

She slumped back against the pillow. It would be a while before she got the chance to speak, whether she was able to or not.

The doctor breezed through, asked a few questions that only needed yes or no head shakes, and exited just as quick. The nurse checked all her machines. Pepper could see the uniformed officer through the clear plexiglass door, waiting out in the hall. Watching the hall with her steady gaze.

Pepper needed to give the female officer a statement. Before she did that, there was something she had to tell Allen. And ask him.

Thankfully she was done breathing with the oxygen mask. "Were those firefighters hurt at my house?"

He studied her. "Yes, but it didn't have anything to do with you."

"I started the fire." Hopefully he heard her. It didn't seem right to admit the truth any louder. A tear fell from the corner of her eye. "I didn't want you to be a part of this."

Allen shifted. She thought he might take her hand, but he just brushed the blanket flat. "A part of what?"

Pepper sniffed. "It was nice. What we had."

"Why does that sound like you think it's a bad thing?"

"I got to pretend I was a different person."

He stiffened, but there was nothing she could do about it. The words were out now. Her confession had seen the light of day.

Like her past.

Allen's jaw flexed. "You pretended to be someone else when we were dating?"

"I wanted to introduce you to Victory so badly. Sage was in a time of being all smothering with her, so I didn't get a chance to have her visit my house and stay, even for a weekend. I had to go see them, or it would've been a couple of years." Pepper sighed. "That time with you? I wanted to be me. None of their baggage."

For a while there, she'd been free of it.

"Victory isn't baggage. I love her so much. It's just the emotion, the drama, and all the stress that comes with having her in my life." Pepper hadn't told anyone this. "I thought about running away with her once. Then I met you and got to be the person I would've been. Without them."

"That's who you are."

Pepper didn't want to lie. "It wasn't the truth. It was a dream."

The best kind of dream. Until she realized it couldn't go on any longer without him finding out she'd withheld so much of who she was.

"I didn't want you to know what kind of person I really am. I wanted you to believe what we were was real, even if it couldn't last." She glanced at that implacable expression on his face. "Because I did."

Allen pushed his chair back, turned it and left the room.

I'm sorry. Pepper swiped the tears from her face.

At least he finally knew. Even if he hated her, Allen would

learn her background when everything eventually came out. He'd realize she'd done the only thing she could—broken up with him.

After all, he'd told her he loved her. Which meant he loved the woman she was, without her messed up family in her life.

He would know she could never be that person. Even if she'd loved him back.

"Knock, knock." The uniformed police officer entered. "Okay to talk?" She had kind eyes.

Pepper nodded. Fresh tears rolled down her face. She swiped them away. "Stupid tears."

"I don't know Frees that well. We never worked together, but everyone seems to respect him." The officer tipped her head to the side. "But did he say or do anything I should know about?"

One of the police officers in town hadn't been poisoned by what the rest of them thought of her? Another dream that wouldn't last.

"Allen Frees never did anything a good man shouldn't do. He's never said anything that a good man wouldn't say to me."

The cop waved a hand. "Girl, sometimes that's the worst part."

Pepper blinked.

She stuck that hand out. "Olivia Tazwell."

"Pepper Miller." They shook.

The officer's expression softened. "Can you tell me what happened at your house?"

"First tell me what you meant. About it being the worst part."

Olivia scrunched her nose. "I don't want to get into my sob story. That won't be fun for either of us when you're supposed to be feeling better."

Pepper nodded. "It was horrible. I'm not sure I'll get

through the story. You'll have to tell me your thing first so I can take my mind off it. Then I'll be able to talk."

"You should've been a lawyer."

Pepper shook her head. "No way. I enjoy treating animals. I want nothing to do with criminals."

"Some of them didn't do it. At least, that's what they tell me."

Pepper managed a smile, even though her heart was breaking. Allen had just left her. Was he coming back?

"Okay, hang on. I'll tell you." Olivia lifted her hands, palms out. "Don't get me wrong. Far as I can tell, all the guys I work with are good guys, and I love them all to death, even if they're trying to little-sister me every minute." She grinned. "But they can't be too good, you know? Or it just makes me feel like I don't measure up."

"I know I don't."

Olivia studied her. "I don't know you, but I think that isn't true. Unless you burned your own house down."

Pepper blanched.

"You should tell me what happened." The cop settled in the chair, and Pepper recounted all of it. The two men. Their questions. The moment she lit the flame. Olivia wrote it all down. "Could you point the men out to me if I showed you pictures?"

Pepper nodded. "I've never met them. But I think they know my sister." Before Olivia could ask, she said, "I filed a police report a couple of days ago." It felt longer. "You'll want to include that information when you contact social services and"—*keep it together*—"find somewhere for my niece, Victory, to stay until Sage comes back."

"Social services." Olivia sat back in the chair and studied her. "For your niece. Because your house burned down?"

"She can't stay with me. It's not safe." Pepper sniffed. "I'm obviously not able to take care of her."

Olivia tapped her notebook against her leg. "I'm going to step out for a minute. I'll be back, okay?"

Pepper nodded, even though it didn't matter. And then Olivia left, and she was alone.

The way she should be.

16

Allen shut the door of his truck so he could answer the phone. The display said *Patterson*. "Frees."

"House is all cleaned up. Mickey and I are headed to the hospital now."

He couldn't push his wheelchair and hold the phone at the same time, so Allen stared at the rear entrance of the police department while the cold made his eyes water and his nose start to numb. "Get the truck back for the next shift. As soon as they come in, call dispatch. Put Truck 14 back into service."

With two men down, they couldn't respond to any fires. Rescue squad had been picking up the slack all evening so far.

"Copy that."

"How's the house?"

Amelia pushed out a breath he heard over the phone line. "Kitchen and dining area need a complete renovation. It's not livable. Her closet wasn't touched—which is why she's still alive since I found her in the bedroom. But everything she owns smells like smoke."

So there was no point getting Savannah to pack a bag for

Pepper out of her closet, a few things she might need over the next few days.

She also needed somewhere to live.

He'd successfully put her words out of his mind for a whole two minutes. Too bad he still cared about her.

"No, park over there," Amelia said. "I've got to go."

"Patterson."

"Yeah?"

"Thank you for saving her."

Allen hung up before she could say anything else. He stowed the phone and headed for the rear doors of the police station, where they brought criminals and suspects in and out. Where the stairs had a side ramp they'd suddenly decided to add a month after he got out of the hospital, along with the post he rolled up to.

He smacked the button on top of the pillar, which looked suspiciously like the disabled access at the mall his cousin Natalie had dragged him to before Christmas. The automatic entry door.

A buzzer went off and the doors swung open.

He had to admit that, as a former cop who'd brought in a lot of unruly suspects, having an automatic door probably helped. Maybe every police department had one at their back door, though he didn't know. He'd only worked at this one.

On the other side of the door, Sergeant Aiden Donaldson and Lieutenant Alex Basuto stood side by side in their street clothes. Trying to act nonchalant. Like they weren't waiting for him—determined to talk to him.

Allen turned his wheels right back around.

"Nope!" Donaldson strode over. "This isn't an ambush."

Allen glanced back over his shoulder. "It's been a long day."

The sergeant lifted both hands. "I'm not going to roll you in myself. I know that's not cool. But I do want you to come in."

From back in the hall, Basuto yelled, "*We* want you to come in."

"If I come in, it has nothing to do with the two of you. It's because I need to be in the police department for a reason." He turned back to them but didn't move.

If the guys wanted him to spill, they could work for it. Allen didn't share easily, and they knew that. Hence, the ambush.

He was surprised Natalie wasn't here to get him to talk about his "feelings."

She was probably seeing clients tonight.

"Get in here." Basuto waved at the doors. "You're letting all the cold in."

Donaldson snorted. "You're so ready to be a dad."

The lieutenant grinned. "Don't hurry it up. Those babies need to stay where they're at as long as possible, even if Sasha's going crazy being static."

Allen didn't know much about Basuto's wife, but she sure didn't seem like the kind of person who enjoyed being passive. They fit, even though they were different. Same with Donaldson and his wife. Both men had gone through some crazy times, fallen in love, and now they were building families.

He'd thought Pepper fit with him. He had no idea what to do with what she'd said to him.

"So what's going on?" Basuto said, not at all fooling anyone.

When Allen said nothing, Donaldson shifted a step closer. "How's Pepper?"

"Neither of you are fooling anyone." Allen sighed. "That's not why I'm here."

Basuto folded his arms. "We'll get to that. Talk first."

"It will take too much explaining."

"So talk fast," Donaldson said.

Allen really didn't want to get into it. The two of them had happy relationships and stable lives. He had two horses, a cousin who was his best friend and his counselor, a job putting out fires that didn't involve any flames, and a nothing-sandwich relationship.

Neither of them said anything.

"She didn't break up with me because of the accident."

Both of them blinked. He'd let this go on far longer than he should have, at first because he'd been injured. Recovering. By the time he realized he needed to clear up their confusion it had seemed pointless to bring it up.

Now it wasn't.

Basuto squinted. "So why break up with you?"

Allen sighed. "She dated me as the person she wanted to be...or was supposed to be. She didn't pretend to be someone else, and she didn't lie. She just didn't tell me anything about her family or let me into her life at all. She said dating me was a dream."

"That's a good thing, dude." Donaldson clapped him on the shoulder. "Especially if she isn't who we thought—in a good way."

"Not if it wasn't real and it didn't last."

Basuto stared at him.

Donaldson whacked his lieutenant's shoulder. "Say something."

Basuto shook his head. "He's not ready. He's processing."

Donaldson lifted his hands and let them fall back to his sides.

"We should get to work." Basuto headed down the hall.

Allen pushed his way after him. "He's right, you know."

Donaldson strode beside him. "You know what Bridget—"

"Yeah, I know. Things were crazy with the two of you."

Allen only knew pieces of their story of betrayal—a story wrapped up with Basuto's wife. Looking at them now, though? No one would guess all that had happened a couple of years ago.

They had peace. They were still the same people, and life was never perfect. It was just that they seemed so content.

Allen knew how to have contentment with what he had. He didn't wish for more, just progress. Even if he knew what it was like to have a happy family. If that happened for him, then it happened. No point in forcing it or wanting what didn't even seem to be on the horizon.

Who knew what God had for him?

Allen wasn't going to demand to know.

The office bustled with energy that seeped into his skin, like being surrounded by a warm blanket.

Donaldson sat at his desk. "Pepper's neighbor has a camera on her back patio to watch her dogs while she's at work. It's up above her patio, and the side of the view has a portion of Pepper's yard. Enough we know what happened to Foster."

Allen frowned. "What happened to Foster?"

"That's what we're getting at." Basuto pulled up a rolling chair and sat.

Donaldson said, "Two guys were hiding in her yard, behind the shed. In the footage we can see Foster go over and check it out. Probably heard something or thought it was a cat."

"They hit him over the head."

Allen hissed. "Same as Pepper."

Donaldson nodded. "Tazwell reports she had a blow to her head."

"Can we ID the guys?"

Basuto shook his head. "They jumped the fence into the neighbor's yard, where the dogs ran after them, barking. They ran to the back fence and hopped it. Too far away to make out their faces."

Donaldson said, "Tazwell is going to get Pepper some mug shots of local guys. See if she recognizes them."

"She saw their faces? I thought they just hit her over the head." Allen frowned. He'd assumed that was all it was. But then, she'd set that fire, hadn't she? Pepper had knowingly destroyed half her house to draw people's attention and circumvent whatever those guys had been trying to do.

Allen shivered at all the things that ran through his mind.

Donaldson winced. "They threatened her. One shoved his gun at her throat."

Allen had seen the bruise below her chin. His stomach rolled over, but he held himself together. Pepper didn't need him flying off the handle.

"Look," Basuto said. "You care about this girl, and now we know it's not that she did you dirty."

Allen had no idea where he was going.

"So why not...stick around? Make sure she's safe. See what happens."

"I'd rather figure out why dangerous men are targeting Pepper and Victory." Allen waved at Donaldson's computer. "Anything on Pepper's former brother-in-law?"

Donaldson and Basuto glanced at each other.

When they said nothing, Allen spoke. "I'm not a cop anymore, but that doesn't mean I can't handle whatever this is."

Basuto lifted a hand. "No one is saying that. It's still early and we're looking for probable cause."

"Tell me what your theory is."

Donaldson leaned back in his chair. "Elijah Burns used to be a doctor. Pepper's sister Sage married him nine years ago. Lived the high life for a while, according to social media. Not much has been updated recently, but it's clear she for one enjoyed that life."

"Meanwhile," Basuto picked up the explanation, "Burns is working at the hospital. Until a series of complaints arise, and his license is revoked."

"He was fired?" Allen had gotten vibes from the guy like he'd been sleeping in his fancy car lately.

Donaldson nodded. "We think he got into business with whoever these people are."

Allen frowned. "The bad batch of drugs?"

His former colleagues glanced at each other again.

"Burns is the one who ripped off the dealers? He's got the money, and they've got stuff that's killing the clientele."

Donaldson glanced at Basuto. "I told you he'd figure it out."

Basuto shot him a look right back. "But Pepper isn't involved, as far as we can tell."

That wasn't enough reason for her to withhold the truth of who she was—extended family included—from him. Allen's family wasn't perfect either. Not by any means.

His mother had been killed when he was nine. He barely remembered her, and what he did recall wasn't good.

He'd roamed military bases for a few years while his dad served, then met and married Allen's stepmom. She had a son from her previous marriage, eight years younger than Allen.

He and Trey got along fine, both then and now. Just not like Natalie, who'd come to live with them when Allen was sixteen. A gangly pre-teen with braids hadn't been on his list of potential best friends, but it'd worked, mostly because she liked the same movies he did.

He saw his stepmom every Sunday at church and had lunch with her after most weeks. His dad...

That remained a different story.

Maybe all the good in Pepper's family was her and Victory. She hadn't wanted him to know about the disaster of the rest of it.

If these guys let him use the computer, he could dig for himself and figure out what she thought was so bad he wouldn't be able to see past it.

Donaldson cleared his throat. "Coffee?"

"I'll go with you." Basuto bumped the mouse with his hand as he got up and followed the sergeant to the break room.

The monitor flickered on, the computer already unlocked. Which was a dense thing to do in a police station. Anyone with access to another person's computer profile could do whatever they wanted. Including but not limited to breaking the law or changing their background picture to dancing rainbow unicorns.

Not that Allen had ever done that to a young, brand-new Officer Aiden Donaldson.

Everyone had to learn how to secure their electronic information.

Unless they left the room to allow a former coworker to do whatever he wanted.

Allen shifted his chair closer and pulled up the database. He typed in Pepper's name first but found nothing. She was clean. As if he'd ever believe otherwise, no matter what her family was into.

He looked at her sister's history and found a reference to their mom. That search proved a whole lot more fruitful.

Mom was incarcerated in a federal prison in Colorado, serving a life sentence for murder. No opportunity for parole.

The victim's name brought a lump to his throat.

He knew why she hadn't told him about her family.

17

The vehicle swaying made her stomach flip over, but Pepper wasn't going to turn and face the front. She'd loosened her seatbelt enough she could turn sideways in the SUV, her legs between the two captain's chairs in the middle row.

"But you got hurt." The tears in Victory's eyes sparked as soon as Pepper walked out of the hospital and got in the Hudsons' car.

"True." Her head still pounded even though the doctor had given her medicine for that. She had a bandage over the wound where that guy had hit her on the head. Pepper had to fight a shudder just thinking about it.

Not to mention everything that happened at the hospital.

They were in the car, with Savannah and Tate in the front. Headed to wherever they were going. Probably a hotel or the bed and breakfast in town.

Pepper and Victory had no clothes and no personal belongings. Tomorrow she would have to figure out what to do. Right now, she had to make sure she and Victory were good.

"I know I don't look okay, and I'm not going to call them 'ouchies' like we did when you were little. You're not a baby."

Victory hadn't been a "kid" for a long time either. Not with the way Sage raised her.

The little girl lifted her chin. "Did someone try to take you?"

"Not the same as what happened to you." Pepper needed to tell her something or she'd wonder why they weren't going to the house. "I knew I needed help, so I started a fire in the kitchen. Now I smell." She sighed, louder than she needed to. "And all our stuff smells. Plus the house has to be cleaned, and fixed up. So we need to stay somewhere else for a while."

Victory reached into her backpack and pulled out her blue stuffed animal puppy.

"I'm glad you have Booper." Pepper ran a hand over the dog's head.

They were both okay, and Victory had what she needed most in the world.

So what if the rest of her life was a disaster? They were alive. She could rebuild her life, and nothing would change. She didn't need to wish for more.

Victory snuggled the stuffed dog and closed her eyes. Pepper would have adopted a pet for her years ago if either of their lives could accommodate one.

She shuddered again. *Thank You.* No one had been killed. Three people were injured—thanks to her fire and the two men she still needed to identify. The police would catch them. Her life would go back to being quiet.

Sage would come back.

Elijah would forget they existed again.

One day, when she graduated—or the day she turned eighteen—Victory would be able to move out on her own. Pepper would be able to support her whenever she needed it. Whatever she needed. They could both pull away from Sage a little bit, just for their sanity. Maybe they would even be friends.

Family.

Pepper ran her hand down Victory's blonde bangs the way Victory had done with the puppy. She was safe.

She turned in her seat, adjusting the belt as she moved. The SUV bumped off the blacktop. "Why are we going up here?"

Not just outside town—she knew this road.

"What do you need from Allen's house?" She didn't want to see him. "Victory and I will wait in the car."

Savannah turned in the passenger seat. "You're actually getting out."

Allen rolled down the ramp off the porch, pumping the arms of his all-terrain chair as though determined not to allow her to escape. This day couldn't get any worse.

Pepper sank back into her seat. Victory didn't need this—and the truth was, neither did she. It hurt too much seeing him come over to her after he'd left her in the hospital. Why be around each other again and make this more painful than it had to be?

Tate hopped out the driver's door and opened hers.

She stared at him. "We can't do this," she hissed.

They didn't know. They couldn't.

Allen turned his chair and came back around, pointing toward the cabin alongside the car door.

"I'm sorry. I didn't know they were going to bring us here." She sniffed back tears and rubbed her nose.

"I asked them to." His face held a shadow despite the sun hanging high in the sky. Maybe a storm was coming.

"Why did you—"

Savannah said, "Come on, Victory. I'll show you what Allen needs help with so you'll know what to do while you're here."

"You planned this." Pepper couldn't believe it. He should hate her.

She hoped none of her shock was visible to Victory. The child didn't need any more upset.

Allen held out his hand. "Come on. You look like you need a nap."

Pepper sniffed, angling her body out of the car. She nearly convinced herself she'd managed to hide from them how much that hurt, but Allen frowned. Tate grunted.

She lifted her chin. "It's not polite to comment on someone's appearance."

"I never put much stock in politeness." The expression on his face was inscrutable. How much pain had he been forced to shove down for this?

"You'd better be nice to Victory."

He tipped his head to the side. "You think I wouldn't be?"

Pepper lifted her chin. It didn't matter. "We aren't staying here."

Surely someone would bring her car. Plus everything else she would need to stay in a hotel. Her purse, keys, and phone had all been in the house when Lieutenant Patterson hauled her out.

Allen had been there the whole time. Waiting to find out if she was alive or dead.

The counselor, Kelsey, had visited her, but Pepper had been exhausted. Not to mention trying to figure out why it wasn't Natalie who came if the Ridgeman Center people thought she needed to talk to someone. But since she'd been convinced Allen, and everyone he knew, would hate her, maybe it wasn't that shocking.

She was supposed to call the center and make an appointment for her and Victory to chat with Kelsey if they needed it.

Allen motioned with his head toward the house. "Let's talk about it inside."

She breezed past him through the front door like she'd been sentenced to prison. That thought hit far too close to home.

A dull thud sounded behind her. She spun back to where

Tate had dumped a duffel and a bulky trash bag full of stuff. "There's more. I'll grab it." He strode out.

"More what?"

Allen pushed through the door in his regular wheelchair, the other left on the porch. "Stuff the women's ministry at church dropped off at his place. They rounded up a bunch of donations, mostly clothes for you and Victory. Some blankets. When you need it, they've got a food pantry, and they'll help fill your cupboards until you get back on your feet."

Pepper's mouth dropped open. Before she could comment, Victory hopped in. She ran right to Allen and wrapped her arms—and the stuffed puppy—around his neck. "Thanks!"

He grinned. "No problem, Vicki."

"That's not my name!"

"It could be your nickname. What do you think?"

"I wanna be called Thunder."

Allen chuckled, the sound so warm it hurt Pepper's ears.

He said, "No can do, Vicki. No one gets to pick their nickname. But I can choose another one if you don't like it."

Victory's lips shifted around. "I like it. Can I watch TV?"

"Sure." He pointed. "Through there."

She grinned and hopped out of the hallway into the living room.

Savannah leaned against Tate's side, and he put his arm around her. "They stayed up until after midnight on their sleepover, and this morning half a packet of cookies had been eaten." She grinned. "Give her five minutes. She'll be napping."

Tate glanced between them. "Well, if you kids don't need anything else, we have things to do."

Were they just going to leave? "Do you know where my sister is?"

Tate shook his head. "I have a few friends looking into leads, but they haven't been able to locate her yet. She's below the radar, that's for sure." He and Savannah turned, holding on to each other. "Allen will fill you in on the rest."

Tate closed the door.

Pepper ran her hands down her face. "What is going on?"

Fatigue felt like a dog-training suit, bulky and heavy.

"Let's go sit."

Pepper nodded. Allen wheeled to the living room, where Victory had curled up in the recliner. A kids' cartoon played on the TV. He turned the volume down, pulled the blanket off the back of the chair, and settled it over her. He waved Pepper through the house.

He opened the door to the back porch, rolled out, and locked his wheels beside a wicker chair.

Pepper sank into it.

"I know how we left it, and it might seem weird to ask you to be here. But I'd like to know you and Victory are safe. I have enough space in the guest room, and I can work from home for a few days if needed."

Pepper stared at his backyard. It was basically a mountainside, with thirty feet of long grass and patches of snow before it dropped out of sight. The peaks beyond were covered with snow. In the mornings, he probably had deer grazing his yard.

Maybe he'd even seen a bear out here.

"I don't want to be anywhere else," she said.

"And you think I hate you?"

Pepper glanced at him.

"I'm right." He frowned. "You do think that."

"What else would I think after you left like that?" She lifted her fingers from her knees. "I don't blame you. I hate myself more than a little bit."

"So why get into a relationship with me if you knew it couldn't last? That you'd never tell me the truth?"

Lord, help me. His voice. She had to fight the urge to fall into his lap and beg for another chance. No one liked that look.

"Pepper."

"I couldn't help it. You were so..." She cleared her throat. "I probably convinced myself it might work. Like we had a chance. Because I wanted it all. Life up here, where the world seems not so close. Where I can pretend everything's peaceful and bask in the beauty of what you have."

She took a breath. "Because I wanted the option of marriage and a family of my own that wasn't so far beyond dysfunctional we're parked in man-made disaster territory. With a sprinkling of 'you did this to yourself' and 'you should've known better.' Now all I have is Victory. Sage is missing, and guys with guns seem to think Elijah gave something to me when you were—"

Allen tugged on her arm.

Pepper turned to him, and his lips touched hers.

She swallowed the surprise, and her brain caught up with what was happening. Everything in her jumped for joy. Thankfully, not out of the seat.

Don't overthink it.

She would always be a terrible person, because Pepper didn't push him away for his own good.

He didn't need her drama in his life.

Instead of doing what she should, she clasped both sides of his neck where it met his shoulders.

Pepper held on for dear life while he thoroughly kissed her.

18

T he lobby of City Hall bustled with people passing through security for their workday. Suits and shined shoes. Fixed up hair. Even in his fire department uniform, Allen felt like a plumber at the White House.

When he took the job, no one told him he had to dress in the department uniform when he was a liaison. But Allen had worn a uniform for every job he'd ever had, and the firefighters needed to see him as one of them.

"Whoa, buddy."

He grabbed the handles of his chair and stopped two inches from the security guard. "Sorry, Tommy."

The older man cracked a smile, bright white against his dark skin. "Someone on your mind this morning?"

Allen had to admit that was true. He hadn't been able to get Pepper and the kiss they'd shared last night—even if it was to get her to quit overthinking—out of his mind. He knew why she'd broken up with him, but he needed her to trust him enough to tell him herself. In her own time.

But resist kissing her?

No way.

Especially if it served to remind her how good things could be between them.

He just hadn't been thinking about her a moment ago. "You could say that."

"Must be quite a woman."

Allen had met Tommy's wife at a Fourth of July barbecue at his lakeside cabin. "I should see if she knows how to make berry cobbler."

"Son, you find a woman who can't cook? That's a catch and release, my friend."

Allen chuckled. "Oh yeah?"

"Good lookin' don't last. Good cookin' do." Tommy grinned. "You hear that?"

"Sounds familiar." Allen scratched at his chin.

His watch buzzed with a calendar notification.

"Meeting?"

"Yep."

Tommy stepped back and waved him to the door off the side of the metal detector and scanner the bags went through. "You packin' today, son?"

Allen smiled to himself. "Yes, sir, I am."

Given everything happening to Pepper, he didn't want to be without his personal weapon. She and Victory were staying home today. They had an off-duty officer watching out for them, and Conroy had a patrol car sticking close to the area where Allen's house was.

"You'll need to check that in while you're inside."

Allen pulled the gun and holster from his hip. Tommy held open a lockbox. He secured the weapon inside, and Allen set his thumbprint on the scanner. Only he would be able to access the lockbox. He could've left the gun in his car, but that would mean a thief robbing his car could score a jackpot, and there would be yet another illegal weapon on the streets.

"Sign here."

Allen gave his autograph and got a ticket. Tommy had him enter City Hall through the side partition, while everyone else had to get scanned. He had so much metal in his body that there wasn't much point in trying not to set off the machine.

"Have a good meeting."

"Thanks, Tommy." Allen pushed down the hall to the room where he was to meet the city council, who provided oversight to his department.

One day he might walk this way on crutches, ambling slower than he could roll right now. He could admit to himself that the adventurous kid in him wanted a flat stretch where he'd see just how fast this chair might go.

As for the meeting, no doubt they'd asked him here to discuss his recommendations for who the next chief of Eastside firehouse should be.

His response to their stack was a stack of his own, with one of theirs at the bottom of the pile. The department had no use for another white-haired paper pusher buying time until retirement.

That wasn't what his firefighters needed.

He had to push the heavy door with his chair, then hold it open with one hand and wheel his chair through with the other. The door clipped the back of his wheel when it closed.

The chatter ceased.

Three men and two women looked over from their seats around the conference room. Beside them on one side, the chief of Westside firehouse sipped from a paper cup, wearing full uniform with all his shiny medals pinned to his coat.

Chief Robert Warrick had known what was happening at Eastside firehouse under Steven Hilden. He'd said nothing, only speaking up eventually in order to save his job.

One of the women got up. Janice had asked him out before. She'd been several years ahead of him in high school, and he recalled one day she'd shoved him aside to get to the water fountain with a group of her friends. Divorced for three years now, she'd gone gray years ago.

She tugged a chair from under the table and pushed it to the wall. "Here's a space for you."

He pulled his laptop from the backpack on the back of his chair and took a sip from his hot cup. Last night's kiss with Pepper should have him jumping on clouds. But so much was up in the air still. She remained in danger. He had to figure out if their relationship could survive giving it a shot or if things would crash and burn like they had last time.

He had to risk his heart getting broken. Again.

Janice sat. "Let's get started, shall we?"

Just because he assumed this meeting would go badly didn't mean that was true. He would rather be at home making sure Pepper and Victory were safe and happy.

The Westside fire chief lifted his cup and smirked behind it, as if no one would see.

"What did you want to discuss?" Allen glanced around.

Janice shifted papers in front of her. "I'm sure you can understand why we have concerns. This is a delicate matter, and I hope you'll be able to see our side of things."

He nodded, trying to be compromising. "Naming the chief of Eastside firehouse will always be controversial. I'm not sure the public can ever lose the memory of what the previous chief did and the damage it caused."

Janice swallowed. *Uh-oh.* "That's not the first item on our agenda this morning. It's been brought to our attention that you've spent time recently with Pepper Miller."

"Yes, she's a veterinary nurse at Brett Filks's practice." What could they possibly have to object to about her? She'd been an upstanding member of the community for years.

"She seems to have had some dealings with the police also. And there were armed men in her house, which she combatted by setting a dangerous fire in her kitchen that injured two fire-fighters."

"One was injured because of the fire. The other was assaulted by the same two armed men who hurt her." Allen held himself very still. "Both firefighters will be back to work this week."

"And in the meantime, my house is providing yours with floaters to cover your truck." Chief Warrick stared him down. "Your Winter Carnival was interrupted by the near kidnapping of a child. Your firefighters are in disarray. And you haven't picked a chief yet."

"You volunteering for the job, Warrick?"

A muscle flicked in the chief's jaw.

Not surprising, considering he was allergic to putting effort into his work that couldn't be followed up by a flashy press conference and a medal.

"Didn't think so." Allen addressed the rest of them. "The candidate for the chief position at Eastside needs to be the right person for the job. Not another placeholder. Not just a safe choice that makes the brass feel good. Their next chief needs to be a guy with the drive to make that house a strong family."

Several of them shifted. The consensus looked like fifty-fifty against him.

"My personal life isn't up for discussion."

Janice shifted in her chair. "It's the view of this committee that your personal life choices reflect on your ability to—"

"And when you brought your concerns to the mayor, what was his view?"

Her lip curled for a second.

"Good. I'll discuss it with him, but that's as far as this goes." He opened his laptop. "Let's discuss the merits of the candidates." That way his trip here wouldn't be a total waste of time.

Janice started talking about his bottom choice—a retired firefighter who'd moved here from Colorado a while back, who'd put his name in the hat. Probably because he'd been invited to do so by someone in this room.

But where had a safe choice got them so far? The firefighters were still a disaster.

Allen had no idea how to fix it apart from giving them a leader they respected. One with the physical ability to do what they did.

Something Allen didn't have.

Warrick—and their previous chief—just wasn't the kind of guy to drop and do pushups with his underlings. Allen figured there wasn't much difference. Except he actually *wanted* to.

As the conversation continued, he couldn't help his mind drifting back to her.

The councilors really thought they could have a say over who he spent time with. He wasn't breaking the law. Nor was his personal life their business.

He might feel like he had nothing to hide, but that didn't mean he'd share everything with people he cooperated with but barely respected beyond their standing. People had put too much stock in their leaders for too long in this town. It had backfired, and now Allen got to clean up the mess.

Meanwhile, men like his father went unnoticed. Let loose from the Marine Corps and left to fend for himself. A hero who had been forgotten.

Allen would go to the end for the people he cared about. With Pepper it might very well mean doing that. If the committee pressed their objections, he could be forced to choose between a relationship with the woman he'd been halfway in love with for years and a job he'd been given because he couldn't do the one he wanted anymore.

As if there was a contest.

The truth was, he wasn't sure he wanted to contemplate how much he'd let burn just for a shot at a future with

Pepper—and a relationship where she opened up and let him in. Completely. For life.

He wanted all of it.

"Let's talk about this next candidate." Janice studied the paper, interest in her eyes.

Chief Warrick snorted. "A wilderness firefighter who just happens to be friends with Lieutenant Crawford?"

"It's time to think outside the box." Allen wasn't going to apologize for bringing a fresh perspective. "Macon James has the skills and the experience, and he doesn't have to think back twenty years to remember what it's like to fight a fire. He might not be the obvious choice, but I see no issues with interviewing him."

He wanted to get to know the guy. After all, Allen was the one who'd have to work closest with him. If they didn't get along, there wasn't much point considering him.

This was about the health of the house.

Even if he burned that bridge for Pepper's sake, there was no way he would leave Eastside firehouse with no one to lead them.

And he definitely wouldn't leave the firefighters with the wrong chief.

That would be a disaster.

19

In the sunshine of the clear afternoon, Pepper could almost forget she'd had a gun to her throat recently. Forgetting the fact Allen had kissed her? Not so easy.

Listening to Victory's steady chatter helped. Her niece skipped beside her through the park. The trunk of Pepper's car was full of shopping bags. They'd had cheeseburgers for lunch at Hollis's diner, followed by ice cream. Now they were stretching their legs until Allen showed up to drive them home.

Which meant she would have to face him after he'd swept her away with his affection.

Pepper's cheeks heated, and not because it was sunny out. There was so much unresolved between them still. He seemed so confident it could work, but she couldn't let herself get caught up in how every part of her wanted to fall into his arms and let him fix all her problems.

The only outward indication she had that her world was currently out of whack was the plainclothes police officer walking ten feet behind them. Olivia Tazwell had stuck with them all day. Part of their activities—to the extent Victory didn't find it strange they had a guard.

"And then we have to shovel out the poopers." Victory had an *ick* expression on her face.

Pepper blinked. "Are we still talking about the horses?"

"Yes, Auntie. Obviously." Victory giggled. Despite the humor underlaid in the conversation, there remained a shadow in her eyes. Things weren't safe.

Knowing it had been Pepper who'd put that there rather than take it away hurt. Like a knife to the chest.

"Obviously." Pepper pushed aside the guilt and focused. "If you want a horse of your own, you'll have to muck out the stall. Just like you'll get to do all the fun parts."

"I hope we can ride this afternoon."

"We can ask Allen if that's okay." Pepper squeezed her niece's hand.

"If I get a horse, I'm gonna get two so I can call them Peanut Butter and Jelly."

Olivia chuckled behind them. "Good idea, kiddo." The plainclothes officer wasn't watching them. She was watching everyone else in the park, keeping them safe.

Allen had told her that if they rode, he'd put Victory in front of him on his horse, and Pepper would ride the other. That would make them feel entirely too much like a family— something that caused heart palpitations. Enough it made her wonder if she should see a doctor.

Since she already knew—even before the kiss last night— that she loved Allen, it wasn't so surprising.

The whole thing was like trying to grasp smoke. But she didn't want to try, because odds were it would slip through her fingers like it'd never had any substance.

She didn't know what it meant that he'd kissed her, and they hadn't talked about it. Victory had woken up, and they'd fixed dinner together, then watched a movie. Allen had kept the conversation light. Pepper had fallen asleep before the movie ended and woke up on the couch after dark with him close and Victory ready to be tucked into bed.

"Heads up." Olivia spoke quietly.

Up ahead on the path, a homeless man ambled toward them. Pepper glanced over her shoulder and shook her head at Olivia. "Not one of the guys from yesterday."

She'd spent time describing them this morning and looking at mug shots on a laptop Olivia brought with her. She hadn't been able to find them in all the arrest photos the Last Chance County PD had.

It didn't feel good to have failed at that.

Olivia said, "Still."

Pepper figured that meant they should keep up their guard.

"Hello." Victory waved at the man, apparently unfazed by the whole thing. Or her finely honed street smarts that Pepper didn't discount told her there was nothing to worry about with this guy.

Pepper wondered which it was. Victory knew what danger felt like. It could be that they were in the park and she felt secure. Or there might be no threat from a random guy.

His distant gaze glanced across them, and he grunted in response.

Pepper angled Victory to the right so the man would pass them on her side and not her niece's. "Good afternoon."

"It is." He slowed, still not exactly looking at her. "Be careful."

Pepper's foot caught on something. He reached for her arm, and she felt strong fingers catch her in a secure grip. She righted herself. "Sorry."

"Apologize when you've done something wrong, and only then." His expression softened. "I doubt that's the case here."

She studied him and the layers of worn clothes. The grime on the side of his neck. Stubble. Hair in need of cutting. Yet he seemed solid, healthy even. Maybe a little on the thin side.

If she had to guess, this guy had an easier life than Sage. Peace seemed to shine through his gaze. Her sister had none of that. Sage might only wear flashy clothes, but they were armor. This man needed clothes that kept the weather at bay. He seemed more at peace than a lot of people she knew.

Her heart squeezed in her chest. "Can I help you?"

Maybe he needed something, and she had it to give. No one should have to live on the streets if that wasn't where they wanted to be. A friend in nursing school had helped her out when she had nothing, offering Pepper a place to stay and a ride to school so she didn't have to bike all year round.

"Heard your house burned down," he grunted. "Looks a sorry state now. Like the spot where I live." And yet he didn't seem disgruntled about that.

Only her mind stuck on him knowing where she lived. Pepper couldn't help the shiver that ran through her, which had nothing to do with the high of forty-five.

Olivia closed in behind her. She felt the shift, but neither she nor this homeless man paid attention to it.

Pepper managed to say, "The important things are safe."

He nodded. "That's right, girl."

Victory tugged on her hand. "Can I play on the swings?"

Olivia said, "We should keep going in that direction."

Pepper wanted to tell the police officer to take Victory to the swings, but no way would Olivia go for that. "Let's do it." She glanced at them, then back at the homeless man. "It was nice talking to you."

He grunted, gave the cop a wide berth, and continued down the path.

She watched him for a second, wondering what had just happened.

"Yeah, it's me." Olivia paused. "No, nothing like that. We just met some homeless guy in the park. And he knew about the fire."

Victory's hand tightened around hers.

"Let's go to the swings." Pepper tugged her toward the playground area.

It served as a sufficient distraction.

Apparently Olivia thought the homeless guy knowing about her house was significant. Pepper didn't know if it was, but she wasn't a trained law enforcement officer. She could tell the rotund puppy racing across the grassy area needed to be fed less than the instructions on the bag of dog food said, but nothing about bad guys and threats.

All she'd wanted was to find her sister. She and Victory were in protective custody. Her house needed a major renovation—if not rebuilding entirely. Elijah was wrapped up in something bad. Criminals had her on their radar.

Victory tugged her hand free and ran to the swings.

Pepper sat on the curbing between the grass and the bark of the play area. All she wanted was to see Allen again, maybe kiss him some more. And take a nap. The kissing part meant opening up more to him, otherwise what was the point? It would only be more of the same they'd had last time.

Connection, but no substance.

This time she wanted more. If it was possible there would even be a this time. Maybe he was only invested in this because he cared and he was a good guy. He'd arguably kissed her just to get her to stop talking. Though she wanted it to mean something, the truth was it might not.

He could keep their relationship what it was for the rest of their lives.

Pepper blinked away tears and looked at the sky. Victory swung as high as she could, chattering to the girl on the swing beside her. The kid needed to be back at school after winter break. At the least, Pepper needed to take her to the library so they could check out another cart full of books to read together.

Maybe she should get some worksheets, and they could make sure Victory didn't end up behind all the other kids in her grade.

Much like everything else in her life, what she wanted and what she got didn't come close. And she wasn't thinking about Christmases as a kid.

Pepper wanted a family.

If she had a shot at one with Allen—she didn't dare dream of keeping Victory forever—then it would come with her fully bringing him into her life.

That meant telling him the truth behind their breakup.

Sure, she'd given him the highlights. However, they would need to wade through the darkness to get to the light at the end of that tunnel.

The idea of it scared her more than that man with a gun to her throat. She knew how to deal with physical threats. Plenty of times her dad threatened her and Sage. But opening up? Showing Allen her heart?

She could fight the fear enough to do that, and he might decide then he didn't want anything to do with her.

Just the idea of doing that made her want to pack her bags and run. Which was how she'd ended up in Last Chance County in the first place.

Her sanctuary had become somewhere she might need to escape from.

Victory ran to the play structure with her new best friend from the swings. Pepper had been that resilient as a child, but life still beat her down. Until she wanted nothing more than to forget who she had been and just be who she was now.

The relationships, without the substance.

But who wanted a shadow of a life when everyone around them said the dream was possible?

Pepper twisted left, then right, popping the tension from

her back. Across the park where they'd entered, she spotted Allen talking to the homeless man.

Officer Tazwell stood where she could watch both Pepper and Victory as well as Allen and the man who'd known about her house.

The homeless man shifted his stance and stuck a hand in his pocket—the way she'd seen Allen do before. The resemblance struck her so powerfully she stood.

Allen nodded to the man, then headed down the path toward them. He spoke briefly to Olivia before coming to meet her.

"Allen!" Victory raced over, her friend forgotten. "Can we ride the horses?!"

"Great idea."

Victory slammed into him and wrapped her arms around his shoulders. Allen patted her back, his eyes wide. "Great!"

Pepper bit her lip. Should she ask who that man was?

Likely they'd met while Allen had been a patrol officer like Olivia and built a rapport. Enough the older man had assumed some of Allen's mannerisms and kept up on local happenings everyone in town was talking about.

She was about to ask when her phone started to ring in her coat pocket.

She pulled it out. Victory had skipped over to Olivia, so Pepper said, "It's Elijah." She swiped her thumb to answer. "Hello?"

"I found her." His exhale rattled across the speaker.

"You know where Sage is?" Pepper frowned.

Allen had his phone out, texting someone.

"The Starburst Motel. On the west side of town."

"I know where the Starburst Motel is." Repeating everything would get obvious fast, but Allen needed intel. "And what kind of place it is. Why is Sage there?"

Allen looked up and nodded.

"How should I know?" Elijah asked. "Just get here. Room twenty-two."

He hung up.

20

"You want to *what?*" Basuto pinned Olivia with a look.

Allen didn't think the suggestion was so out there. After all, Pepper for sure wasn't going into a dangerous situation. If anyone was, it would be a trained law enforcement officer. Which he no longer was.

Olivia shrugged. "We're similar enough build. I can wear clothes like hers and put a hat on. I show up in her car, and I go in. All y'all are outside, ready to bust the door down and save the poor undercover officer at a moment's notice."

Basuto shook his head. "Jessica all over again."

Officer Tazwell set her hand on her hip. "What's that about Detective Ridgeman, Lieutenant?"

"Nothing."

She eyed him and wandered back to her desk, where her partner—a guy Allen hadn't met—stared at the computer monitor with reading glasses and those strings dangling behind his head to secure the specs.

A lot had changed in Last Chance County in the last few years. There were six detectives now instead of two. And a K-9 and his handler—the ones walking in right now.

Basuto lifted two fingers in a salute. "Officer Stuart."

"Puppy!" Victory jumped up and grabbed the inside edge of the front counter so her body lay across the top.

"Whoa, kiddo." The K-9 officer grinned.

"Can I pet your dog?"

Stuart said, "Do you know what a working dog is?"

Victory shook her head.

The K-9 officer glanced at Pepper. "Is this munchkin yours?" He pointed to the side, at Victory.

"Yes."

Allen heard the tone in her voice and wanted to hold her hand. But what they needed to do was hash out the plan to go to Elijah so the police could detain him—and hopefully find Sage in the process.

"Is it okay if Titan says hi to her?"

Pepper said, "Yes. Thanks for asking."

Officer Stuart headed to the front lobby, where Victory had been playing a game with the receptionist on duty.

Basuto said, "Okay, Tazwell. It works in a pinch, and we don't have much time."

"Thanks for the vote of confidence." She hopped off the edge of the desk. "I'll go do something with my hair." She asked Pepper, "Is it okay if I drive your car?"

Pepper nodded.

Allen squeezed her hand. "If you have objections, it's okay to voice them. But no one is okay with putting you in danger."

"I know." She held on when he'd have let go. "Can I at least be there and watch what's happening?"

He nodded. "We can follow in my truck." He glanced at Basuto, who had a look on his face. A look of *I caught you.* "We'll stay out of your way."

The lieutenant nodded, a grin on his face. "Sounds good." He sent a side-glance at Allen's hand holding Pepper's.

Allen ignored him.

Basuto coughed. "So I'll head out with SWAT."

Pepper spoke with Victory for a second, and they headed out back to Allen's truck. As they crossed the back parking lot, she said, "The police here have SWAT? I thought they weren't that big of a department."

"We still need an armored division for certain circumstances when the response is necessary. So a handful of officers have been trained for that, and they're on call on rotation."

"Did you do it when you were a cop?"

He nodded, hauling the driver's door open while she stood watching. Allen did the transfer into the seat. Every time he tested the strength of his legs, putting a fraction of weight on them for a second. Some days were fine. Others not so much. Today he felt like he should be able to hop up and hit the gas pedal with his foot.

Which probably had more to do with her watching him.

Retrieving the wheelchair from the ground required him to brace a hand on the door and lift it from the ground. He drew it across his lap and put it in the back.

"That's probably more hassle than it's worth." She folded her arms.

He knew that look. Allen wasn't going to admit that he both loved and hated needing the upper body strength to haul himself up into the seat. But it wasn't as if he would ever admit defeat.

"You could drive a van."

Allen sent her a look of his own. One she would not mistake.

"It's not a commentary on your manhood to drive a van."

"No, it isn't. Now get in the *truck*, Pepper." He slammed the door.

Through the glass he heard her chuckle. When she was buckled in, he drove to the motel—two stories and a revolving sign that twirled around at the corner of the rutted concrete parking lot.

The structure had been built before he was born. It hadn't been good quality then, and the years hadn't been kind, though the doors were freshly painted cherry red. The last time he was here, arresting a drug dealer who'd kidnapped his sixteen-year-old girlfriend, they'd been a nasty tan color.

Tazwell had already parked Pepper's car outside when they pulled up.

Pepper shifted in her seat so that her body angled toward him. "I wasn't making fun of you."

"I know."

"I think it's great that you've made your life what you want it to be."

"Some things are nonnegotiable."

"Like the truck."

He nodded.

"This seems too normal, being here with you." She eyed him. "Domestic even."

"She's about to go in." Allen lifted his radio from the dash and turned up the volume.

"...upstairs now." Tazwell's voice came through loud and clear over the police frequency. She trotted upstairs to the second floor. Given the sway, the rickety stairs didn't look like they'd been repaired since Allen was here last time.

Basuto responded, "Copy that. Eyes open."

"That's the idea," Allen said in answer to Pepper's comment. "Normal. As much as it's in my power to do."

He realized that what he'd done with his truck might be similar to her dating him the first time. Doing it the way she wanted, so she didn't have to deal with the pain of something she couldn't have.

"It cost a lot of money to make the modifications." Allen watched the motel door as Tazwell approached. "Conroy got word of a foundation for disabled law enforcement officers, and they paid the bulk of it. I used savings for the rest."

To her credit, Olivia could pass as Pepper. She lifted a fist and knocked on the third door of the second floor rooms.

Allen spotted the SWAT truck, an armored vehicle he'd loved to ride in. The officers piled out but kept to the shadows, splitting up and moving to the second floor to be close if Olivia needed backup.

"So you got to keep driving your truck. That's amazing."

Memories of being in his dad's truck, driving—it didn't matter where. Those were the best memories he had.

He liked that she thought something about him was amazing. It felt good. Like their kiss the night before, the one they still needed to talk about. "After Victory is in bed later, can we sit and talk some?"

"I'd like that." She squeezed his arm. "Do you think Elijah left? Maybe neither of them is here."

Allen shrugged. Before he could make up an answer for her, Olivia twisted the door handle for the motel room.

"It's open." The radio crackled. "Headed in."

"Copy," Basuto said. "SWAT is responding."

Olivia pulled her gun and held it in front of her in a way that caused a pang of grief in Allen. She stepped into the motel room. SWAT raced along the upstairs balcony after her, disappearing through the door seconds after she had with Basuto right behind them.

Allen held out his hand, and Pepper took it. He laced their fingers together.

"Got Burns." Olivia paused. "He's DOA."

Pepper's hand squeezed his. "What about Sage?"

"They'll tell us in a second." He wanted to get on the radio and demand more information. Telling Pepper they needed to wait helped him slow his roll—literally and figuratively.

The radio crackled. "This is Officer Tazwell. There's no sign of Sage Burns."

Allen lifted the radio and depressed the button. "Copy that. Thank you. How did Elijah Burns die?"

There were several options. A few meant something significant to this case. Since they'd discovered he might be the person who ripped off a local dealer, a major player on the drug scene, he'd wondered if Elijah would simply turn up dead.

Either way, they'd find Sage and figure out who was behind all this.

"Elijah is dead." Pepper sniffed back tears.

He said nothing, just held her hand. She would take care of Victory regardless. That was the kind of person she was.

He wanted that directed at him and the freedom to kiss her whenever he felt like it. Did she want to be married to a man with his problems? He could take on hers if she were willing to reciprocate. But given everything happening right now with her family, maybe it was better to leave it until after things settled. Like with their conversation later.

A box van, riding low—full of heavy items—drove slowly through the lot. Dark gray, the dumb color that looked like primer, like car manufacturers had run out of imagination. No license plate on the front.

He twisted as it passed. No plate on the back either.

Allen's instincts pricked. Basuto headed into the motel room on the second floor. He lifted the radio. "We might have company. Gray van."

The police lieutenant came back immediately. "Copy that. Eyes open, everyone."

A few cops would still be on the ground floor, but Allen couldn't spot them. The van eased out of the parking lot onto the street. Could be someone related seeing as there were cops crawling all over the motel. They might be leaving to go inform the boss this avenue was done—the location had been burned.

Like a lead that fizzled to nothing, or an informant who suddenly refused to cooperate.

Pepper shifted in her seat. She leaned across the center console to see what he was looking at out his window. "What is it?"

He shook his head. "I don't know yet."

The van started to drive away, then made an illegal U-turn in the middle of the street. Screeching tires. Smoke out the back.

It picked up speed, bumped the curb by the entrance, and raced across the half-empty parking lot.

Faster.

Faster.

"All of you out. Now!" Allen gripped the radio. "Get—"

The van drove at the stairs. Wood splintered into a million pieces, and the van barreled into the corner of the building. A deafening crash rattled Allen's truck across the lot as the van plowed through the lower corner room—took it out completely.

The upstairs had no support.

Everything gave way, and the end of the motel collapsed in on itself. From inside the truck, he heard people screaming. Pepper and the victims inside.

Allen fumbled for his phone and called 911.

"What is your emergency?"

"Building collapse." He had to fight to take a breath. "Starburst Motel. Multiple people trapped." His mouth tripped over the words. "This is City Liaison Allen Frees. We need rescue squad, any fire truck available, and ambulances. Any you can spare." He gasped. "There are people in there!"

21

A fire truck bumped the curb and turned into the parking lot. Pepper tried to take a breath, caught a lungful of grit, and coughed it out.

The man on the ground gasped.

"Easy. Just hang on." She pressed both hands against the man's stomach. The first person she'd pulled out.

As soon as Allen had called 911, she'd jumped out of the truck. It didn't feel right leaving him to get out and rushing in, but everything in her screamed to help. She'd seen this man right away. Getting him out meant lifting a couple of pieces of what had been the stairs, but she uncovered him. *Blood.* Pepper put pressure on the wound. It seeped through her fingers.

He had to have been in the top-level room on the end.

But what about the cops and any other occupants? A nighttime winter breeze brushed over her skin, flushed and clammy. *Shock.* As if she had time for that. "Just hang on."

Another fire truck pulled in. This one had a ladder on top, but it wasn't Truck 14. The rescue squad from Eastside firehouse jumped out of their vehicle. Her ears rang. Four guys, but then a fifth hopped out followed by another person—Amelia.

"Help!" Pepper didn't want to seem helpless, but why pretend? Half the motel had been destroyed. The other half emptied of people. About half had their phones out, recording video. Probably live streaming.

Other motel guests ran to their cars with bags and pulled out of the parking lot seconds later.

Amelia ran over. "What have we got?" She landed on her knees on the man's other side.

"He was right there." Pepper pointed.

"Put pressure back on." Amelia grabbed her other hand and placed it on the first, covering the man's wound.

Pepper didn't look. Wet, warm blood seeped between her fingers.

"Keep it there."

She looked at the man's face. His skin had paled and looked almost gray now. "Is he..."

Amelia touched Pepper's cheeks with her gloved hands. "Keep doing what you're doing. The ambos will be here in minutes, and they'll take care of him."

Pepper nodded.

"I'm going to help the others, but I'll come back and check on you."

"I wasn't in there when the van hit. I was in the car with Allen." Where was Allen? Pepper glanced around, but Amelia's gloved hands stopped her.

"I'll check on you."

"Okay."

Amelia let go, hopped up, and headed for the others. Pepper needed to find Allen. It didn't take long. He watched the scene, holding that radio. Directing people. The pained expression on his face wasn't one she liked, but regardless, neither of them could do anything but what they were doing. He probably wanted to be in the thick of it, pulling people out. But he wouldn't do nothing. He would help.

Pepper watched rescue squad lift pieces of debris. In the midst of chaos, they seemed organized. Things were shifted in one direction, wood and drywall. Even furniture.

One firefighter with *Crawford* on the hem at the back of his coat bent down and pulled out a woman in a dress.

Pepper winced at the blood on the woman's head.

Bryce bent his knees and put the woman over his shoulder. He carried her past Allen, off to the side, and laid her down.

Pepper looked at the man under her hands. Sightless eyes stared across the street. She moved two bloody fingers to the side of his neck. Nothing.

She hung her head for a second. Bit her lip. Tried to breathe. To think. *Lord, help us.*

Pepper closed the man's eyes and headed for the woman. She hadn't made it either.

The next person Bryce pulled out was alive. An older man he assisted, since the guy seemed to be able to walk on his own. Amelia also lifted a guy and half carried him over rubble. The others kept clearing debris away.

She met Bryce. "I can take him."

He let her get under the man's shoulder. "Over there. We triage in three groups." He held up a finger. "Didn't make it, or won't." He added a second finger. "Requires immediate treatment." Then a third. "Minor wounds, stable. Got it?"

"Copy that." Seemed like the appropriate thing to say.

Pepper was a licensed nurse—just not for people. There were minimal things she could do, but she wasn't without the skills to help.

Bryce turned back. As he passed Amelia, he said, "Two-one to me."

Pepper blinked. The injured man needed her help, and she assisted him walking. But her mind wanted to figure that out.

They were keeping score of the people they rescued?

Pepper figured if it got victims out of the debris fast, their competition wasn't necessarily a bad thing. But it also didn't seem good.

"Here. I think you should sit down." Pepper helped lower the man to the ground but didn't crouch. "I need to help others."

The man waved a hand. "I'm good." He didn't look it, but she took his word for it.

She remembered Amelia's words to her. "I'll be back to check on you."

An ambulance pulled up to the curb behind Allen's truck. Trace and Izan jumped out. More relief rolled through her than she anticipated, and she shivered.

They ran to her. Trace's assessing gaze roamed over her face, and he pulled on a pair of gloves.

Pepper lifted a hand. "I wasn't in that."

She turned to look at the end of the motel. *Sage.* Was her sister in there somewhere? She hadn't been in the room when the cops entered.

"*Oh, Lord.* Tazwell." She turned back to Trace. "The SWAT team went in. And Lieutenant Basuto."

Tears burned hot in her eyes. She sniffed. Dissolving under the weight of all this right now would not help her. She could cry later, because right now there were things she could do to help, considering all these people were hurt because of her family and their messed up drama.

"Bryce said triage."

Trace patted her shoulder. "Got it. You have some medical experience. Why don't you help me?"

Izan glanced over with a puzzled look. Pepper nodded. "I'd like to."

Someone yelled, a woman. Two firefighters pulled Olivia

Tazwell from the rubble. Pepper ran to her. Trace tugged on her arm and stopped her.

Olivia had a piece of metal sticking out of her thigh. She cried out but seemed more like she was mad about it than in pain.

One of the firefighters said, "Easy."

They walked her over to Trace but had her sit down.

"Got her." Trace knelt beside her.

The firefighter ran back. Pepper laid her hand on Olivia's shoulder. "Doing okay?"

Olivia turned her head. "Peachy. You?"

Pepper wanted to laugh but couldn't. "I think we should go out for ice cream later."

"You should bring it to me in the hospital."

"I can do that." Pepper watched Trace pack the metal piece with gauze and bandage around it. For some reason, he taped the whole thing like he was trying to keep the shard of debris steady.

"You need a surgical suite, Officer Tazwell," Trace said. "We'll get you to one as soon as possible."

"Just get the others out." Olivia spoke through gritted teeth. "Is the chief here?"

Pepper glanced over at Allen, talking into his radio. Beyond him she spotted Chief Barnes climb out of his car and jog over. "Conroy's here."

"Good."

Another ambulance pulled up, and then two police cars. Another fire truck, probably from Westside firehouse. This was an "all hands on deck" kind of situation. The type where personal conflicts went out the window and everyone focused on helping the injured.

All because Sage and Elijah got themselves into a situation with the type of people who would drive a van into a building and then race away, leaving destruction behind—not to mention who-knew-how-many dead.

"Go update them."

Pepper frowned. "I'm with you right now."

"Go find out if they called the lieutenant's wife. Report back." Olivia's eyes darkened. "I need to know."

Whatever lived in her mind and heart, it wasn't a fun place to be. Pepper nodded. She understood needing to know. The impulse to exercise her control over an out-of-control situation. Like Bryce and Amelia, two lieutenants going head-to-head. They'd save people, but it would be about their rivalry—a place to funnel their emotion into determination and work the problem in front of them.

Pepper wanted to do the same. To look on this almost dispassionately and not be affected by the destruction.

"Go, Pepper."

She stood without realizing she'd responded to Olivia's order. After this was over, she planned to follow up on that ice cream with the cop. They could end up friends.

Until Olivia found out where Pepper had come from. The kind of people whose blood ran in her veins. Even if she already knew about Sage, it would be over after she learned the rest of it.

Pepper was probably better off not getting into a friendship.

Allen studied her as she picked her way through the chaos to him and Conroy. The EMTs raced around, calling orders to one another. Cops and firefighters hauled rubble away behind her. Another dead body had been laid beside the other.

Pepper didn't look at him. "Olivia wants to know..." She couldn't remember. "I..."

Allen lifted his hand. Someone behind her yelled.

Pepper spun around and nearly toppled over. Allen grabbed her back pocket, held on until she steadied herself, and then let go. His fingers squeezed hers for a second.

Two firefighters pulled a uniformed police officer out of the debris.

"Conroy!" That was Amelia's firefighter. Mickey, she thought his name was.

They walked the cop over and sat him down. Conroy met them—beside the other victims classified as minimally injured and stable.

Pepper let out a breath. She hadn't realized she'd been holding it.

Allen tugged on her hand. "Hey."

She wasn't sure she could face him. "People are dead."

"I know that." Allen paused. "Pepper, this wasn't your fault."

She turned. "This is my family." She waved a hand, encompassing the destruction. "This is exactly what happens."

Allen shook his head. He started to speak, but she couldn't let him try to change her mind.

"Olivia wants to know if Basuto's wife has been called."

His expression softened. "Sasha is very pregnant with twins. Conroy has Aiden, the sergeant, and Basuto's mom going over there to stay with her. Otherwise she'd be here trying to help. They all would."

Pepper nodded. "Okay, I'll go tell Olivia that."

"Pepp—"

She kept walking, chin up. No thoughts were allowed to enter her mind. The last thing she needed was to collapse crying right now. Except that was exactly what she wanted to do.

Her limbs felt as though they weighed twice what they should. Just looking at the destruction made her chest squeeze like when that guy had grabbed her.

She lifted her fingers and rubbed the bruise on the underside of her chin. The wreckage of her house was down to her. This was because of someone else. *Not you.* But Sage was in the middle of it, and Pepper was supposed to be here. This could be retaliation.

Elijah was dead.

She sat beside Olivia. Except her legs gave out halfway down, and she crumpled to the ground beside the police officer.

"Whoa." Olivia stopped her from falling to the side.

Pepper planted both hands on the pavement. Bile rose, but she fought back the sensation.

"Hey." Allen's hands gathered her up. He'd come over with her?

She shook her head and tried to tell him no. She didn't deserve to be comforted by these people. This was all her fault. *So many* people were dead.

He lifted her off the ground with all that strength he used to make his life what he wanted it to be. Refusing to compromise or give up what he didn't want to lose.

Had she ever had that much strength?

Allen lifted her onto his lap. Pepper tucked her head in his shoulder. "All my..." She gasped. "Fault."

She wound her arms around his chest and held on as tight as she could.

For as long as he would let her.

22

Allen set the mug of coffee on the table in front of the mayor's desk—reluctantly, he had to admit. It seemed like hot java was the only thing keeping him going this morning. Coffee, and seeing Pepper when he got home.

He looked at the tablet on his lap. "We believe that whichever local dealer Burns sold the tainted drugs to retaliated and executed him."

After last night's tragedy, they'd finally made it back to his cabin before two. Pepper had still been crashed out asleep when he headed out this morning, leaving Victory with his cousin Natalie. He didn't like the child being without a familiar face, but his cousin would be kind, keep her safe, and listen if Victory wanted to talk at all.

If anyone could help Victory feel safe, it was Natalie.

He hoped she did the same for Pepper when she woke up. He hadn't slept well. Nightmares woke him several times, covered in sweat and tangled in the sheets.

Just the idea that he might've been inside when that building came down brought back memories of the day he'd been injured. An entire building had collapsed on the cops in the basement that day.

He cleared his throat. Back to business. "Likely, when he realized the cops already found Burns, he decided to take them out as well."

"Five dead. One, a cop."

Allen looked up. "That's right, Mr. Mayor. Officer McNamara's family has been notified of his passing. The rest were civilians." He fought back the lump in his throat. He'd been so grateful when they pulled out Lieutenant Basuto—spitting mad, with only minor injuries.

The next man hadn't been so lucky.

No one needed big bad Allen Frees breaking down into a puddle of tears. He tried to reserve that for three a.m. showers.

His job right now was to do his job. Which meant being respected enough to be left to take care of things and get them done.

The door opened. Janice walked in, followed by Conroy. The chief looked as tired as Allen felt. He walked right over while Janice headed for the water and glasses on the mayor's side table. Conroy squeezed Allen's shoulder and sat in the wingback chair Allen had rolled up next to.

The mayor glanced at Janice, who took a drink of the water with a shaky hand. "Everything okay, Janice?"

She inhaled a choppy breath. "This woman has caused destruction all over town. It's unbelievable. Someone needs to be held accountable, and as far as I can see that person is Pepper Miller."

Conroy shifted. A subtle signal to Allen not to wade in. The mayor didn't miss it, glancing between them and Janice.

Conroy said, "The police are investigating, and we haven't had the time yet to draw any conclusions. However, I can tell you right now that Ms. Miller isn't a person of interest. She's barely a witness. People are innocent until proven guilty, and not the other way around."

"Let's get back to our briefing, shall we?" The mayor's tone left no room for argument. "Allen?"

He nodded. "The debris will be cleared out today. All guests checked in have been accounted for. There's always the possibility someone had an additional person not listed on the registry present in their room at the time of the incident. However, the local search and rescue team has brought over cadaver dogs."

Janice let out a whimper.

"If anyone remains in the rubble, they will be found."

"Good." Mayor Harrelson nodded.

Allen continued. "We believe the dealer took out Burns, as I already stated. Sage Burns is still in the wind. However, we recovered Elijah's phone in the rubble." He turned to his former boss. "Chief?"

Conroy nodded. "Our preliminary download of the phone revealed a text message thread. Someone posing as Sage lured him there, or the woman herself did. When he showed up, he was executed."

Janice whimpered louder.

Allen bit down on his molars. The woman was distraught and didn't need him getting aggravated at her. He'd always had a temper that flashed hot and then burned out fast. She hadn't been there last night, but that didn't mean she didn't feel the emotional impact of what had happened.

Janice should be escorted calmly out to go home and rest. Take the day off.

"We need to find Sage Burns." The mayor's face remained impassive.

Conroy nodded. "At the least she can tell us who these people are. If not testify against them."

Allen wanted concrete evidence to surface so the conviction

didn't hang on the word of a woman who'd proven herself unreliable. Add to that the weight of wanting to protect Victory from her mother and father and what they'd been up to. If he wasn't careful, he'd be persuading Pepper to marry him and go to family court for custody of her niece.

She should've done it years ago, if anyone wanted to ask his opinion.

No one had.

He needed to keep his dreams to himself. Just because he wanted a family of his own didn't mean he should push the people he cared about into a situation he thought was best.

Allen said, "The fire department will keep working the scene, looking for evidence. After they're done clearing up, the arson investigator can have a look around. As many eyes on this as possible will help us gather as much as possible."

Conroy nodded. "Based on evidence found that we believe came from a different room, we've opened an unrelated case. My people have their assignments as of this morning, and everyone is working today."

Allen said, "Same. Unless they're in the hospital, they're on the clock."

Ridge was back to work, in fact. Zack needed another day, but Allen figured the kid would be at the firehouse anyway— probably making sandwiches for everyone. He hated it, but the fact was, a situation like this one helped bring people together. They were all focused on a common goal—cleaning up and solving this scene.

No one had time for petty interpersonal squabbles.

Allen had to make time for a video call with Macon James later. Since the guy was in Australia, that meant late afternoon before he started his day fighting bushfires with Bryce's twin brother.

Lieutenant Crawford had asked him to drop a hint to Macon to see if he could also persuade Logan to come home.

Allen wasn't sure Bryce understood the concept of an interview, but if he could drop it naturally in the conversation, he was going to.

Adding not just one but two quality firefighters would make this department even better.

The mayor blew out a breath. "Okay, keep me posted."

Fifteen minutes later Allen rolled out the open doors, Conroy right beside him. Allen turned for the ramp rather than the stairs, and the chief did the same.

"Sleep okay?"

Allen said, "I wasn't caught in that blast."

"But you watched it happen." Conroy shrugged a shoulder. "Unlike Janice, you were there through the whole thing."

"I get where she's coming from. It hurts, thinking about how many people got hurt. Who lost their lives. Being so grateful someone is alive when someone else is dead." Allen realized what he'd voiced and quickly said, "But we still do our jobs. Push through and get the work done."

Conroy slowed. When Allen stopped on the sidewalk, the chief turned to him. "Don't keep it all bottled up."

"I've got a cousin who is a trauma counselor, remember?"

"Free therapy?"

They both grinned, but there was no humor in either of them. He could see as much on Conroy's face and had no doubt it was mirrored in his own.

Allen glanced around at the busy street. "People go about their lives, no matter what. Only some people are brought to a standstill in a tragedy. This one was small, relatively speaking. Yet for some people, life will never be the same."

Across the street he spotted a familiar figure and lifted his hand to wave. The homeless man simply stared back.

Something in Allen eased, just a fraction.

Conroy held out his hand and Allen shook it. "I think I might call Dean. No point risking one of my officers burning out or spiraling. Might as well get them all someone to talk to. Even if I don't make it mandatory."

Allen huffed. The firefighters could use a little interpersonal training, that was for sure. "If only I could pull that card."

"Depends how much power you give the new chief." Conroy eyed him. "The right guy will take your advice. And I know you'd never use it to manipulate people. You're not that guy."

"Thanks." Allen had worked long and hard to earn the respect of people in this town. His stepmom was a woman people looked to in crisis, a solid member of the church family who was always helping folks. His younger stepbrother, Trey, was an EMT in Benson, Washington. He had a cousin, Wyatt. Enough people to sit around a Thanksgiving table and be grateful.

The homeless man had moved on. Allen would see him around, and things in his life would have shifted slightly each time. It seemed like his world constantly moved. What he wanted was for something to stabilize.

He had his faith. Or as much as he invited that stuff into his life when he needed more answers than he had. What he wanted to do was pray that Pepper stuck around this time. It seemed too risky, like if he voiced it even in a prayer, God might not give him what he wanted. She might leave again, cut ties but stick around where he had to see her.

And every time, it hurt a little more.

Hope caused too much pain. Like venturing into uncharted territory with no map and no idea the place was overrun by wolves.

Conroy flicked two fingers. "Keep me updated."

"Same." Allen headed for the parking lot, where he'd left his truck in the accessible space. The drive home felt far too long. He should visit the firehouse but wanted to work from home for a while. Pepper had to report to the vet's office in a day or two. She planned to take Victory and keep things light.

Moving on.

She trusted him to work the problem, and he would. But he wanted more from her than respect. He wanted a hint of what they'd had before—with a promise they had a future. Too many things were happening, and so far there hadn't been enough time to talk.

Yet.

He turned around in his yard and pulled up to the end of the porch that stuck out, basically a dock like on a lake. He could use it to get in and out of his truck without going to ground level. He also used it to dismount a horse when he wanted to forgo the harness lift in the barn.

The barn door had been left open, which Natalie did when she was inside. Better than going all over trying to find her. He watched for a second and saw Victory skip around inside. They were safe, and the child had found a way to be happy today.

He took a moment and thanked God she'd been nowhere near the motel last night.

That left Pepper inside his cabin.

Allen didn't find her in the kitchen or the living room. It was barely lunch and fatigue weighed down his arms, so pushing through the house was hard. "Pepper?"

She stuck her head into the hallway and waved, her other hand holding her phone to her ear. A deep frown on her face. "I know that, but..."

She ducked back into the bedroom. Allen moved to the doorway and saw her turn and lean against the wall.

"People *died*. How can you say that?" Tears filled her eyes.

Allen palmed his cell phone, wondering if the police department would run a trace if he asked. And if they could do it fast enough to find out who Pepper was talking to before the call ended.

"So that's it? I've got no choice, and we all have to live with the decisions you made?" She swiped a tear from under one eye. "I'm sick of it."

The caller must have said something. Pepper shook her head. "You tell me where you are, or you don't come back. Victory and I don't need you in our lives. Not now. We've got enough to deal with."

Allen braced, praying her sister gave her a location.

"We won't be going anywhere. Victory is going to be safe, Sage," Pepper said. "Even if that means keeping her safe from *you.*"

23

P epper gripped the phone. *Am I really going to do this?* Her resolve hardened like resin. "We both know this has been a long time coming."

"Your betrayal?" Sage laughed, but it sounded dead. "I guess we did know. I've been wondering when you were going to take her from me. You've probably already got her calling you *Mom*."

Her stomach hurt, she had it clenched so tight. The aches and pains from last night, running from person to person administering basic medical care. She got barely any sleep between the nightmares and dreams about the kiss she'd shared with Allen—which then twisted into a horrific facsimile of what it had been.

"Don't be ridiculous." Pepper sank onto the edge of the bed, no longer able to hold her legs up to pace. She would fall to the floor. "I'm her auntie. I'll always be that."

The truth was, they wouldn't be closer if Pepper had Victory call her *Mom*. They would have the exact same relationship with each other—the one they both needed.

Support. Peace.

As much as she could give that to Victory, the child effort-lessly gave the same back to her. So long as Victory didn't feel the weight of it, Pepper would soak up what she needed.

"You'd better not disappear with her."

"The way you have?" Pepper clenched her jaw. Sage could make it so Pepper never saw Victory.

"You kidnap her, I call the feds. Don't forget that."

Pepper didn't doubt her sister would cause all kinds of trouble for her. But she did doubt it would involve calling the FBI. Sage wouldn't want them looking too closely at her life.

She squeezed the bridge of her nose. "Neither of us wants the cops up in our business. That's never gone well for us before."

Sage huffed. "Because we don't mean squat to the cops. Victory? She's an innocent child caught up in our battle."

"We're not at war."

"They'll believe what they want to believe. We're the bad guys, remember?"

Pepper winced. "You know it doesn't have to be that way."

"Pretending to be some upstanding, do-good citizen never did you any favors. Why would I wanna be like you?"

Pepper lifted her gaze to blink away the burn of tears.

Allen had stopped in the doorway, his phone out. She stared at him. He lifted his free hand and made a circle with his finger. He mouthed, *Keep her talking.*

Were the police tracing the call?

Pepper's stomach rolled over. "Ditto on that."

She and Sage had agreed to disagree about how to live their lives. Sage did whatever she wanted. Meanwhile Pepper tried to do what was right, and her sister seemed to think it meant nothing. But if Pepper wanted a shot at peace, and hope for the future, leaning on God as her Lord was going to be the *only* way it happened.

"Sometimes you being a goody-two-shoes comes in handy."

Pepper said, "How's that?"

"You'd better keep her safe, you hear me?" Sage shifted, and Pepper heard a door close. "Maybe you should disappear. That would at least keep her safe. But you'd better not steal my kid, Pep. I'll never forgive you."

Pepper bit her lip. "What's going on? I thought you'd been kidnapped. Either that or you were dead. Why else wouldn't you have come back to get her?"

"I'm working on some things. She's safer with you until I've ironed it all out."

"How long is that going to take? Victory needs to go to school."

"So homeschool her," Sage said. "People do it all the time. And she's in first grade. How hard can it be to teach her to read?"

"She already knows how to read."

"Whatever. You know what I mean."

Pepper pressed her lips together. She couldn't resist the temptation anymore, and shifted her gaze to Allen.

He shook his head.

She didn't know what that meant. "Why are they targeting Victory? Because of you?"

"They think Elijah gave her something."

"They thought that about me too. You're going to let bad guys shove her around and terrify her?" Pepper swallowed the lump in her throat. "She's a frightened child."

"No one did us any favors, and we turned out fine."

Pepper blew out a breath, trying not to be sick. "What did Elijah give her?"

She wasn't sure it had happened, but any information Sage could provide would help. She hoped.

"Whatever he tried to buy his freedom with, or her safety." A low voice rumbled in the background of her call. Sage said, "I know that, baby. I'll be right there."

Pepper pressed her fingers to her mouth.

"Gotta go, sis. Think about what I said."

The line went dead.

Pepper dropped the phone to the bed, covered her face with her hands, and moaned.

Allen closed the gap between them. "Come here."

He probably figured she could use a hug. She wanted one more than anything but couldn't accept. Not when he didn't know. When he found out, he would wish she'd told him from the start. She couldn't even voice it out loud.

He would hate her.

Pepper jumped up. "I can't do that again. I have to withstand this on my own, not fall apart just because I want to let you be the strong one."

"I *want* to do that for you." He shrugged one shoulder. "Is it so bad to let me?"

"I can't." She shook her head. "Because it's what I want more than anything."

He studied her. "I had the police department try to run a trace, since they have a warrant to dig into Sage's life and it covers her cell phone. They said it's not a model that has GPS. Whoever called you, it was from a burner phone."

"It was her." Pepper sank back onto the bed so they were at eye level. She wanted to feel like they were on even footing. "I'm sorry." She winced. "Thank you for helping Victory and me. We'll be out of your hair as soon as it's safe and I can get people in my house to repair things."

"Why does this conversation suddenly sound a whole lot like when you broke up with me?"

"I can't..."

Allen leaned forward and laid his hand on hers. "Whatever it is, I need you to tell me. Not necessarily right now. But at some point."

"Or you're done looking out for us?"

"No."

Pepper didn't want to let hope be born in her heart. "You'll never want to see me again."

"How do you know that for sure?"

She couldn't decipher the look on his face. "Because I feel the same way about it."

"You're allowed to move on from the past." He paused. "Unless it was you who did something, and me being formerly a cop poses a problem to your freedom?"

She shook her head. "It wasn't me."

"Then you don't have to pay for it. Someone else did something wrong, and it affected you, but it doesn't have to define you."

"I want that to be true."

"So whatever it is would destroy this?" Allen waved his hand back and forth between them.

"You won't want me in your life."

His expression shifted then, and she read exactly what was written there. *Try me.*

He wanted her to take a chance on him—on *them*. But he didn't know, so how could he be sure this was something he could get past? No one deserved what she'd done to him.

What her family had done.

"I should go check on Victory."

He waylaid her with a hand on her arm. "I know you're scared. There's a lot going on. Whatever it is? I want you to give me a chance." The hard line of his mouth softened. "Maybe even the benefit of the doubt that I can be understanding. Forgiving, if the situation warrants it."

He let go of her arm.

Pepper walked down the hall, out the front door, and down the porch steps. She stopped on the gravel by his network of paths to wheel himself everywhere on his property.

Unyielding. He hadn't wanted to give up the parts of his life that he loved just because he was paralyzed.

He brought that same determination into a relationship.

Now he was determined to get her to give him the benefit of the doubt. To believe he was the man he was, who she wanted—needed—him to be.

Pepper ran her hands through her hair, still damp from her shower, elbows bent and splayed out. She stretched her back while she stood there, just for good measure. Her life was a shambles.

She was staying with her ex-boyfriend and caring for her niece whose mother had abandoned her. She needed to go to work. Instead, she couldn't do anything but shiver with fear that more gunmen would show up.

Or it was just cold out here.

Allen seemed to think she could handle more. He didn't know how close she was to packing everything in her car and fleeing in the middle of the night. He would probably want to be the designated driver.

And she would let him.

Can I really tell him, Lord? She wanted the truth out. But the stain of what her past meant to them hung like a gavel, ready to pronounce a sentence the moment her confession got out.

He didn't know. He couldn't understand her hesitation.

Pepper was about to test their entire relationship, and it had barely begun. There couldn't possibly be a solid enough foundation to weather something like this.

He would want to forgive her but wouldn't be able to get past it in the end. She would know he tried to do the right thing just because he was a good guy. She'd have to watch it all fall apart the way she always knew it would.

Maybe Natalie had an answer. She was a counselor, and Pepper had certainly been through some trauma.

Her last counselor had told her she needed to get to know

God better if she thought He targeted people for failure just for the fun of it. Maybe that was true, but she'd quit that counselor and the ministry she represented. Was Natalie like that, or did she bring compassion?

That counselor had been no different from the FBI agents Sage always brought up. Like they were representative of the whole bureau.

What a mess.

It was easier to be alone than take a chance, fall flat on her face, or be disappointed.

Again.

Pepper stepped into the barn. "Natalie? Victory? You guys in here?"

A horse shifted, and she heard that snuffle they did when they exhaled out their nostrils. She didn't know much about horses, but she liked them, even if they were intimidating. For Victory's sake she would get over that. The same way she would try not to remember what it had felt like riding in front of Allen when they were dating.

The feel of his arms around her.

Pepper sighed. "You guys in here?"

"Auntie!" Victory's voice came like a cry.

At the end of the barn, where the door to the storage room stood open, a dark-dressed figure stood with his back to her.

"Shut her up." His voice was low and lethal.

Pepper said, "What are you doing?"

He swung around and pointed his gun at her. A man she'd never seen before.

Pepper lifted her hands. "Whatever you want, we don't have it. Elijah gave us nothing." True in more ways than one, but this guy didn't need to know that.

He backed out of the doorway and waved the gun between her and the storage room like he could shoot either of them whenever he wanted.

Inside the room, Allen's cousin stood in front of Victory, guarding her from this man. Those telltale thick blonde bangs hung over one side of her face but didn't obscure the look of determination in her eyes. She would take a bullet for this child.

Pepper prayed it didn't come to that.

24

Allen pulled a package of ground beef from the freezer and set it in a bowl of water in the sink to defrost. He was prepared to pull out the big guns to get Pepper to trust him. If that meant making his stepmom's recipe for lasagna, so be it.

He'd loved it as a kid, so much she'd often made one for the fridge so he could get a piece whenever he was hungry. She'd called it "snack lasagna."

Which was his stepmom in a nutshell. A good woman who took care of the people she loved. It just hadn't been enough to keep his father from self-destructing. Natalie had lived with them for a while, around her junior high years. Both of them had seen his father fall down the slippery slope that led to him isolating himself from them.

Because he was broken, and they deserved better.

He couldn't help thinking the same thing was happening all over again, this time with Pepper.

A shuffle in the hallway pricked at the edge of his awareness. Every instinct he had flared to life. He catalogued a number of options in the first split second. Gun under his jacket in the shoulder holster he preferred. Knife in the block on the counter. Scissors in the drawer.

He could do some damage if it became necessary.

Allen set the package of pasta on the counter and reached to unsnap the gun. He didn't pull it out. Yet.

Just in case he was wrong.

He didn't turn. Using the phone pocketed beside his leg, he called 911. A nonresponse from a caller warranted police, fire, and ambulance rolling out in answer. After all, the dispatcher would have no idea what the problem was. He wasn't incapacitated and didn't plan to be.

Hopefully they'd hear him talking.

Allen called out, "Everything okay?"

"That depends on whether you plan to cause trouble." The voice had a slight accent.

Allen eased his chair around but kept his gun out of sight. If this guy didn't think he planned to cause trouble, he'd neglected to do his homework on Allen Frees. At the least, he might know Allen had been a cop. At best, he figured Allen posed no threat because he couldn't walk.

"Seems like you're the trouble," Allen said. "Since you broke into my house armed with a gun. Intent on what?"

He let that hang, hoping the dispatcher sent a patrol car.

"Give us what Elijah gave to his family, and we'll leave."

There was more than one. "How many of you are there? If you hurt the people I care about, I will kill you."

The guy cracked a smile, flashing a gold cap. Gold watch on his gun hand. Designer clothes with a gangster flair. He was entrenched in the life. He'd paid his dues if the tattoos on his neck were anything to go by.

Not someone Allen needed to get complacent with.

"Yeah? You'll kill me, cripple?"

"You'd be surprised." Allen bit down on his molars. He didn't need to antagonize this guy into shooting him. He needed to disarm and detain—if that was at all possible. Then get to the barn so he could help Victory, Pepper, and Natalie.

"Give me what I want."

"Tell me who you work for."

The guy motioned with the gun. "Let's go find your lady friends in the barn. See what they have to say about you asking questions instead of talking."

"It's a flaw. I'm trying to work on it."

"Get moving."

Allen turned his chair and headed the opposite direction around the table. Shoot the guy, no more fuss?

Tempting.

Throw something, draw his gun, and finish this?

Too noisy if another gunman had the girls hostage.

Tackle and subdue meant he had to stand and take at least one step—doable, though he'd already be falling at that point—and take the guy down. That sounded a lot more fun than just putting a bullet in the guy's forehead. Allen had some pent-up aggression to work out. Starting with payback for the bruise on Pepper's jaw.

Hopefully she never found out he had a lethal side. Even if it fell within the bounds of what qualified as legal according to the penal code, she could get frightened if she saw it. Then she would never open up the way he wanted her to.

She just didn't need to see him kill anyone.

Maybe Natalie would help out, keeping Pepper and Victory from seeing too much.

The gunman shifted to follow him out into the hall. Allen stayed in the doorway for a split second. Long enough to swipe one forearm crutch, swing it around, and slam the guy in the side of his shoulder.

The gun went off.

No time to pray he didn't get hit. Or duck out of the way.

The sound cracked like a firework and the guy dropped the pistol.

Sound in his ears warped into ringing.

Allen tossed the crutch, pulled his own gun, and said, "Don't even think about it."

The guy froze in his crouch, halfway to his weapon on the floor.

Allen saw the split second of indecision before he swiped it up. He'd seen that look before. He knew what it meant. He moved his finger to the trigger.

The guy brought the gun up.

Allen squeezed. His gun went off.

The guy fell back and his weapon hit the floor a second time, fingers open. Unmoving. Blood pooled behind his head.

Allen hit the porch, sped down the ramp, and shoved the wheels forward double-time. *Go. Go.* His heart pumped along with the movement of his arms, propelling him down the path. The ringing in his ears subsided a little, enough that he could hear police sirens in the distance.

Backup.

He'd been a cop long enough to know he should wait out here for them. But he'd been a man longer than that, not to mention a marine. A son. A brother. A friend. He wasn't going to allow Pepper, Victory, or Natalie to be in danger one second longer than necessary. Not if he had anything to say about it.

He eased his chair to the side of the door and listened first. Wheeling in without getting an idea of what was happening made for potential disaster.

"You will tell me!"

Allen made a quick assessment of the voice. A man who thought he was on the side that would win this. He had to have heard the gunshot from the house but probably figured it was Allen lying dead in the hallway.

Maybe the two women and the child in the barn did as well. Allen could hear the subtle sounds of crying.

Then Pepper's voice. "We can't tell you what we don't know."

The sirens were louder now, but the cops still had to drive up the mountainside to his house. It would take time.

Which they didn't have.

"Then you die," the man yelled. "I will tell Hector I had no choice, and we will be done with this."

There was a little tidbit he didn't have before.

"Fine!" Pepper yelled the word, but there was a note in it. One that didn't resonate right. Was it fear under the bravado? He wasn't sure. "Do what you want. We don't know anything!"

That didn't sound right.

Allen eased forward to look at what was going on.

His stomach flipped over. She was going to get them all—

Natalie, almost behind the man, swung a shovel into his back.

He cried out and fell to his knees. Pepper cowered in the corner, Victory behind her. Natalie readied for another swing.

The man came up, gun first, way too fast.

Allen aimed his gun and squeezed off his second shot of the day.

The man fell to the ground, dead. Natalie dropped the shovel. Pepper and Victory screamed.

That police car sounded much too close now. Allen's head swam. Natalie helped Pepper and Victory to their feet and brought them to the door. "Come on. Let's stand outside."

Allen nodded even though she wasn't talking to him.

Victory hiccupped a sob. The kid had one shoe, the other lost. She slammed into him and wrapped her arms around him. Allen held the gun away from her and felt the prick of tears in his eyes. "Victory."

Pepper joined the hug, sandwiching the child between

them, her forehead on his shoulder. Natalie took the gun from him.

Allen found his cousin's gaze and mouthed *thank you*. She shook her head and walked away—probably to meet the cops.

He wrapped both his arms around Victory and Pepper. "My girls." A statement of relief. A cry of his heart. Both, or either. Did it matter?

Pepper pulled in a breath and let it out with a shudder. She kissed his cheek and eased back to a crouch. She laid her hand on Victory's back. "You okay, Nugget?"

The child didn't lift her head from Allen's sweater. "You killed that man." The words were muffled against the material.

He glanced at Pepper for guidance and saw no concern on her face, just sadness. "Sweetness." He rubbed his hand on the child's back, trying to warm her with some reassurance. This child lived in an uncertain, dangerous world. "If someone is trying to hurt you, I will *always* do whatever it takes to make sure you're safe."

Victory shifted. She lifted her head and looked at him. Unsure.

"Hop on. I'll give you a ride so you don't get your sock dirty. Okay?"

She climbed onto his lap and curled against him, her legs tucked up so her feet were on his knee.

Pepper walked beside them to where Natalie was relaying the entire experience to the two uniformed officers. She'd been in the military like him, but not in combat. She was a therapist, but she'd had training and knew how to defend herself. They were cut from the same cloth.

He should've given her the full set of *Castle* DVDs for Christmas, not just the first couple of seasons. He'd have to figure out what else he could do to thank her for risking her life to save Pepper and Victory.

Victory shifted on his lap, her coat unzipped but wrapped

around her. They probably needed a blanket. Pepper was shivering. But going inside meant dealing with the dead guy in his hallway.

Victory wore the same coat that had hung from the closet door handle when Burns had showed up at Pepper's house, which felt like weeks ago but was more like days.

He lifted the bottom of the zipper, where the pocket met the hem. He didn't like thinking those men had been right, but Elijah could have slipped something in here at Pepper's.

Something "Hector" wanted back.

His fingers closed around a small object. He'd have to get to that later.

"...statements from you. Unless anyone needs to see a doctor." The cop looked each of them over. His partner headed up the porch steps into the house.

Pepper shook her head.

"They're just shaken up, I think," Allen said. "But I've got a recipe for that."

Victory said, "It's too cold for ice cream."

"How about hot chocolate?"

She lifted her head. "With marshmallows?"

"They have big ones at the firehouse. And little ones." He leaned his head close to hers and whispered, "I like to use both."

Victory smiled, just a glint of humor in her eyes. No movement of her mouth. There had been too much danger today for that. She was okay, though. It could hit her in full force later, and they would deal.

For right now, he needed to get both of them to the warmth and safety of the firehouse. And then look into that jacket.

25

Pepper pushed back the blanket and remembered there was a top bunk just before she smacked her head against it. She eased to standing and stretched her hands above her head. Victory wasn't in her bed, and Amelia had a spot to sleep set up in her office.

Out of the four bunks, Pepper's was the only one occupied in the girls' room.

She had to push down the worry that wanted to consume her. Victory was in a safe place—and once Pepper found her, she would know for sure.

The door from the bunk room led right into the engine bay where the trucks were parked. The rescue squad fire engine. The fire truck with its ladder on top. Another truck in the lane farthest from her, over by the storage rooms, had half its engine spread across the floor. Out of service.

Pepper felt like she'd been out of service for days. It was time to get back to her life, but how could she do that when there were bad guys out there looking for something Elijah had given her? Or Victory. Bad guys and someone named Hector.

She shuddered and doubled back to her bed, tugged the

blanket off, and wrapped it around her shoulders. Voices at the other end of the engine bay, followed by a child's laughter, drew her. Pepper wound around the front of the rescue squad truck to see the open front doors on the fire engine.

Zack, in full turnout gear, climbed into the passenger seat. "Ready to go, Lieutenant."

The truck wasn't running. Pepper walked to the front and looked through the windshield. Victory sat in the front seat, both hands on the steering wheel.

"*Vroom, vroom.*" She swayed in her seat, and Zack matched it. "Gotta go save the kitty from the tree."

Zack spotted Pepper. His eyes widened like she'd caught him with his hand in the cookie jar. "Step on it, Lieutenant!"

Victory took a particularly sharp imaginary turn.

Pepper grinned and left them to it. Instead of taking the hall that led to the common room and kitchen, she figured it more likely Allen was in his office and headed down the hall at the end of the engine bay.

Maybe she would get her coffee and go up to the roof. The place had an elevator, so Allen could go with her. Did he want to have that talk? There wasn't much point, considering it had become painfully clear to anyone watching that her family stuff only hurt people.

She'd destroyed her house. His was a crime scene.

Now they were hiding out at the firehouse in protective custody—until the firefighters were called out.

She glanced down toward the elevator and the hall that led to the door on that side. Pepper caught a flash of movement. Had to be one of the firefighters over there, working in the storage rooms.

She wandered down the hall to Allen's office, hoping he would go with her to get some coffee so she could fully wake up.

The first hall that branched off to her left led to the gym.

Someone was in there in the throes of a tough workout. Maybe two people, sparring. Or wrestling. She could see the firefighters here doing that to get some of their frustration out.

Straight ahead on the right were the two lieutenants' offices and then Allen's at the end before the hallway turned to the chief's office and the conference room. She could walk circles around this place all day and keep finding rooms and offices. Or storage she hadn't known was there before. This place was huge.

Allen's chair sat empty in the center of his room. Allen stood up between the parallel bars. Feet on the ground. Arms braced, muscles strained. The man could lift his entire body with just his arms and shoulders. Like one of those Olympic gymnasts on the bars and rings.

She'd never been attracted to guys obsessed with sports before but had to admit the fact he possessed so much strength made her face flush.

Sometimes it seemed like he could do anything.

Pepper eased the door open. "I don't want to break your concentration."

"Distraction is good." He stared at the floor in front of him. He moved one foot, then the other, lowered himself in a semi-squat, and then took another step. Another squat. Another step.

"Wow."

"Because I can walk while holding on to something?"

"I was so worried it was an all-or-nothing injury. Not that you might be able to one day work your way back to walking."

"I'll never walk normally, without assistance."

Did he think she cared about that? "But you're working on it."

"The alternative is giving up. Or being content with where I'm at—which isn't giving up at all. It isn't even surrendering. It's just being happy with the situation and making the best of it. But my muscles need to be worked to keep up my strength. I need to be moving forward, at least figuratively."

"I bet your physical therapist likes that."

"She told me to slow down."

Pepper chuckled. "Why does that not surprise me?"

"I don't do slow. I like being content with my forward progress." Allen got to the end of the bars and turned around using his arms, his legs swinging under him, and she got a flash of the Olympics again.

Who'd have thought that would be her weakness? On the heels of him protecting them yesterday, she found him a bit irresistible this morning.

"You're gonna stare at my back now?"

"I'm going to back gracefully away from that comment. As I am a lady."

It was his turn to chuckle.

"I'd like to go back to that contentment thing, though."

"You think progress means I'm not content?"

"You tell me."

"I was content when I could transfer myself couch to chair, solo. Then I was content when I could do it faster. In a few months, I'll be content when I'm up on crutches, taking steps and not falling on my face. And at the end of the day, I'm content to lie down and not have to move anymore."

He turned and lowered himself back into the chair with a sigh, grabbed a towel from the shelf beside him, and mopped his face.

"I'd be content with a cup of coffee right now."

"Some wins are easy. Some are harder." He smiled. "That's an easy one."

She said, "Did you know Victory is in the fire truck with Zack playing make believe firefighters?"

Allen grinned. "I had an inkling he was the man for the job."

"He's back at work?"

"They all are. Probably in the kitchen throwing breakfast around again."

Pepper said, "Making a hot mess."

"Something like that." He studied her for a minute. "I'd rather not bring up the bad stuff, but I do want to know if you're okay. After everything that happened yesterday."

Pepper didn't like the "why" of what'd happened.

But the rest of it?

She crossed to him, leaned down, and touched her lips to his. "Thank you for keeping us safe."

He kissed her back, and the scent of his exertion filled her nostrils as he tugged her close with those strong arms.

She planted a hand on his biceps and felt the corded muscle beneath his skin.

There was so much more she could say, things fear would never let her voice aloud. All of it was there in the exchange, the softness of that simple touch. The certainty of what she wanted, even if things weren't settled and she didn't know what the future would bring.

He still didn't know.

Pepper pulled back. "I get sucked in by you, and I forget reality."

He touched her cheek. "This is what's real. Everything else can go away for all I care."

"You won't say that when you—"

"I already know, Pepper."

She backed up. He reached for her hand and didn't let her get far.

"I know your mother is serving a life sentence for murdering another woman in a fight behind a bar."

Her head swam.

"Your mother killed my mother."

Pepper gasped. "I'm sorry."

"Me too." He frowned, but he wasn't distraught.

She shook her head. "How can you say it like that? My family—"

"Did you ask for that woman to be your mother?"

"No."

"Do you visit her or write to her? Are you close?"

"Of course not. She went to prison and we were taken away from her."

"That was at least a year after I was removed from my mother's home and full custody was given to my dad. I was half the world away, living on base with marines." A tiny smile curled the edges of his lips. "I barely remember. And what I remember wasn't good."

"Murder isn't good."

"You and I had nothing to do with that. It was two women we barely know in a fight behind a bar. We weren't involved."

Pepper shook her head.

"If we don't want it to be between us, it won't be. Don't use it as an excuse because you're scared I'm going to be anything like those people who call themselves your family."

She frowned.

"Sit for a second. Then we'll get coffee."

She slumped into the empty desk chair.

Allen pushed his chair over so they were almost knee-to-knee and locked his wheels so it didn't roll.

"You've decided it's fine?"

"I did a...deeper dive on your background days ago, Pepper."

She frowned. "You could have said. I've been *freaking* out."

He touched her knee. "Sorry."

She took his hand. "Was it before you kissed me at your house?"

He nodded.

"So you've declared everything is nothing to worry about?"

"It's up to you to decide. I'm fully aware of the situation and content to make this work without putting that between us."

"Ugh." Pepper slumped back in the chair.

Allen said, "What did I say?"

"Why do you have to be so *reasonable*?"

"You'd rather I was irrational and flew off the handle?"

"It might make me feel better if you did."

"You don't need to feel bad, though. Life happened and we're connected, but only indirectly. It didn't have anything to do with you."

"My mom killed your mom." Pepper had to make him see this. He couldn't pretend it wasn't a big deal.

"My mother's name is Audrey. She married my dad the year before I turned eleven, and she is everything a mom should be. Including the kind of woman who sends a box of chocolate chip cookies in the mail for my entire squad of marines. Did you know if you put a slice of bread in, the cookies don't dry out?"

Pepper frowned. "What does—"

"It's a tragedy. I won't say it wasn't. But it feels like something sad you'd read about in the newspaper. Not something that happened to me personally. I barely remember that woman. She was never a mother to me. My mother is Audrey." A shadow passed over his expression.

"What is it?"

"I was just thinking about my dad." He reached back and squeezed his neck. "And how things aren't perfect, even if we have the best of intentions. Life is hard. We have to find the good and trust that we can make it work."

"You really think we can do that?"

"I know I want to try. In a way I've never wanted with anyone else."

Pepper bit her lip.

"What do you say?"

The door flew open and hit the cabinet behind it. Victory raced in and climbed on Allen's lap without invitation. "Mr. Zack showed me a cabinet on the fire truck so big I can fit *inside* it. But he wouldn't close the door."

Pepper grinned. "You wouldn't want to get stuck in there."

"I want to bring my friends here for a sleepover." She shifted to look at Allen. "Can we have a bounce house?"

The look on his face made her wonder if Allen wanted to give Victory anything she asked for.

Pepper said, "Let's figure out what you want to do. Then we can ask the fire department if it's okay for you to have your birthday party here. If we're not allowed, I bet we can find somewhere else good to have it."

Allen nodded. "But first, coffee."

26

A llen's desk phone rang. "Frees."

He was feeling pretty satisfied with how things were going. Until Lieutenant Basuto said, "Got something for you."

"I didn't know you were back to work already."

"Sasha is camped out in the break room, and I'm supposed to 'take it easy.' But I have intel for you. I'm sending you a file. Listen to it."

"What is it?"

"Voicemail Burns deleted. Sent before he called Pepper the day of the motel incident."

"I'd rather ask if everyone is fine than talk about this." Things had been peaceful today. He was trying to forget he'd killed two men yesterday and keep his mind on Pepper. Making sure the two of them felt safe today. He'd nearly told her about his dad and would at some point. But they didn't need to deal with everything in one day.

"We're burying a member of our SWAT team on Friday," Basuto said. "Everyone else will be back next week... Yes, I know, Sash. I was about to tell him."

Allen's lips twitched.

"I'll be taking another week off before I'm back to full duty. Sasha's orders."

If she had the twins anytime soon, Basuto would be taking even more time off.

"So let's get this case wrapped up."

Allen said, "I'll listen to the message."

He leaned back in his chair and looked at the hall. He could see the entrance and a corner of the common room from his chair. Not enough to check on everyone, but things had been quiet since Pepper and Victory went with Zack to help make pancakes for breakfast.

They'd aired their biggest issue and come out of it with a tentative agreement. He wanted to see where it went, but Basuto was right. They needed to get this case wrapped up.

He said, "What about the flash drive I found in Victory's coat?"

He'd waited until she was asleep last night and then looked in. What he'd found had him calling the nonemergency line and getting an officer to take the evidence to the police station.

Basuto blew out a breath. "Now there's a thing. We're trying to figure out why Burns put that in her pocket. Seems like he's passing information to this Hector that was mentioned, but the question is why."

"Run it all down for me."

He did. The drive was full of shipment information, times, and routes. "Do we know who Hector is for sure?"

"We've ID'd who we *think* Hector is. I've got detectives figuring out where to find him. After you listen to the voicemail you'll see more. Basically we think your suspicion was right. Hector is on the warpath, after revenge for that bad batch and his money."

"So he comes after Pepper and Victory."

"We think he already has Sage."

"Seriously?" She'd been on the phone with Pepper the day before. Could she be a captive even after that?

"We think she's making her own deal. Doing what she needs to do to protect herself and not end up like Burns."

"Which leaves Victory as a target."

"Nearest we can figure out," Basuto said, "he was under the radar, maybe about to disappear. He finds out Hector nearly took Victory—or at least that his plan was to take her and disappear. So he shows up at Pepper's and drops the flash drive in Victory's pocket so when, or if, Victory is taken by Hector, she has that information on her. Maybe he won't kill her."

Allen shook his head.

"So he's about to skip town, but Sage calls. She says she'll meet him and they can disappear together. But when he shows up at the motel, it's a trap. He gets executed, and whoever did it sticks around to take out the police when we show up."

"Sage lured him to his death?"

Allen heard a noise at his office door. He whipped his head around and saw Pepper in the doorway.

He held out his hand and mouthed *come here.*

She took his hand and settled on the edge of the desk beside him. Allen put the call on speaker and replaced the handset in the holder.

Basuto said, "We think Sage is hedging her bets, using Hector for protection."

"That won't last," Pepper said. "She'll make a run for it and try taking Victory with her. Or she'll screw up and he'll kill her. Right?"

She glanced at him. Allen figured she might not be wrong.

Basuto said, "Uh, hey. Pepper. How are you this morning?"

"Full of pancakes. How is Sasha?"

"She's got her feet up on the break room couch, reading a novel." Basuto chuckled under his breath. "It's almost like she's become domesticated."

Allen snickered. "Don't count on it."

Surely the stories around town about Sasha's antics weren't all true. But given the woman's condition, he hoped she took it easy this time. He much preferred a sweet woman who took care of animals for a living and was an amazing auntie. Who didn't get flustered when bullets were flying and dangerous men invaded her house.

No, Pepper had shown she had strength in her, and they were all alive because of it.

She had so much resilience it made him want to catch her all the more when she let go of her guardedness and he got to see the soft underneath. "Do you think Sage will survive this?"

She bit her lip. "My sister has always lived close to the edge. I knew one day it would catch up with her."

"It always does. And the outcome is hard to say in situations like this," Basuto said. "But we'll do everything we can to so this doesn't end with more bloodshed."

"Even when this Hector person cost you an officer and injured even more?"

Allen squeezed her hand. "Yes. Even then."

"Gotta go," Basuto said. "Later."

"Bye." Allen hit the button on his phone to end the call.

Pepper stood. "Food time."

If she didn't want another heavy conversation, that was fine with him. They'd be able to do that. Over dinner, on his back porch—after the cleanup people took care of the blood that'd no doubt stained his hallway.

He winced.

They could work miracles, but he still prayed the blood wouldn't remain forever on his floor the way it would in their minds.

Pepper shook her head as they headed for the common room, her gaze catching on a metal artwork scene of two mountain peaks. "I still can't believe what Sage got caught up in. And at the same time, I'm so not surprised it isn't even funny." She ran her fingers along a meadow at the bottom.

"I found a flash drive Elijah put in Victory's coat pocket. He had to have slipped it in there when he was acting weirdly at your house."

She frowned, her steps slowing. "What did it have on it?"

"According to Basuto, valuable intel. Shipping manifests for freight trucks, routes and delivery times." Allen pulled up short of the doorway in case she wasn't ready to go in.

Pepper turned to him. "What are they transporting?"

It wouldn't be long before she had something close to cop instincts. "Controlled substances. A couple of truckfuls. You know that superstore they're building on the highway at the other end of town?"

She nodded and leaned against the doorframe.

"They're stocking it for opening day. The trucks are full of all the meds for the pharmacy and a couple of deliveries for local hospitals."

Her eyes widened. "Elijah handed that information to Hector?"

"He planned to." Allen took her hand. "I think it was there to save Victory's life. If it came to that."

"It didn't save his. He probably just wanted to get away himself."

Allen nodded. He didn't say aloud that the man hadn't exactly tried hard to make sure Victory went with him. If he were ever a father, he couldn't imagine there being anything he wouldn't do to spend time with his child.

"*I* want to steal her and run away." She glanced at him, a sheepish look on her face. "If it wasn't illegal."

Allen smiled. "As long as I can come too."

"Coming through." Amelia squeezed between them and headed into the common room.

"Lieutenant Patterson, I need your timesheet." He followed her.

She glanced back at him. "It's not due for three days."

"Just a check. Make sure no one is pushing their hours, spending more time here than they should." Allen turned back and had to wave Pepper in.

Patterson headed for the coffee pot, tension in her shoulders. "I know what the requirements are."

Allen knew she'd also worked more hours than she should have this week, accounting for her firefighters who'd been out sick. And she'd pitched in off shift as well. "I don't want anyone burning out."

Zack turned from the griddle. "Where's Vicki?"

Allen frowned, even though the question was directed at Amelia. Around the room, firefighters looked up from what they were doing. Half the currently-on-duty shift was in here.

"I thought she came back from the bathroom before me." The lieutenant turned, coffee in her hand. "Did she not?"

Zack motioned to the room.

Allen said, "Vicki?"

Zack nodded. "She asked me to call her that. Said it was the nickname all her friends called her."

As far as Allen knew, he was the only one.

"I'll go check the bathrooms." Pepper left the common room.

"We'll check the halls." Jayson patted Eddie's shoulder and they headed out.

Allen rotated his chair, wanting to do the same in favor of sitting here while everyone else looked. *Lord, don't let her be lost. Or taken.*

He wheeled out into the hallway.

Overhead, the alarm went. "Rescue 5. Truck 14. Ambulance 21. Residential fire, two units of fourplex fully involved. Multiple people trapped."

Zack unplugged the griddle and dropped the spatula to the counter. He jogged over to Allen. "Find her."

"I will."

The firefighters sprinted down the hall, pulled turnout gear and boots on, and climbed into the fire truck.

Seconds later they pulled out, and Allen heard the sirens begin.

"Everything okay, Mr. Frees?"

He glanced back at Meredith. "Have you seen Victory anywhere?"

She shook her head. "I'll help you look if you'd like."

"Thanks."

Pepper rounded the corner, wringing her hands together. "She's not in the ladies' room, so I checked the men's after everyone left, if that's okay. I hope it was. I was worried she went in there by mistake, but there's no one in there."

Allen didn't like the sound of this. "Split up. Look in every room and every closet. Just in case she's playing hide-and-seek and we're supposed to find her."

Pepper nodded. "I'll run up and check the roof first. She was talking about it earlier."

A shadow shifted behind her, but when Pepper moved, Allen saw nothing in the engine bay or the hall beyond that on the other side, which led to the ambulance bay.

They split up and he searched the rooms around his office, calling out for Victory. Meredith checked the parking lot.

He wheeled out of Bryce's office and heard the buzzer over the door go. "Find anything, Meredith?" He went to the corner. "Meredith?"

She came into view from the entrance, a pinched look on her face. Before he could ask her what was going on, a man moved right behind her. He had a hand on Meredith's shoulder, a gun to the back of her head.

The guy spotted Allen down the hall. "They told me you

were in a wheelchair. You're really the one who took out two of Hector's guys?"

"Let her go."

The guy sneered. "Hector gets paid. And you cost him, so you're going to pay."

"Fine. I'll pay." Allen pushed his chair closer, still several feet from them. "But she's not part of this, so let her go."

"We'll see about that."

Before Allen could figure out what to say next, he heard someone behind him. He whipped his head around but it was too late.

A gun came down, and pain cracked his skull.

Everything went black.

27

Pepper closed the door to the men's bunk room, not exactly surprised Victory hadn't gone in there. But she'd needed to check anyway so they didn't miss the girl. No one wanted Victory to be the victim yet again. After what happened the last time Victory was at the firehouse, Pepper and Allen were both determined to keep her safe.

As a team.

Now that Allen knew the worst about her and everything had come to light, she almost couldn't believe how things seemed to have settled.

Still, even while hope flickered to life in her, stronger than ever before, there remained that disquiet. The disbelief that kept her where she was, refusing to take risks.

Had God really led her to this, through all these things? All so she and Allen could get to the place where they were free to be with each other? To see where it might go?

She knew where she *wanted* it to go.

She turned the corner by the engine bay but headed toward the front door.

A man grabbed on to Meredith, holding a gun to her head.

Pepper froze, but it was too late. The guy had seen her. He shifted the gun from Meredith to her. "Found her."

He wasn't talking to her or Meredith, so there had to be someone else...

A man rounded the corner from Allen's office. "You grab her. I've got to take this guy."

Pepper turned and ran for the engine bay. She heard Meredith scream and then a thud. Pepper shoved through the doors and skidded across the engine-bay floor. The doors were still up, the trucks gone. Except for the broken-down one, that was. There were plenty of places to hide, but not enough time to get somewhere fast enough that she wouldn't be seen and immediately discovered.

She raced for the driveway.

Heavy footsteps came up behind her. Entirely too fast for her to figure out what to do but pump her arms and legs faster and try to outrun—

He slammed into her back. Pepper toppled over and hit the ground, a heavy weight on her.

One arm bent underneath her. She cried out and he pulled back on both elbows, dragging her to her feet. "Nice try." He chuckled.

"Help!" Pepper screamed as loudly as she could. "Somebody help me!"

Victory. *Lord, she needs to stay where she's hiding.* If her niece even was hiding. Where had she gone? Nausea roiled in her stomach at the thought of these guys getting their hands on her.

The man dragged her back through the doors to the hallway, all the way to meet his friend. Allen wasn't moving, slumped over in his chair. She spotted blood on the back of his head. Oh no.

Pepper let out a whimper before she could pull it back.

Meredith lay unconscious on the floor, her body up against the reception counter she worked behind. They'd hit her too.

Please don't be dead.

"Let's get them out of here." The guy who'd been holding Meredith grabbed Pepper's arm and shoved his gun in her face. "Don't try anything. I can kill you whenever I like."

The other man went to the back of Allen's chair. "What about the kid?"

"Do you see a kid around here?" The guy glanced around as though Victory would pop out. He shot his associate a look. "You heard them looking for her. She probably ran off."

"Fine. But you can tell Hector that." He started to push Allen out the front doors.

Pepper sniffed. "Is the fire everyone got called out to even real?"

"I have a better question for you. But if we get going, Hector can ask you himself." The guy sneered. "I'm sure you'll enjoy the experience."

A shiver rolled through her.

He dragged her outside into the chill afternoon. Wherever Victory was, Pepper hoped she had put on her coat. The little girl didn't need to go through another dangerous situation.

Even the coat was connected to everything that'd happened.

Such a simple thing, and yet her niece lived on the edge of danger with no end in sight.

Maybe it was for the better that she had disappeared. Pepper couldn't even imagine where Victory had gone. All she could do was pray. *Lord, keep her safe.*

An undercurrent of fear moved through Pepper, even though she realized if these guys didn't know where Victory was, it meant Hector's men didn't have her.

Pepper prayed all the way to the SUV, the pleas to Jesus coming much easier now in her desperation. She prayed that she would continue to be safe no matter what happened next. That Victory had someone watching over her, keeping guard.

The gunman shoved Pepper in the middle row and got in behind her, which apparently necessitated him being handsy. Pepper winced. She slid all the way across the bench seat, aware of someone in the front. She didn't look to see who it was. She just got out of the way of the man who'd grabbed her.

Through the open rear door, she saw the other man haul Allen out of his chair and dump him in the back, where the third-row seats had been folded down.

He flicked a lever on the wheelchair and got it partially folded. Cursed. Hit it a couple of times and then just dumped it by Allen.

The guy by her shifted. "You're bringing that?"

"I'm not carrying him when we get there." He yanked down the back door and slammed it shut.

Pepper shivered. There was a sense of finality being enclosed in the vehicle, and it got worse when they set off. Way too fast. She grabbed the door handle to hold on. *Seat belt.* She pulled it across her and buckled in.

"Where is Victory?"

The sound of the woman's voice washed over her.

She leaned across the middle far enough to look. "Sage." Her sister sat in the front seat. "I guess I'm supposed to believe you just got a ride with them."

The guy beside her shifted. The other drove the car. Sage sat there like the queen of everything, except for the telltale note Pepper could see in her eyes—one no one else likely noticed.

Sage said, "I asked you where my daughter is." Lethal, but also scared.

Pepper wasn't going to lie to her, no matter how much she wanted to rage. Blame. Scream. None of it would get them out of this.

She shook her head. "I have no idea where Victory is. I kept her as safe as possible, considering everything that's happened."

"Elijah." Sage muttered her ex-husband's name.

"This might be mostly his fault, but you are definitely involved." What was it the police called it? Oh, yeah. She was *an accessory.* Still just as guilty of the crime—at least, as far as Pepper could tell. "Meanwhile, I have to figure out how to tell a scared eight-year-old that her father is no longer alive."

Sage snorted. "Half of this wouldn't be happening if your friend back there didn't shoot two of Hector's guys."

"You really want to get into this?" The car turned a corner, and Pepper braced a hand on the seat in front of her. "Because that happened *yesterday.*" Her stomach burned like someone had lit a fire in her. "Allen only did that to save our lives."

"That's him?" Sage peered over Pepper's shoulder to look in the back of the car. "Seriously? Allen?"

Because yes, Pepper had explained everything to her sister in the throes of her breakup. She'd told Sage all about the man she'd loved and the relationship that had to end. His breakup. Their shared history.

She expected the gunmen in the car to tell them to shut up. They didn't.

She expected to find herself drowning in fear.

She wasn't.

All she had in her was that hot anger bubbling up— directed at her sister.

Pepper said, "Are you really going to malign my choices, after all you've done?"

She was so over her sister and the way Sage lived her life, uncaring about how the things she did affected those around her. People she was supposed to care for and protect.

Pepper had to convince a judge that *she* was the right choice to raise Victory. Not the girl's mother. Sage wasn't going to walk away from this. Not when she had gotten herself so deep with this Hector person and whatever he was into.

Pepper wouldn't be surprised if her sister wound up in prison like their mother when this was over.

Or worse.

"You're never getting Victory back."

Her sister shifted in her seat and rolled her eyes. "Whatever, Ms. High and Mighty. I do what I need to. It's how I've survived. Not just burying my head in the sand and pretending everything is the way I want it to be. My life is real."

The driver hit the brakes and pulled the car into a driveway. All the way into the garage, where he hit the button on the sun visor and the garage door rolled down behind them.

It clattered against the concrete.

"Real scary, maybe," Pepper said. "I don't know how you don't go crazy with the fear."

Sage rolled her eyes again. "You always were a baby." She shoved out of the car.

The guy next to Pepper grabbed her elbow and dragged her out. She barely managed to get her feet under her before he set off for the house.

She tried to turn around. *Allen.* He needed to wake up. "What are you going to do with him?"

"He killed two of Hector's guys. What do you think the boss is going to do?"

"No." She shoved against his grip on her arm.

"Cut it out or you'll end up there first."

She had nothing to give these people. They had no reason to keep her alive after they saw her face.

She tripped into the empty house.

He dragged her past Sage, down a bright white hallway. No furniture. Brand new, some fancy house on the market that had never been lived in. No one would buy it with their blood all over the floor.

She twisted in his grasp. "Sage, you have to help me! I'm your sister!"

Sage just stared at her.

"Why are you doing this?" Tears rolled down her face.

The man opened a door in the hall and shoved her inside. Pepper stumbled off a step, started to tumble and caught the railing. Pain flashed like lightning up her arm. She screamed.

He kicked her back and she fell down the stairs.

The door slammed shut.

28

Allen groaned. His face had been used as a punching bag, and the taste of blood tinged his mouth.

He heard the rustle of clothes, and Pepper's face swam into view above him.

"Allen?" Her voice shook. "Are you awake?"

He blinked in the semidark, head pounding. It took a second to focus while his tongue found a sore spot on the corner of his mouth where a tooth had cut his lip when Hector's guys punched his face.

He took a couple of long breaths, taking stock of everything. "Pepper?"

He sat up. One leg lay under him, bent at an awkward angle. What sensation he had didn't spell out anything good.

She held on to his shoulders. Allen didn't like the look on her face. There was no time for him to contemplate their bad situation—she would read it all in his expression. Pepper had to keep what hope she still had in her.

"Tell me what happened while I was out."

Pepper bit her lip. "I need you to tell me what they did to you first."

He planted both hands on the floor and shifted his hips to lean back against the wall. He had to grab his pant leg and adjust his foot to the right angle. The dull throb in his foot probably meant something bad had happened, and the limited sensation he had gave him enough of a clue that he knew trying to walk was going to be more difficult than normal.

"They wanted to know who I am. How come I killed those men at my house. They could've done a web search, but whatever." He shrugged a shoulder. *Ouch.* "They're going to kill me. They'll drag it out, though."

Unless he figured a way out of this.

Allen looked around what was a partially finished basement. The drywall had been taped but not mudded and painted. Windows along one wall, high up and difficult to escape through.

They might be able to break one and get Pepper out, if they had something to take care of the glass with.

"What are you doing?" Pepper glanced around. "There's no way out of this. What are you looking at?"

"There's always a way out." That was what he told himself in his nightmares, in the thick of the fear. When his heart screamed as much as his mind, trapped back in the lower level of that house in complete darkness, unable to move. Powerless. Waiting to die.

Suffocating.

He pushed the encroaching claustrophobia away.

Inhaled a long breath the way Natalie had taught him. He pushed it out slowly and counted. He held it for four seconds at the bottom of the breath, then inhaled for four.

Repeat.

Pepper needed him to support her and not succumb to the fear. Allen needed her as much.

He touched her cheeks.

She winced. "They beat you good. Your face is a mess."

"So you're not going to kiss me?"

"I don't know where I'd put one, considering the mess of bruises on your face."

"Shame." He ran his thumb over her lower lip.

"Maybe we could focus on this situation rather than getting distracted."

"Where's the fun in that?"

She rolled her eyes. "They're going to kill us and you're making jokes?"

"It's called gallows humor."

"You've told me that before."

He had. It was a tactic cops often employed—even if they didn't realize it—to diffuse tension and help cope with the horrible things they saw every day. He'd done it.

What Natalie thought about it as a coping mechanism wasn't relevant.

He looked at Pepper. "What do you need?"

She stared right back. "You."

He didn't let go. "Same."

The edges of her lips curled into a smile. "So romantic."

"Let's get out of this, and I'll show you romance."

She chuckled. "Deal."

He wanted to draw her into banter again by complaining about her opinion of his ability to be romantic, but they should figure out a plan to escape. She was right about that. He'd been plenty romantic when they were dating, thank you very much. Maybe he was a little rusty, but rediscovering all that would be half the fun of being back together.

"Did they say anything when they brought you in?"

She shook her head. "Sage talked to me in the car, and they have your wheelchair upstairs, by the way."

"Good. I want them to think I can't walk at all. Gives me an edge over them if they're not expecting me to be able to stand a little."

Tears filled her eyes but didn't fall. "They have guns."

"Don't worry about me." He rubbed up and down the outside of her arms. She was the kind of woman who needed physical reassurance—a hug, a touch. She also needed the words. "I want you to focus on getting *you* out of this. Because Victory needs a parent, and the one God has given her is you."

She bit her lip. He knew what she was thinking. They had no idea where Victory was or if she was safe. If Hector's guys would find her and bring her here. Threaten her. Terrify her. If they would be killed and Sage would take her daughter—disappear, never to be seen again.

"I need you to promise me something."

Pepper frowned. "What?"

She wasn't going to like this, but he had to say it anyway. "If it comes down to you or me, I need you to save yourself."

She started to argue.

Allen didn't let her. "Promise me. If I can't get out but you can, you're going to go. Run. Save yourself and don't worry about me. You need to stay alive for Victory. Regardless of what happens."

"I don't know if I can promise that." She glanced to the side. "I might not be able to leave you if I think you're going to die."

He probably was. "They have no reason to kill you, Pepper. Sage could vouch for you. That you're not a threat to them. Whatever they want, tell them and get yourself out of this."

Meanwhile, he'd killed two of Hector's men. Whoever the guy was, it didn't appear he was the kind of drug dealer to let that slide. He wanted revenge.

And they were going to drag it out. Make him suffer.

If he had to suffer, he was going to figure out how to get Pepper out of here before it happened. No way did she need to watch it. Or hear it from down here.

Or see it.

There might not be anything he could do to stop it. Like

lying in that basement, thinking he would die trapped down there, unable to move. Everything he'd been in his life taken away. All his weapons. His fighting skills. His mind's ability to problem solve had come up with nothing. Everything he was, overcome by fear.

Those minutes had felt like hours. His darkest moments.

If he could keep Pepper from suffering like that, he would gladly die just so she went on living.

If he wanted to get out of here, he would have to fight one of them and get a weapon. Or find something to draw attention to the house—like Pepper had done by setting the fire in her kitchen. The options were limited, and each move was a risk. A tell Hector and his men would pick up. Allen intended on fighting. He wouldn't give up easily.

"If I tell you to go," he said, "you go."

Pepper's expression hardened.

"It's nonnegotiable."

"I'll go find a phone and call for help. Get the police here."

He nodded. By the time they got here, it would be too late. But that wasn't the point. "Good idea."

Maybe there would be some evidence to collect when they arrived.

"What will you do?"

Allen said, "I have some ideas. There are supplies upstairs from the cleaners. I could do what you did and start a fire if the gas is on. Or fight back somehow."

"There are three of them plus Sage."

"That could make all the difference, depending on how badly Hector wants to keep her around."

Pepper shuddered. "Running sounds good."

"I'll make sure you're clear before I try anything big."

She frowned. "Wait. You're going to kill yourself?"

"It's one option on the list, and not ideal." He had to have several plans, depending on how this went.

"You're going to take them out and kill yourself in the process?"

It was essentially the same question as the previous one, but he didn't point that out. "I don't expect you to accept it as the best idea for a solution—"

"Good. Because I won't." Pepper shifted back a little, not quite out of reach but close. "You cannot kill yourself, Allen."

"I'll be taking out these guys. Murderers, kidnappers. People who killed a cop and attempted to murder the entire SWAT team, the lieutenant, and our undercover officer that night at the motel. You can't mess with people like this. Or bargain. I have no leverage, and they want revenge."

"Well, so do I. They tried to hurt Victory." She folded her arms across her chest, pulling back from him in more ways than one. "I'm not going to let them hurt you."

"There might be no choice, sweetheart." He hadn't called her that in a long time.

"I don't want to leave you."

He leaned close and dipped his head. "Promise me you'll do it anyway."

Her lips shifted and she started to speak.

The door at the top of the wooden stairs opened. Two men thumped down in boots—the guys who had kidnapped him from the firehouse. Both now had abrasions on their knuckles. Allen was just glad they'd stuck to fists and hadn't used anything else on him.

No doubt that would come soon.

A new man strode down behind them. Sage didn't. This had to be Hector. The guy moved like the boss. Every inch of him screamed, *in charge.*

Pepper twisted around and put her body between them and Allen.

He clenched his jaw. She wasn't going to take a hit meant for him. He wouldn't let that happen. "What do you want?"

She stiffened, probably because he'd barked right behind her. Whatever fear she felt, Pepper was doing a great job keeping it in. Showing her strength, and the source of that strength, in her ability to appear calm while she no doubt shook inside.

The two men stood on either side of his legs. Hector moved between them.

Allen figured the distance to the stairs and how fast Pepper could jump up and run. He grabbed her hips and pulled her back, partially on his lap. She could get her feet up more easily this way. As anticipated, she bent her knees and planted one foot.

They both knew she was going to have to make a run for it. Surprise the guy between her and the stairs, shove past him and go.

He squeezed her hips.

Hector drew a gun. "The two of you are going to tell me what Elijah Burns said to you. You're going to give me what he gave you. And then you both die."

Allen pushed Pepper's hips up. She got the message, planted her feet, and he shoved her toward the stairs.

She slammed into the guy in her way. He nearly went down, grabbed for her and missed. He spun and grabbed her shirt.

Pepper screamed, dragged back by his grip on the sweater.

Allen gritted his teeth.

Hector turned to her. She struggled against the hold, face-to-face with the man responsible for all of this.

Allen needed to get the focus back on him. "Worth a try. Can't blame a guy for that, right?"

Hector pulled a gun from the back of his belt. He leveled it at Allen without looking. In fact, he stared at Pepper with murderous intensity.

"You tell me what I want to know or watch your boyfriend die."

29

Pepper's entire body quaked. No doubt the guy behind her could feel it. But she wasn't about to let them know exactly how scared she was. "How about I tell you and you *don't* kill us?"

They had nothing else to bargain with.

The scary guy in front of her wasn't someone she would've run into at the veterinarian's office. At least, he wasn't the kind of person who normally brought an animal in. What did she know? Maybe he had a Pomeranian.

She pushed aside those ridiculous thoughts. Unfortunately, that left the runway clear for Sage to take up space again. The way she always did. What was that phrase people used? *Real estate in her head.* Sage had occupied her thoughts for years. Pepper figured that was what happened with family.

Maybe it didn't have to, though.

Hector studied her. She might as well have been a mosquito that landed on his arm. Not a threat, just a curiosity that needed to be eradicated. "You think I'm the kind of man who would submit to a bargain?"

"You did it with Elijah. I can see how him selling you

tainted drugs might give you cause to rethink business arrangements. But this transaction can be mutually beneficial."

His gaze drifted down her, then back up. "I doubt that."

Rude. She started to speak but couldn't think of the words to say, because he'd flustered her. She didn't need to feel desirable to anyone other than Allen. However, a little appreciation might've been nice.

Then again, given the caliber of these guys, disdain rather than interest was probably a good thing. She really did *not* have anything to offer them.

"Good." She lifted her chin. "Because that's not what I'm talking about." Pepper took a breath to try and draw strength. *Lord, You've helped us this far.* "You want to know what Elijah gave us? I'll tell you where it is and what it says. But you'll get nothing if you murder us in cold blood."

"I assure you, my blood is not cold."

"Agree to disagree." Where all this bravado was coming from, she had no idea. Other than that she was at the end of her patience. The end of her strength. God holding her up didn't make her sarcastic. But if she didn't get through this with His help, then Allen was right.

Victory would have no one.

"You want me to kill your friend?" His dark expression shifted.

"No. If you want leverage, there it is." She wasn't sure he even knew Sage was her sister. "I will tell you what you need to know. But I'd rather you didn't kill us after. We won't tell anyone who you are. We won't say a thing."

"Our secret?" His expression betrayed no interest in what she'd proposed.

Didn't matter. She had to try. "This doesn't have to go bad just because you're worried about the police catching up with you. Or the feds. We're not affiliated with either. Allen works for the fire department, and I'm a veterinary nurse. We're not a threat, and we're not competition."

She'd negotiated with disgruntled customers before. Maybe she could talk him down to being reasonable.

Also worth a try.

"So I take your word for it that you won't tell anyone where to find me?"

"I have no idea where to find you." She looked around. "I'm assuming this isn't the main hub of your operation."

"Correct."

"Aside from my sister, Sage, I have zero connection to any of this," Pepper said. "Except that you tried to kidnap my niece. Sent your men to threaten me. Nearly destroyed people I care about. Which means I have every reason to give you nothing."

"Except you will." Hector glanced at Allen. "Or he dies."

"Elijah gave us a flash drive intended for you."

Pepper gasped. "Allen!"

The man holding her shook her by the arms. "Shut it."

She pressed her lips together.

Hector crouched in front of Allen's feet, the gun held loosely aimed at him now. "And what was on this flash drive?"

If Hector learned they'd given it to the police, he would probably kill them right here and now.

What was Allen doing?

Whatever it was, he counted on her to trust him. The way she hadn't when she didn't want him to know that her mom was the person who'd taken his mom's life. Now that had been resolved. Not that he didn't care. It was simply that the news had no bearing on their relationship as far as he was concerned. The incident was a tragedy but didn't prohibit them from getting closer. Or building a future.

As long as the two of them weren't another tragedy themselves.

"Key information. A shipment of narcotics headed for the

new superstore at the edge of town." Allen's face remained impassive. "Enough drugs to fill the shelves."

Hector said, "Where is this information now?"

"I destroyed it."

Pepper held still, not wanting to give away the truth while Allen did what he needed to do in order to solve this. She'd set it up, and he would do what he could to save them.

Or just her.

Part of her wanted to hate him for even suggesting she save herself and leave him behind to die. She'd wanted to slap him. What had they fought for this whole time if he was just going to throw it away for the sake of her life? Alone. Without him.

She'd done that for nearly two years. Why would she give up what they had now—and could have next—after knowing what loneliness felt like?

She didn't want to be alone.

Even for the sake of taking care of Victory, she couldn't imagine having to live knowing Allen gave his life for her.

"So the information is nowhere?" Hector shifted to stand.

Before he did, Allen said, "The truck leaves the warehouse in Salt Lake City at one a.m. Tonight. I can tell you the route it will travel, but not until you let her go." Allen tipped his head toward her.

"I have a better idea." Hector stood and looked at his guys. "Get him out of here." He took a step back. "She stays here. Javan will be upstairs. You go with me, and if I suspect any funny business, she dies. Got it?" He lifted his gun and pointed it at Pepper.

Hector's men hauled Allen up to his feet, which she noted he pretended could only dangle under him. He needed them to underestimate him.

Whether it worked or not, the fact was he played a dangerous game.

They dragged him up the stairs, leaving her alone in the

basement. She didn't know where Javan would be, but maybe she had a chance. She moved to the bottom of the stairs.

Hector turned at the top. "Don't even think about it. My man will put a bullet in you. You mean nothing to me."

Pepper stilled. *God, don't let them hurt him.*

She could do this. Two men gone and one left? She could sneak upstairs. If he wasn't right outside the door, she could maybe subdue him—or even sneak out. She'd have to figure out how to get help. Like steal his phone or find the closest one she could use.

Call the police and tell them what Allen was doing.

She didn't even know if the shipment time was correct and if whatever route he took them on was real. He knew what he was doing. *God, I hope he knows what he's doing. Please, can You help him?*

She'd just gotten him back.

Her dream felt more at risk than ever before. She and Victory. She and Allen. It was just out of reach and could so easily be taken from her, while she could do nothing to keep it.

Pepper listened long enough she heard a car pull away from the empty house.

She walked slowly up the stairs, avoiding the one step that had creaked when the men left. She bit her lip to keep from crying. She couldn't afford to succumb to the fear.

She had to get out of here.

Pepper twisted the handle slowly. She prayed it would stay silent as she eased it open, adding an additional prayer that she didn't get shot straight away. Javan probably didn't plan to kill her right away now that the boss was gone. Or do worse things and then end her life.

She shivered, listened to the hallway for a second, then stepped out.

Sage stood at the end of the hall. "What are you doing?"

Pepper snuck over to her sister. "Give me your phone." She

waved her fingers in a *gimme* motion. "I need to call the police and get Allen help."

"There's no way to help him."

"I think there is." Pepper glanced around again. "So I'm leaving, because I need to get help. I refuse to give up."

Sage grasped her arm. "Hector won't let you get away."

"He's not here."

"Javan is..." Sage swallowed. Despite the nerves, she gripped Pepper's arm hard.

Pepper winced. "Let go. Come with me, and we don't have to worry about him."

"He'll know. He'll hunt us down." Sage shivered. "I've seen what he does to women. Just go back down into the basement and don't provoke him. Don't give him a reason to hurt you."

"Come with me." Pepper tugged on her arm, but Sage didn't let go. "I'm sorry, but I will leave you. I'd rather you come, but I can't stay here. Victory needs me."

A hard look crossed Sage's expression.

"I have to make sure she's safe. No matter what." If it cost Pepper her life, she would keep Victory protected. As much as she had the power to do, at least. "Why aren't you letting me go?"

"That's not how this is going to work."

Pepper moved close enough they were practically nose-to-nose. "Let go of me. Now." She shoved her sister away with her free hand. Sage's grasp slipped from her arm.

Pepper turned and ran through the entryway to the front door.

She grasped the handle.

Sage slammed into her back. "Javan! She's escaping."

Pepper cried out, not caring how loud it was. She got the door latch flipped and twisted the handle. Sage tried to grab her.

Pepper shoved her away with all the anger and pain she had

in her over the person her sister had turned out to be. "How could you!"

Sage stumbled back, caught herself, and rallied to come at Pepper again.

"Enough!" His voice echoed through the entryway.

"I told you she'd try to sneak out." Sage sashayed over to him.

Bile rose in Pepper's throat.

Sage plastered herself to Javan's side. "What are you going to do to her...Hector?"

Pepper stared at them. *This* was the man in charge. Not the guy who had taken Allen to the truck full of drugs.

He stared Pepper down, ignoring Sage for the most part even though she was still close to his side. "Whatever I want. Isn't that how it goes?"

Sage chuckled. Pepper grimaced at the sound, nothing like humor. "Let me go."

Her sister laughed louder.

"I'm not sure I will," he said. "After all, you and your friend cost me considerable time and personnel."

Somehow, she didn't think he cared all that much about the people who worked for him.

"Like this one." He shoved Sage off him and lifted his gun.

She held up her hands. "Baby—"

Hector squeezed the trigger. Her sister's body jerked, and she fell.

Pepper didn't wait to see her hit the floor. She turned and raced outside, crying out because she couldn't hold it back. Her sister was dead.

His deadly chuckle followed her out into the night.

Pepper ran as fast as she could, knowing each step could be her last one.

30

The SUV rumbled down the road, that steady hum of tires on asphalt. The two guys in the front talked low to each other about football and someone's brother-in-law who supported some team. Which they thought was crazy.

Allen pushed off the carpet between the seats and sat up. One of them made a noise and got the other one's attention, motioning toward Allen with a whispered, "The invalid's awake."

He shifted on his seat and moved his legs where he needed them. His face throbbed like he'd been attacked with a couple of clubs—and now he had a bunch more bruises.

The men kept talking while the guy in the passenger seat looked back to watch what Allen was doing with an expression like morbid curiosity.

Allen didn't put his seatbelt on. What he needed was a phone, or some other way to let Conroy know things were going full speed ahead. Not exactly as planned, because all they'd had was a bunch of what-ifs and the contingencies for each. He hadn't anticipated everything. But when did that happen?

He blew out a breath. His mind wanted to analyze all the variables that would play out when Meredith woke up. Or the firefighters got back to the house.

When everyone realized he and Pepper were gone.

God had brought him this far. He'd put everything Allen ever wanted right in front of him, in a way he could believe it was meant to be. *Lord, keep her safe.*

Allen had to get through this.

He didn't have a chair. They hadn't brought it with them when they dumped him unceremoniously in the middle row of the car. They'd swung him back between them and tossed him over the seat between the captain's chairs.

Now everything hurt.

He lifted his hands and gently probed his face. He probably looked like a gargoyle because everything seemed to be puffy and swollen. His cheekbone smarted. The orbital bone too. Probably something chipped when he'd been punched. Miraculously, his nose wasn't broken. It had happened so many times before, he wouldn't have been surprised to find it obliterated.

He could breathe. He could see—mostly. *Thank You for that.* Both of those were kind of necessary for what he had in mind.

The guy in the passenger seat shifted. "You're going to take us all the way to that truck."

And then they'd kill him, take the drugs, and...

Allen's nascent thought dissipated as fast as it came. He glanced between the two guys and tried to figure out what was off about this.

The one in the passenger seat was the boss—Hector—with those perfectly unmarked knuckles. His friend the driver had bloody knuckles, cut from punching Allen in the face.

A ring on his right hand probably matched the cut on Allen's cheek.

The gun appeared then. A low voice said, "The truck."

"I know." Allen let fear tremble his tone. Hopefully it sounded real. He wasn't so certain things would work out, just quietly confident. Trying to trust in God.

But he still understood the stakes. These two guys were dangerous. Allen could do everything right and still lose his life. Lose Pepper.

He tapped the side of his leg.

Phone. Gun. He needed both.

"Start talking."

"The truck is supposed to stop for gas at the station on Lincoln. Just off the freeway."

The driver glanced at his passenger. "How'd you know that?"

They were headed across town in the direction of the new superstore being built. "The truck is coming from Salt Lake City. They'll need gas when they hit town, and there was a recommendation based on price on the flash drive. It's the same gas station I use. That's why I remembered it. They'll stop." He'd never been a truck driver, but that sounded reasonable enough. "If I'm right, we'll see the truck there."

"After that, it won't make a difference if you are or not, because you'll be dead." The passenger, Hector, thought that was hilarious.

Allen looked out the window. He spotted a familiar vehicle two cars behind.

It took work to keep the smile from contorting his lips. "I guess we'll see."

Allen realized what instinct had been trying to tell him. Neither of these men was the boss, despite the fact one pretended to be Hector in that basement. The underling who'd stayed behind with Pepper? Could be that was the boss. A guy who liked to get his hands dirty and wanted the police chasing someone else.

"You guys haven't thought of taking the drugs for yourselves?" Allen said. "We could make a deal. Split the product three ways."

The two of them started laughing.

What can I say? I'm a comedian. Allen waited for the right moment. Just a little more, and—

He swung his left arm out and punched the blade of his fist into the driver's temple. The other guy lifted his gun hand. Allen grabbed him by the wrist. The gun went off, acting like a flash-bang in the close quarters of the SUV's interior.

The bullet hit the driver, who screamed. The car swerved.

Allen pulled on the other guy's wrist, dragged him out of his seat by his arm, and punched him in the head.

He slumped, out cold.

The vehicle crossed the left lane of traffic. Someone honked their horn. Police lights flashed, and sirens filled the air around the car.

Allen pulled the seatbelt across his body.

The SUV bumped up the curb, hit a bench, and plowed right through it to glance off the brick building. The impact sent them over to the right-side wheels. The vehicle flipped and metal scraped concrete. Allen clapped his hands over his ears.

The SUV hit something, and they stopped.

Finally.

The whimper he let out would stay between him and the Lord. No one else heard it, and he would never mention it to anyone.

He unclipped the seatbelt even though it would make him fall out of the chair. He landed with his shoulder smashed against the door and adjusted his body so he could be hauled out, whichever way they did that.

"Frees!"

More than one person called his name. Allen looked around the front seat and out the windshield. The gun lay within reach, so he grabbed that just in case one of these guys woke up.

"You okay?" Basuto pounded his palm against the window. "Allen!"

He called back, "Yeah! I'm good."

"Rescue squad is on their way to get you out."

Allen leaned back against the roof of the car. The whole thing was on its side with a dead body hanging from the driver's seatbelt. The unconscious guy was slumped in front of him. If he woke up, the cops could take care of him. Neither of these guys was Hector—the real threat they needed to worry about.

The one with the woman he loved.

"We need to go get Pepper," Allen yelled. "I'll tell you where the house is." He could describe the location well enough they'd get the idea and figure it out. "Hey, Basuto!"

He held on to the gun and prayed for Pepper. Prayed they would get to her in time. He wanted to go as well, but she needed to be rescued. He didn't have to be the one to do it. Someone. Anyone could go to that house and save her from Hector.

"Frees!"

Allen lifted up to look. Lieutenant Crawford crouched at the window. When he spotted Allen, Bryce said, "We'll have you out of there in a minute."

"Get Basuto—"

The lieutenant smashed the window from the frame and pulled out the whole thing in one piece.

Allen punched the back of the seat and yelled out his frustration. "We need to get Pepper!"

Bryce crouched in the opening. "She's in there?"

"No!" All of them needed to listen. "A bad guy has her."

Bryce turned to Jayson and Eddie. "Let's cut this, pull the roof back, and get him out."

"She's back at the house." The whir of machinery drowned out his words.

They pulled the roof back a foot and bent the window opening so it was wider. Bryce said, "I'll be in there in one second. We've got to get this guy out first."

Allen spotted Trace and Izan and their ambulance. They'd better not put him in that thing.

The firefighters hauled the passenger onto a backboard.

Allen reached between the door and the passenger seat and found the lever. As soon as the guy was out of the way, he pushed the chair forward so far it touched the dashboard, then started to crawl over it.

Eddie frowned. "You're supposed to stay put until I get you."

"Doesn't mean I don't need a hand to get out still." It wasn't like he could get out of this on his own. He needed their help.

"Basuto has your other chair."

"Does he have a phone?" Allen tried to keep the frustration from his voice. "We need to go get Pepper, and there's no reason to wait around for me to get pulled out of here. He needs to save her. *Now.*"

They laid a blanket over the glass.

Eddie glanced to the side. "Guys, we have to go save Pepper. Basuto!" When he looked back at Allen, he winced. "You don't look so good."

Allen said, "I'll be okay when we find her."

Eddie grabbed Allen and hauled him out. He bent his knees, shifted Allen's weight on him, and straightened with Allen over his shoulder. Eddie started walking. All he could do was stare at the back of the guy's turnout coat. "Seriously, dude?"

Basuto jogged after them. "I'll be in the police car in front of you guys."

More than one set of hands got Allen upright and sitting in

the passenger seat. His face flamed, but he couldn't deny the transfer had been expedient.

Eddie had an arm out the window. He tapped the outside of the door behind him. "Let's go save your girl, boss."

Bryce handed Allen a phone so he could call the police lieutenant, then steered the fire truck away from the crash after Basuto's car, already speeding down the street with lights and sirens going. Allen got on the phone and gave him directions to the house so the police lieutenant would know where they were going.

Minutes later, they pulled up outside the house where he'd been held. The entire neighborhood was brand new, some of the houses just frame. Others had a sign on the lawn that read *Available.*

Basuto set Allen's chair on the ground beside the rescue squad truck. The guys got him into it while the cop jogged to the house.

Allen pushed his wheelchair up the front walk. His heart squeezed in his chest. Jayson and Eddie lifted his chair over the front step, and he wasted no time wheeling over to where Basuto stood.

"Blood."

Allen said, "A lot of it." Someone had been shot here.

"We need to search the whole neighborhood." Allen turned for the door. He had to find Pepper.

The rest of them stood around in a huddle. Bryce, Eddie, Jayson, and Charlie. His team. Not one he'd been looking for or thought he would get again, but they were here for him anyway. The way he was here to find Pepper. The way the community in Last Chance County pulled together.

Brothers. Friends. Coworkers. The family he'd always dreamed of.

Eddie said, "Where would this guy have taken her?"

Allen pushed aside the family thoughts, just grateful he wasn't alone here—even if he was also surprised they'd come.

"I never saw more than one vehicle. She could still be in the neighborhood." He didn't like any of the ideas his mind came up with as to what she might currently be suffering.

Bryce nodded. "Let's go door-to-door." The rescue lieutenant strode out, already on his radio, getting their truck out of service so they could assist the police.

Allen wheeled outside and stared at the dark neighborhood under the night sky.

Where was she?

31

Pepper raced across whatever room this was. The walls and floor were wood boards, the doorways open and unobstructed.

She didn't know how far she'd gone from the original house. She could barely see where she was going. Nowhere to go. Nowhere to hide.

Her heart cried out to God, but the words didn't find her lips. She had no time to think. All she could do was run from this guy long enough and far enough to get help. She'd made it this far. God knew if she would survive. Or not. If Allen would make it out of his situation alive.

If Victory would have a parent left alive tomorrow.

Tears blurred her eyes. She sailed off a step and landed on the dirt between two houses.

Pepper stumbled but caught herself before she went down.

She gasped and swiped at her face, moving grit around with the dampness. *Move.* Hector's boots thumped through the house, steady and relentless. She couldn't let him catch her. Somehow she had to make it far enough the police caught him. Or killed him. There was nothing Pepper could do except what she'd done in her house when his men threatened her and she'd set fire to her kitchen.

Cry for help.

She would die out in the open.

Pepper raced for the neighboring house and had to turn right immediately. This house was a maze of rooms and hallways. She couldn't hide. It was far too tempting, but there was no cover in any room and nothing to fight back with.

Just bare walls and bare floors.

Her foot caught an obstruction and she tumbled over. Her knees slammed the wood floor. She couldn't hold back the cry. Surprise. Pain. All of it rang through the room, echoing against the bare walls.

He would hear her.

"So much running." Hector's voice rumbled through her. "Your sister won't make it far either."

Pepper shuddered. She tried to get up. Pain whipped through her shins like lightning. She touched it, unable to see much in the dim glow from the streetlights outside. Sticky. Wet. Her shins throbbed, streaming blood.

He stepped into the room, that gun pointed at her. The one he'd used to kill her sister. Or so she'd thought. Sage had been shot. Was she alive?

Pepper screamed all her fear and frustration, praying someone heard before she died. She took a breath and started to do it all again. There was plenty of fear in her to draw from. The sound of it rang in her ears like the time she'd tried to learn how to play the trumpet.

Hector stared down at her. His finger on the trigger.

Pepper braced herself for the pain that would end her life.

A dark figure slammed into Hector. The gun went off—a flash in the room and the accompanying pop. She screamed again but didn't hear the sound.

The dark figure had a yellow band around his jacket and on the hems of his pants.

A firefighter.

Hector elbowed back and hit the firefighter in the face. Eddie. He cried out. Hector rolled the rescue squad firefighter off him with another elbow and a punch.

They both scrambled for the gun.

Hector kicked the firefighter. Eddie rolled to his back, blood running from his nose.

"Rice!"

Boots rumbled down the hall.

Hector jumped up and ran to the window. He swung his legs over the edge and dropped out of sight.

"Help!" Pepper wanted to have the strength to get up. "Eddie!"

Firefighters thundered into the room. Then Lieutenant Basuto from the police department. "Where did he go?"

She pointed. "Out the window."

Basuto raced from the house, yelling into his radio.

Allen rolled into the room. The gasp turned into a whimper as he moved around them toward her. "Hey."

Relief tugged her under its current until she was drowning in tears.

"Come on. Let's get out of here."

Over his shoulder she saw someone move past the window. Maybe Basuto. Allen had her stand, but her legs shook. "Are you really okay?"

She blinked at him. "I was worried about you."

"These guys got me out of the car."

Eddie said, "Yeah, after you crashed it." His voice sounded like he had a heavy cold, a shirt pressed to his mouth and nose. Covered in blood.

"And you all came?"

Allen squeezed her hand. "I would have regardless. They tagged along."

Bryce glanced over. "You think we'd pass up the chance to be heroes?" He grinned. "No way."

Pepper wondered if it was more that they wanted to help their friend. But they were guys, so maybe they didn't want to admit they cared about each other.

"We'll take this guy to the hospital and go back, clean up that crash scene."

Behind Bryce, Jayson and Charlie hauled Eddie to his feet. He shoved them away. "I didn't break my legs. Just my nose."

Bryce held out his hand to Allen and they shook.

"Thanks." Allen nodded. "Watch each other's backs. This might not be over."

Bryce gave him that guy nod. The chin lift that expressed so much respect and care she didn't know how they weren't aware of it.

Pepper swiped her cheeks. "Ugh." Dirt covered her hands and now her face as well. Every part of her ached. Shook. Her mind spun, but she purposely didn't think about her sister and what had happened back at that house. Allen had been taken away by those two guys. Was he really okay?

Hector was still out there. This wasn't over.

"Are you all right, Pepper?"

She turned to Allen. "I was about to ask you the same thing."

Allen smiled. "Let's get out of—"

A tang on the night breeze drifted past her nose. "What is..."

Flames whooshed up outside, through the windows. Allen pushed his way down the hall. The front door was engulfed in flames. His firefighters were nowhere to be seen, taking Eddie to their truck.

Her sister's killer had to have done this. Faced with their rescuers, he'd set fire to the house.

"He had to have poured gasoline or something around outside." Allen turned. "All the way around the house."

"We're trapped."

"No, we're not." His jaw flexed.

"Allen..."

He moved through the house. "Basuto either went the wrong way or he's been neutralized."

She gasped. "Is he dead?"

Allen patted his pockets. He reached for his backpack and tried to tug it around.

"Let me get it."

"See if there's a phone or radio in there. It won't take them long to see the fire, but we should try and call for help."

She knelt and rummaged in his pack hanging off the back of his chair. "There's no radio. Or a phone." She found an electronic device. "What about your tablet?"

"It has no cell signal. Only Wi-Fi. We won't be able to use it out here."

She tucked it back in. "What are we going to do?"

"Smoke rises, so we get low. We find a center room, and they get us out before the flames get inside to where we hide." He sounded so calm.

Pepper stuffed down the urge to try and jump through the flames now working their way in the front door. The windows. This place was going up like tinder. They would have minutes, maybe. Not much longer than that.

She moved through rooms where smoke laced the air.

Pepper lifted her grimy sweater to cover her mouth and nose and looked for a good place they could hide.

The hall closet wasn't big enough for both of them. There was no upstairs. A bathroom, maybe? She eventually turned into what she figured might be the bathroom—where plastic pipes stuck through the floor.

The exterior wall glowed with flames, already black under the heat that made her face flush. She went back to Allen, her steps labored.

"Frees!" The yell came from outside.

They moved to the hall, where they had a decent view of the front entryway, engulfed in flames. The firefighter outside yelled from behind his helmet, "Hang tight! The hydrants aren't connected, but we've got a water truck coming!"

Allen yelled back "Copy that!" so loud she started. Allen took her hand. When she looked at him, he said, "Come on."

They moved to the center of the house, where the linen closet provided a pocket of space not big enough for him to get his chair inside.

He tugged her to it. "Hide here, okay?"

He set the brakes on his chair.

She shook her head. "It's not big enough for two."

"I'd stand up in there with you, but it wouldn't last long, and then you'd be holding me up." He tried to smile, but it didn't reassure her. "I have no idea if they'll be two minutes or twenty getting in here."

"We'll be dead by then."

"We just have to hang on." Allen took both of her hands. "Together. The way we're supposed to be."

"I thought you were dead. Things are *supposed to be* okay, and now Hector got away." Too many things rolled through her mind. She couldn't keep it all straight. "I don't even know if Victory is okay."

Allen shook his head. "I'm sorry. Between crashing the car with Hector's guys in it to finding you...I forgot to ask." He hesitated.

"What is it?"

"Your sister."

"Hector shot her." Pepper swallowed back the lump in her throat. So much had happened.

"You look exhausted. I'm sorry, you don't need this." Allen glanced at the front door, though he didn't have line of sight. "But when we got to the house, there was only blood. No one was there."

She could hear sirens and yelling in the distance but had no idea what they were all doing. Pepper couldn't hold up her legs. "Where is Sage?" And Victory.

Her heart squeezed in her chest.

She slumped to the floor. After all, she was already filthy. What did a little more construction dust matter on top of everything else? She sighed and leaned her shoulder against the inside wall of the cupboard. Looked up at him.

"They'll get us out."

"I'd feel better if you could sound convincing."

"I don't like heat or tight spaces."

She frowned. "You work in a fire department."

"They roll out, put out the fires, and then come back. They don't bring it back to the house with them," Allen muttered. "Just their squabbles."

She'd seen enough to know that was true.

He swallowed. "When this happened"—he motioned to his chair—"it was dark and oppressively hot. For a while I thought I was going to die down there."

She reached up and touched his knee.

"Until they rescued me." He pushed out a breath. "After, I slept with the light on for a while. Natalie helped me work through it. She knows what it's like to experience something like that."

"I'm sorry." This was bad enough.

"You're here this time. I'm not alone."

She squeezed his knee, and he laid his hand on hers. Pepper said, "You're *not* alone, and neither am I. It feels odd.

I'm not sure what to do with the feeling sometimes. It's so foreign."

He smiled. "I know what you mean."

The house creaked and moaned around them.

Pepper shuddered. Fatigue settled over her, and her eyes began to drift shut.

He shook her hand. "Hey, don't fall asleep, okay?"

She fought the black of sweet naptime and shifted on the floor, moving around so her brain woke up a bit. Twisting back and forth. "I'm awake."

He chuckled. "They'd better get in here quickly."

Sweat rolled down his temples.

"They will."

He nodded. It didn't look like he believed her.

"I love you."

"Don't do that." He shook his head. "This isn't the end. We're not doing deathbed confessions."

"Maybe it's way past time to tell you." It had taken her long enough. "Maybe we won't die. I certainly hope not. And I have no idea how to make everything work out, but it might be past time to quit trying to figure that out myself."

She'd done what she thought was best. But right now, the still, small urging to let go and allow God to do what He wanted in her life wouldn't quit.

It was time to surrender.

Allen squeezed her hand. He started to speak. The house creaked around them. It grew to a groan, and the whole structure listed to the side.

Pepper screamed as the house came down on top of them.

32

Fire heated his whole body. Sweat dampened everything. Allen fought against the drywall, beams, and debris that locked him in place.

"Easy, bro."

He shook his head, unable to string two thoughts together.

Trapped. He couldn't move. Not just the partial paralysis, but so much worse. He would die down here. He would never get out.

"Frees, listen to me."

"Allen!"

He didn't want to listen to either man, no matter how insistent their voices.

"He okay?"

Allen fought against the fog of the past, blinked his eyes open, and spotted the stars overhead. He inhaled a lungful of clean air. His chest spasmed.

The EMTs rolled him to his side. "Get it out." That was Trace.

Izan stood in front of him, a hard expression on his dark

features. Might just be the light. It also could be that something terrible had happened.

Allen fought the cough and got out one word. "Pepper."

They rolled him to his back and lifted the head of the gurney. The street around him moved like cars at a busy intersection—one of those awful ones in the city, where overpass stretched above overpass like a mess of spaghetti.

"With me?"

He blinked at Trace. "Yep." Given their expressions, neither EMT seemed to think that positive. "What? What's going on?" He coughed against the sandpaper in his throat. "Where's Pepper?"

"They haven't pulled her out yet."

Allen reached down and unbuckled the strap over his hips. There were two more, over his thighs and his lower legs. They might think he was ready for transport, but there was no way he was leaving when he had no idea if she was dead or alive.

"Nope." Trace pushed his shoulder. "You're not going anywhere."

Izan set his hand on Allen's other shoulder.

"I don't need to be babied."

"It's called support," Izan said. "It's what happens when you have friends who know what you've been through."

Trace turned and got something from his duffel.

"We're not leaving until she's out. I need to know."

Izan started to object.

Trace cut him off. "We understand. You're not critical, but you have some injuries that need to be treated."

Allen didn't care about that. He could feel pain in his right leg, below his knee. As welcome as that was, it seemed the fire had gotten to his pants after the house collapsed above them. And his back on the right side, given it stung when they'd rolled him.

Izan said, "The other ambulance is here as well. And Truck

14. They'll find her. But if we're waiting, I want to put gel on your back."

"I don't care."

"Maybe not," Trace said. "But you're going to lean over anyway."

Allen pressed his lips together. Better than chewing these guys out for doing their jobs just because he was a bad patient and worried about Pepper. "Where's Basuto?"

"He got hit over the head." Trace motioned where Allen couldn't see. "But he doesn't have a concussion. The cops who showed to back him up found him a couple of houses over. They figured this Hector guy did that and then doubled back to set the fire. He doused the outside of the framing with accelerant, and while rescue squad walked Eddie back to their truck, he ignited it."

Allen hissed out a breath.

"Exactly."

He didn't correct Trace and confess that what Izan was doing on his side hurt as much as it felt better. The cold gel stung but quickly dissipated into a numb sensation.

Pretty much what he'd tried to do with his heart after Pepper cut things off between them.

Now he could lose her for an entirely different reason.

"Got her!" Zack lay on his stomach on a pile of wood, debris that was still smoldering. "She's down here!"

Rescue squad moved in. The kid helped them get charred pieces aside, uncovering the spot where they crouched and Zack lifted her out. The others grabbed arms and legs.

Allen's stomach turned over. *Lord.*

Izan set his hand on Allen's shoulder again. He thought it was about solidarity, but the EMT eased him to his back. It felt like there was a bandage taped to his side, that spot he wouldn't be able to see in a mirror without twisting around—which was going to hurt for a while.

Allen shook his head. "I need to know if she's okay." His next prayer fell from his lips as a plea. "God, don't let me lose her."

Trace stiffened.

Allen didn't have time to ask what that was about. The two EMTs from Westside firehouse pushed their stretcher to the group of firefighters. "Let's get closer. Move the bed." These guys could get him near her without being in the way. He just wanted to hear what they said.

"Stop trying to get up."

Allen twisted around and grabbed Izan's shirt. Pain screamed across his back. "Go find out if she's *alive*."

"Okay." The younger man blanched, backed up a step, and headed over there.

"Keep praying." Trace didn't move, he just kept that brown-eyed gaze on the other two EMTs and Pepper.

"You could get me an update on Hector."

Trace said, "Not leaving you."

Izan called back over his shoulder, "Unconscious but alive."

Allen nodded. He mouthed *thank you*. Which was pretty much an apology for how he'd acted. Or as good a one as he could muster right now. The adrenaline coursed through him like a buzz he didn't like the feel of at all. Later, everything was going to *hurt*. But he'd be hooked up to all those machines at the hospital, poked and prodded. Again.

Not his favorite.

Considering how many surgeries he'd had, they should give him time-share points—or shares in the hospital stocks.

"Are the cops looking for Hector?"

Near as he could tell, the guy knew he was almost caught. One last-ditch effort had him burning down that house. Which not only got everyone focused on the fire and getting Allen and Pepper out but also brought more firefighters, police, and all kinds of emergency personnel around.

"I can field that question."

Allen glanced quickly enough to see it was Conroy, then looked back at Pepper. She hadn't regained consciousness. He knew what it was like to have his entire life changed in one moment. He didn't want her to go through it, but she was strong.

Allen remembered they'd been unable to find Victory before all this happened. "First, where's Victory? Does anyone know?" He looked between Conroy and Trace.

Trace nodded. "She snuck into a cabinet on the fire truck. When they got to that call—which was a false alarm by the way—she popped out. Said there were men in the firehouse with guns."

Allen said, "She saw them?"

"And hid in a safe place," Trace said. "We brought her back to the house with us, and you guys were gone. We found Meredith and got her to the hospital. She'll be okay, but she was banged up." Trace took a breath. "Natalie came and got Victory. She's taking her to Tate and Savannah and will stay with her until you let them know otherwise."

Allen let out the breath he'd been holding. "Okay, that's good. That's really good."

Conroy nodded. "Now for Hector, who subdued Lieutenant Basuto—who was not ready for active duty again despite what he said. He ran off as far as we can tell. We're contacting the company who builds these houses to see if they have security cameras, and my K-9 officer is looking for Hector. We'll find him."

"Basuto wasn't wrong about being ready." Allen knew better than anyone how quickly things could shift, and there was nothing to do about it.

"He had a motel fall on him the other day. In a scene that looked an awful lot like this one."

"Okay, so that's not wrong."

Conroy said, "He'll take a few weeks off, conveniently around the time his twins will be born, and I get to write up a reprimand."

"Suspension?"

"And medical leave, going into family leave. Plus vacation. He'll be tanned and need to go on a diet by the time he comes back to work."

Despite everything, Allen found himself laughing. "With twin newborns?"

"Hm. Maybe not."

Andi Crawford strode over from the other gurney, peeling off a pair of rubber gloves smeared with dirt and blood.

Allen touched her forearm. "Tell me."

She nodded. "A bunch of abrasions. She's still unconscious, which I'm a bit worried about. But mostly I think she's been through a trauma and her body's answer to all the adrenaline and exertion is to shut down so it can repair itself. She'll wake up in a few hours in the care of skilled doctors."

Allen swallowed down the lump in his throat. "Thank you."

She nodded. "Catch you at the hospital. I'll be the one doing paperwork."

Conroy chuckled.

Allen watched his firefighters work. There was a harmony to their movements he could appreciate. The efficiency of working toward a common goal brought them together. It just didn't do the same in the kitchen when they felt it necessary to argue over whose chili was better.

"Is it me, or are they actually getting along?" Conroy shook his head and strode away toward several police officers congregating together beyond the fire scene.

Trace chuckled. "For now."

Allen groaned. "Don't remind me."

Andi and her partner pushed their gurney to the second ambulance. Izan jogged back over.

Trace patted his shoulder. "Time to go."

He needed to find them a new chief, but that could wait until tomorrow. He needed a day of sleep, a hug from Pepper, and a pizza. "Backdraft does delivery, right?"

"Sure does." Trace pushed the gurney from the back. "But text me. I'll get what you want and bring it over."

"Thanks, bro."

Izan said, "Get enough for all three of us."

Allen glanced once more at the two teams of firefighters, clearing debris enough to put the fire completely out and ensure nothing was left burning. The cops, looking for a dangerous suspect. His past and his present, working together. Allen got to feel like part of one team instead of a guy who'd lost a job he loved and a woman he loved in the same week.

As though God knew that and had given him this gift.

Thank You.

Part of him would remain a cop regardless of the fact he'd never wear a badge again.

Now he was part of the fire department—a different kind of family but capable of the same strong bonds the PD had.

A latent instinct prickled at the edges of his awareness. His gut. God giving him a check in his heart.

"Hold up a second." Allen twisted on the gurney, trying to see what had caught his attention.

"No chance." Izan tugged harder.

At the edge of what he could make out, beyond the firefighters. The cops. Noise and chaos. Flashing lights.

A shadow moved.

Allen registered the intention a split second before he yelled, "Gun!"

Everyone hit the ground. Izan leaned over, but Allen shoved him away.

The muzzle flashed and the sound of a gunshot broke the air, aimed at the cops. The K-9 raced at Hector, jumped, and knocked the guy to the ground. All the officers ran to subdue the guy, roll him to his face, and cuff his hands behind his back.

The police chief stood. "We're clear!"

Firefighters started to get up, brushing off the shock.

"All in a day's work." Trace chuckled.

Izan blinked. "Right. Happens to me all the time."

Allen's laughter dissipated some of the tension in his chest. "Let's go."

"Of course." Izan waved a hand at the ambulance. "Right this way, sir."

33

Pepper fought the lure of the hospital pillow. Instead, she raised the back of the bed so she was a little more upright. They hadn't admitted her, just kept her in a bay in the emergency department. After the last few days, she needed to sleep for hours, but they would release her soon. Where she was going to go, Pepper had no idea.

Victory lifted her head and lay down one side of Pepper, dark circles under her eyes. "Do you like that movie with the mouse? I forgot what it's called."

Pepper said, "It's a cartoon?" After everything that'd happened, normal was a nice change of pace.

Victory's mouth stretched in an exaggerated yawn. She settled her head back down on Pepper's shoulder. "Yeah."

"Wanna watch it again?"

She nodded against Pepper's collarbone. Would the nurses and doctors let them stay overnight if they had nowhere to go? Pepper didn't want to impose on anyone else, and she didn't want to let her niece out of her sight right now. Given the way Victory had climbed on the bed as soon as Savannah brought her here—and hadn't left that spot—she'd guess her niece felt the same way.

The police didn't know where Sage had gone. Pepper had thought Sage had died when that bullet hit her and she fell, but she hadn't waited around to find out. She'd been running for her life.

Her heart squeezed in her chest.

The war of care for her sister and fear for Victory threatened to send her into a tailspin.

Until they found Sage, Victory and Pepper would always be looking over their shoulders. And then there was the hurdle of paperwork and interviews that would come when Pepper officially stepped up to adopt the child.

The curtain swished back. Allen pulled his chair all the way up to the side of her hospital bed, looking like he'd been used as a punching bag.

Pepper said, "Hey."

He gave her a soft smile despite the bruises. "Anything yet?"

She shook her head, about to speak, when Victory shifted and said softly, "Hi, Allen."

"Hey, kid. Doing okay?"

Victory let out a soft noise and settled in to sleep.

Pepper waited a moment and whispered, "Did you talk to CPS?"

Allen nodded. "Her name is Tosha. Nice lady. I've met her before working for the police department. She's going to start the paperwork for you to become Victory's guardian. Officially. Until you can get the ball rolling on adoption."

Tears ran down her cheeks until he had to hand her a tissue because swiping them away didn't work.

"This is a good thing."

She sniffed. "I don't even have a house. My life is a disaster."

Pepper closed her eyes and felt Victory's rhythmic breathing, so thankful the child was able to rest.

"I'd offer you a place at my house, but it's a crime scene." He looked at his watch. "The cleanup crew should be done by now. Except, taking Victory back there might stress her out with bad memories."

They wouldn't know unless they tried. She bit her lip. "I have no idea what to do."

"Are you going to love and protect this child?"

Pepper frowned. "Of course."

"Then you know what to do. Everything else is just logistics."

"You won't be saying that when we move into the firehouse because we have nowhere else to go."

Allen chuckled. "The firefighters will love it. Plus it'll distract them from squabbling."

"It's not a real solution. I just have to call my insurance lady and get renovations started, I guess." And yet, everything in her wanted to curl up and ignore the world.

He squeezed her hand. "You'll figure it out."

"I'd rather go on vacation."

"I happen to know the Ridgeman Center has a couple of open rooms for long-term residents." Allen shrugged one shoulder. "Worth a call."

"I love you."

His expression softened. He started to speak, but her phone vibrated across the table beside her bed.

Allen looked at the screen. "Ready?" He handed it to her.

Of course the cops had been right when they'd said her sister would call. Pepper wasn't ready, and she never would be. She'd barely accepted that her sister was alive, but she still answered the phone. "Hello?"

Her sister didn't speak right away.

"There was blood." She'd seen her sister get shot but didn't know how bad it was. "Are you hurt? Do you need help?"

Sage said, "As if you care."

The hatred in her sister's voice cut through her. "It literally kills me that you think I don't. Where did you ever get that idea?"

Her sister huffed.

Allen handed her the notebook where she'd scribbled down their advice on what to say. How to lead her sister in the conversation. Maybe not so far Sage turned herself in, but Pepper would do her part.

Pepper said, "Why did you call?"

"You don't know why?"

Her stomach clenched. "You expect me to just hand her over?"

Victory shifted against her side and breathed deeply. Pepper loosened her arm.

"She's my daughter."

"You're right." Pepper closed her eyes. "I have no legal claim on her unless you relinquish your rights."

"As if I'd do that."

But her sister thought she would turn Victory over to her? Sage didn't know her if she thought Pepper would subject a child to a life on the run from the police. Victory had been through too much upheaval. Not to mention the distress of her parents skirting the law and making deals. Getting in with bad people. The child had been passed back and forth, and the only normalcy she'd ever experienced was life at Auntie Pepper's house.

Sage said, "I'll never give her up."

"I know." Her sister had never believed she was the source of the problems in her life. It was always someone else's fault. Pepper blew out a breath. She had to keep the hardness from her voice. And the sarcasm that wanted to come out, which would only antagonize her sister. She had to stick to the script the police had walked her through.

She said, "Are you safe?"

"I can take care of my own child."

"I just want to know if you're hurt."

"I'll live." Sage hissed like a wave of pain overcame her. "Which I'm sure you're sorry about, since it means you can't raise my child as yours because you refused to trick that cop into marrying you to make a case for custody."

Pepper squeezed her eyes shut. That's what Sage thought of her relationship with Allen? "I'm glad you'll be okay." She swallowed. "Victory needs her mother."

"Yes, she does. Which is me, in case you forgot that." Sage made a noise that sounded like she'd moved and she was in pain.

Despite everything, Pepper did care for her sister. Enough to know Sage needed to face the consequences of what she'd done in the hopes she'd see her error. Realize the kind of sister and mother she'd been. Do the right thing.

Let them both go.

As if their mother had taught them something different than precisely what Sage was currently doing. Pepper ignored her mother's repeated attempts at contact. Her sister hadn't been quite so determined to break away from the pattern.

Sage said, "I want my daughter."

"I know she's not mine." Pepper blew out a breath to steady her pounding heart, surprised Victory hadn't been woken by it. "We can meet. I'll say goodbye and she can go with you."

"Just like that?"

"My house is a wreck. I have nowhere to go, so I have no way to take care of a child. And I'm not her legal guardian." Pepper let herself feel all the grief wrapped up in her current situation. Even though things seemed to be settled with Allen, the fact was, she'd have to find somewhere to live while her house was repaired. And as fun as that sounded, it wouldn't be the firehouse.

The truth clogged her throat.

Sage said, "Just as long as you don't try anything funny."

"I'm in the hospital, Sage. I don't have the energy to think right now, let alone come up with whatever crazy plan you imagine I'm brewing up."

She looked at Allen, looking for assurance she was doing this right. He nodded but said nothing. Still, she could read enough in the expression on his face. On his tablet, he was getting a transcript of the conversation from the police department.

He'd read every word Sage said.

The confidence he had in her and the care he felt for her was a gift she would cherish. She wondered if he'd been about to say that he loved her back before the phone rang. She'd said it to him twice now, and neither time had he been given the chance to say it back.

If she let it, her mind would spin with worry. He'd loved her before. Did he love her now?

She had to focus. Get Sage to walk into a trap the police had set for her. "I'll meet you."

Sage huffed. "You give her to me, and you never have to see me again."

"How do you want to do this?" She was supposed to let her sister think the meeting place was her idea, then steer her toward the spot they'd scoped out.

"We meet somewhere public but quiet. You come alone. You don't tell anyone, least of all that cop boyfriend of yours."

Pepper bit the inside of her cheek. "What are you going to do?"

"Take my daughter and leave, what do you think?"

It had almost sounded like Sage would try to kill her. But as the police had assured her, neither Pepper nor Victory would be in danger. They would be across town, completely safe the entire time, while someone else pulled up pretending to be Pepper.

Except, the last time they'd done that, a cop had died.

Allen squeezed her knee.

"I think you'll need her car seat. Her things." Pepper let out an audible sigh so her sister would think she'd resigned herself to what was happening. "Why don't you take my car? For now, at least. You'll have to switch it for a new vehicle so the police can't find you, but you'll be states away by then."

"That's right. They'll *never* find me." Her sister scoffed. "Unless you're putting a tracker on your car so they can follow me."

Actually, it was more that the officer would be driving with a lifesaving training dummy wearing a wig that looked like Victory's hair in the back seat, but Sage didn't need to know that. By the time she realized it wasn't Pepper and Victory, the police would have already sprung their trap.

"I'm trying to help," Pepper told her. "I can pack some things in my trunk that were donated after the fire. Stuff you might need."

"And money. You have emergency savings, right?"

Pepper always had. With the life she'd lived, she'd thought essential as soon as she learned what financial literacy meant. Sure, sometimes she funded a weekend break with the money, but she could generally cover an emergency.

And Sage knew it.

"Yes, I can bring you what was in my safe." This had to happen tonight. No way could she tell Sage she had to make a withdrawal when the bank opened. The police officer taking her place wouldn't pass for Pepper long enough in the daylight—and neither would the lifesaving dummy pass for Victory.

"In your house that burned down?"

Pepper said, "It's a fire safe."

"Good. 'Cause *you* burned your house down." Sage chuckled, a hollow sound that dissolved into groans. She coughed.

Pepper winced. "You aren't okay."

"I can take care of my daughter."

Pepper said, "*Good.*"

She gave Sage cross streets and the store where the officer would pull into the parking lot. Far corner. Where the police could swarm them, box Sage in, and make the arrest.

Then Pepper said, "Give me an hour."

"Fine."

"Goodbye." Pepper hung up the phone.

Allen lifted it from her shaky fingers. He reached up and touched her face, gently turning her chin so she looked at him. "I love you."

She fought back the cry. "You're just saying that."

"Things will never be perfect. Our lives will be one thing after another, but I want to weather all of the ups and downs together, trusting in God to bring us through it all stronger than we went into it."

"Thank you."

He shook his head. "You don't have to thank me."

"I'm never going to stop thanking you. No matter what happens."

"Good. Because I'll complain about my coworkers, and I'll drink all the milk and then forget to throw out the carton. The heating will go out. Or worse, the air conditioner in the middle of summer."

Pepper knew what he was doing, and she loved him for it. "I'll burn dinner. Or be grumpy because I'm hungry but can't be bothered to make anything. I'll complain I have nothing to wear. You'll point out I have half a closet full of clothes, and I'll want to smack you for it."

He grinned. "I'll forget what you asked me to pick up on the way home."

"I'll leave my shoes in the middle of the floor."

"I'll kiss you and tell you I love you every single day."

"I'll be there for all of it. Nothing hidden. No plan B." She touched his cheek. "Just gratitude because I get to share it all with you."

He smiled. "Sounds like a plan."

Victory shifted, and in her sleepy voice said, "I'm coming too."

34

Lights flashed around them, courtesy of a police car in front and another behind. Their own convoy.

"Almost there." Allen reached over and squeezed Pepper's knee.

She checked Victory, asleep in the back seat, for the hundredth time. He didn't blame her. He'd angled the rearview down so he could keep an eye on her. Make sure she didn't have a nightmare.

Pepper and Victory had an appointment with Natalie in a couple of days, after they'd rested. Time would tell the repercussions of what they'd been through. He prayed there was something he could do to help them instead of feeling powerless.

"If we're clear to go to my house tomorrow, I can make hamburgers on the grill."

She squeezed his hand. "That would be nice."

He wondered if that was true or if the woman was simply too tired to formulate an argument right now. It would take some doing, but they would eventually get to the point that neither of them remembered the fear when they spent time at his house. Pepper's house would be renovated, and they could live there again. They wouldn't be there too long if he had a say in it. Now that he and Pepper had finally reached the place where their relationship could start, he wasn't planning to play it slow.

Maybe she just needed to talk about easier, simple things.

Allen glanced over. "You're sure Brett is okay with us spending the night at the vet's office?"

"We're down a staff member, and he gets to go home to his family." She shifted in the seat and checked on Victory. "The animals will be taken care of, and the place is big enough we can have cops there watching out for us."

"Okay, then." He didn't like the idea she would spend the night working, but they hadn't had many options after the doctor decided she didn't need to stay at the hospital overnight.

"Victory loves the animals. She'll be more comfortable there than in a strange hotel room."

"Okay." He took the turn. The vet's office wasn't in the center of town—more on the outskirts. Another plus, considering that meant they'd more easily see someone coming. It was unlikely anyone would venture onto this road tonight.

"And by tomorrow, Sage will be in police custody."

By his calculation it should be more like an hour or two from now, but he knew what she meant. The dawn would bring a new day. A new chapter for her and Victory. After they met with Natalie, they would meet with Tosha. The CPS caseworker could observe them and begin the process of approving Pepper as Victory's guardian.

In a way, she'd been raising her niece since the girl was born. Only now it would be official.

"You can start a new phase of your life now, Victory with you full time."

She shifted. "That doesn't...bother you? Like me having criminal relatives."

In a way, they'd been over this. How he felt about her mother wasn't so far from how he felt about Sage being behind bars. Neither of their actions had any bearing on Pepper and who she was. She'd never been an accomplice to anything they'd done.

"I know you and Victory are a package deal." He shrugged. "You accept a lot with me that isn't normal. Things you have to adapt to. Like an accessible bathroom, for instance." There was a lot more, but she got the gist.

Pepper shifted in her seat. "It's not like you can change it. And it wasn't your fault."

He enjoyed the little bit of fire in her words. Even with how exhausted she was, the woman still had strength in her.

"I'm working on progress, so hopefully things will continue to change in that sense." He glanced over. "But I know what you mean. And I know there's no way you'd choose not to do this, but I'm not going to begrudge you for doing the right thing. Victory shouldn't be dumped in the system with CPS."

"Thanks." More than one word, he heard all the feeling behind it. Like a simple squeeze of the hand that meant so much more, he caught the wealth of emotion in her tone.

Allen pulled his truck into the parking lot and took a space right by the door, since no one else was around. One cop car idled. The other parked. Brett's truck would be parked around back, where they had a staff lot.

Allen blew out a breath. "I think I'm more tired than I thought. My thoughts keep drifting off."

"I know what you mean." She chuckled. "We can all get some rest, hopefully."

"And pizza." Maybe they could get a fresh pie delivered from Backdraft.

One of the cops grabbed Allen's chair from the truck bed since Victory occupied the back seat. Allen motioned with his hand, and Officer Ramble gave him an extra assist down.

"Thanks."

He'd probably have felt awkward any other time, but accepting help when needed should never be a shameful thing.

"Anytime, bro. Of course." Ramble rocked forward and back on his uniform shoes. "Heard you saved everyone's lives earlier. For weeks, they've been telling stories from your glory days as a cop. Now it'll be ten times as bad. You'll probably get a medal."

"Apparently there's nothing interesting happening at the police station." Allen shook his head. "Anyone who saw Hector would've called out."

"You've still got the instinct." Ramble stepped back, a note of something in his expression.

"How long have you been on the job?"

"Just over a year." The cop shrugged. "I figure I'll get there."

"Keep doing what you're doing."

Pepper rounded the car. "Thank you for being here to keep us safe."

"Sure thing." Officer Ramble opened the back and lifted Victory into his arms.

Pepper led him inside, where he laid the girl on the lower bunk in the room night staff used to get some rest, or Brett Filks, the vet, took a nap in after a particularly long day—or surgery. They could take a shower here, and Pepper had told him they had clean scrubs, so she could put on fresh clothes.

Allen did a circuit of the place and found Brett in his office. He knocked on the open door. "Hey."

Brett rounded his old metal desk and came over.

"Thanks for letting us stay."

Brett nodded. "Anything for Pepper." The vet stuck his hand out. "I should be thanking you for keeping her safe."

"Of course."

"Do I have to ask your intentions?"

Allen said, "I don't know. Do you?"

Brett eyed him, a slight smile on his mouth. "I guess not."

"Good call." The vet would figure it out pretty quickly when Allen put a ring on Pepper's finger.

Brett blew out a breath. "Let me know when they've caught her sister?"

"Will do."

"She's a slippery one." Brett leaned against the wall. "Met her a couple of times. She hit on me both times, even though she was married." He ran a hand across his jaw. "It'll be better for them when she's out of their lives."

Allen wasn't sure Sage would ever be completely out of their lives, even after she went to prison—which seemed inevitable at this point. But he got the idea.

"I'll go brief her on the patients." Brett pushed off the wall. "Shouldn't be a lot of work, just monitoring an old dachshund and making sure the cats are fed in the morning."

Allen nodded. He went back to the lobby and found the two officers.

Ramble said, "The other patrol car took off. We're going to take a look around outside." He handed Allen a radio. "Let us know if there's anything. You shouldn't need to find us to tell us."

He figured it was a concession to his chair, but it was also a solid idea. He'd want a radio even if he could get up on his two legs and run.

For right now, he'd settle on standing while Pepper walked down an aisle, wearing a white dress. That sounded like the best thing he'd ever heard. And if it didn't happen quite like that, he would take it any way he could get it. Life was life. They accepted what each other came with, and they would go forward together. Lord willing, that plan would last a lifetime.

His phone rang.

A quick glance at the screen showed an incoming video call from one of the prospective new chief candidates. Allen had texted earlier to say they were headed out of the hospital and to call anytime, since it was daytime in Australia and Allen had figured he wouldn't be sleeping anytime soon.

At least, not until he got word Sage was in cuffs.

Allen said, "Macon, hey."

The guy's face filled the screen, ear buds in. Younger than Allen anticipated, though his date of birth had been on the application. Whether or not he'd make a good chief remained to be seen, regardless of whether Bryce and his twin brother Logan thought Macon James would make a good boss for the Last Chance County Fire Department.

He would be on probation for the first few months— enough time to find his feet with a new team.

"Mr. Frees. Everything settled down finally?"

"Almost, sounds like. And you can call me Allen." He hadn't told the prospective new chief much about what had been happening, just that they'd had a busy week.

Macon nodded. "I'm hoping I can call you *boss* pretty soon."

Allen would have to figure that part out. "So you're taking the job?"

Truth was, no other candidate that had applied jumped out at him the way this guy did. Most were existing brass in the department—guys who figured they'd been in the job long enough they deserved the position as their due. Allen didn't work like that. They might be officers, but that wasn't what his firehouse needed.

The list of reasons they were unsuitable in each case was far too long, while Macon's had been a whole lot shorter.

He had roots here. The fire department needed someone new. A fresh face with ideas to get them all working together— as firefighters and colleagues. This Macon guy wasn't anything like the others.

"I'd like to come home to Last Chance County," Macon said. "It's time for me to face home again."

Allen nodded, wondering if the guy had been running from

something and that was what landed him in Australia. "That's good to hear."

"I'll send you an email when I make travel arrangements." Macon grinned. "And tell Bryce I'll talk to Logan."

They hung up, and Allen typed out a quick email to the committee. This wasn't going to be a popular choice, and he'd have to do some convincing.

Hopefully Macon James proved up to the challenge.

His phone pinged with a text from Conroy.

CONROY

Sage never showed.

Allen stowed the phone and pushed the wheels of his chair down the hall, looking for Pepper. She wasn't in the bunk room, where Victory still slept. *Good.*

He lifted the radio. "Heads up. We might have a problem. The sister never showed for the meet." Allen wasn't about to put a child at risk. "One of you needs to find Pepper. I'm with Victory."

"Copy that. We'll keep our eyes open."

Allen turned and backed up slightly so his chair blocked the doorway. No one was getting past him. Pepper could be taking care of the animals, but he wasn't leaving Victory unprotected.

Whatever spooked Sage, she wouldn't be taking Victory.

Not tonight. Not ever.

He got on the radio again. "I want to know the second you find her."

35

Pepper hauled the trash bag up and tossed it in the dumpster. She wanted to get back inside, but the nighttime chores still had to be done—and they would keep her awake just in case her sister showed up. Who knew if she even would. There were cops around just in case, but something about being out here had her on edge.

Inside the vet's office, she would at least be able to relax, do some menial tasks. Keep things moving so she didn't fall apart waiting to hear if Sage was dead or alive.

She turned to the back door. A shadow shifted, the lines familiar. Almost a mirror of her reflection.

Pepper stilled.

"You thought I was going to fall for that act? You're a worse liar than you are a sister." Sage moved out of the shadows with her arms folded loosely. Blood on her shoulder.

"You didn't get that looked at?"

"I'm a criminal. I can't exactly walk into a hospital." Sage slumped against the building. She winced even leaning her uninjured shoulder against the siding, pain in the lines around

262 | LISA PHILLIPS

her mouth and the dark brown of her eyes. "You sent the cops to pick me up so you can keep Victory for yourself."

Instead of that familiar frustration, an entirely different sensation rose in Pepper. Things were new. She wanted to reach out a hand—even if it would probably get slapped back. Maybe nothing had changed for Sage. Pepper knew what she should do. But it didn't seem right to cry out loud enough for the cops to hear and take Sage to the hospital in cuffs.

Pepper wanted to be the one who helped her sister surrender peacefully.

She wasn't sure she'd be able to verbalize exactly why things had changed for her. So much of her life had settled into a good place over the last day or so—even with all the fear and, at times, believing she wouldn't survive. Now she could contemplate a future with Allen, and yes, Victory too.

She wanted to drop to her knees and pray aloud. Just say *thank You* over and over again until she had no breath left.

She was alive. The people she loved wanted to be with her. She might have no home and no things, but she also had everything she needed.

"Come inside." Pepper wanted to do right by her sister whether Sage hated her for the rest of her life or not. "Let me look at that for you."

Sage didn't move or speak.

Someone snuck around the fence at the far end of the rear parking lot. Probably one of the cops, but she couldn't make him out. If he thought he could tackle her sister and throw her to the ground, he would quickly realize Pepper had no intention of letting Sage get hurt. Not any more than she already was.

She motioned to the door. "Come on. I want to help you."

"Just another trap."

If her sister had anywhere else to go, that's where she would be right now. "We can do this quietly. After I've taken a look at your shoulder."

No way would Pepper wind up an accomplice. Her sister had to decide if she planned on doing the right thing or if this was just another manipulation.

Sage shifted off the wall, leaving a dark smudge on the siding. She swayed slightly as she moved.

Pepper got under her good shoulder and slipped an arm around her waist. "I've got you."

Sage huffed. Whether about her statement or because of the pain, Pepper didn't know. She ignored it and pushed the door open.

"This way." The surgery suite would be empty right now. She got Sage settled on the metal table. "It'll be easier if you lie down."

"Easier for some cop to sneak up on me."

Pepper gathered supplies from the cupboard, including a freshly prepped needle she slid between two gauze packets. Would Sage consent to pain medicine? Her sister had rarely accepted anything from Pepper—a fact she now felt the urge to cry over. But the time for tears had passed. Things were the way they were, and neither could do much about it now. Both of them had made their choices.

Same mother. Same foster homes. At least similar experiences, and yet she'd never understood the different paths they'd taken.

Pepper put pressure on Sage's wound, still trickling blood even though she'd been shot hours ago. Her sister's face prickled with sweat, her skin pale. Her shirt was soaked with blood and sweat.

"You're enjoying my suffering."

Instead of responding to that, she said, "I'm sorry for your loss. Elijah might have had a lot of problems, but he loved

Victory, and the two of you cared for each other. At one point at least."

Sage huffed.

Pepper heard a shift behind her, low and quiet. Someone was listening, but she wasn't surprised. "I can give you something for the pain."

It would knock out her sister and make this entire experience more pleasant for everyone. Victory could see her mom was okay—in a couple of days, at the hospital. The cops could hide the cuffs while her niece talked to Sage. They needed the chance to say goodbye.

"Just clean it up. And stitch me closed or whatever you do."

Pepper motioned for her sister to turn. "Let me see the back."

Sage leaned over just enough.

Pepper hissed. *Not good.* The bullet hadn't gone through. "It's still in your shoulder. Which means you need surgery."

"You do that stuff. Fix this."

Pepper frowned. "The bullet is still in your shoulder. I'm not going to go digging around in there. It will hurt." She also had no qualification to do so.

"Not the first time you've stabbed me." Sage lifted her chin. "Just won't be in the back this time."

Pepper hoped the cops let them get through this important conversation before they stormed in, guns blazing. "That wasn't ever what I did to you."

"No? You didn't leave me at the Wilsons'?"

Her stomach flipped. "I aged out of foster care. They wouldn't let me stay." She took a breath. "Did he hurt you?"

"Mrs. Wilson slapped all the kids with her slipper. Who cares?" Her sister's expression hardened. "You got to escape. I had to stay there."

"I'm sorry."

"I never needed your pity. Don't start handing it over now." Sage huffed. "You just feel bad I'm going to jail because of you."

Pepper bit back what she would have said.

She wanted to tell her sister about the peace she'd found getting right with God, even with her hang-ups and all the questions she still had. She'd taken a step on the journey. Part of it meant not defaulting to the kind of sister she'd always been—the one who would point out it was Sage's relationship with Hector that got her shot.

Maybe one day Sage would want to hear about what Pepper had found.

"I'm sorry." Pepper had to say it, regardless of fault.

Her sister had shown up here knowing Pepper's intention was to turn her over to the police. She'd come anyway. Not to get medical care and then run off again, living looking over her shoulder for the rest of her life. She had shown up for Pepper to help her. To see Victory, as well, she guessed.

Because she needed her family.

Her sister brushed off her pant leg. "Can I see her?"

"She's sleeping, and there are cops between you and her."

Sage's expression hardened.

"I'm not saying that because I don't want you to see her. I think she'd like to say goodbye to you if it's going to be a while." Pepper motioned to her sister's shoulder. "If we can put a blanket over you."

"Victory!"

Pepper whirled around. Allen was down the hall, and her niece raced into the room before he could call her back.

She needed to keep things as calm as possible and ensure Victory didn't get scared. "Hey, Nugget."

"Mommy!" The little girl skidded to a stop, wide-eyed like when she woke from a bad dream.

Pepper whipped a blanket from the shelf like Victory and her bath towel. She fitted it over her sister's shoulders.

Sage touched Victory's cheek, smearing dirt and some blood there. "Hey, baby."

She started to sway. Victory bellied up to Sage's knees. Pepper moved so her sister could lean against her. The three of them stood there, in that moment, the way Pepper had wanted them to be the first time Elijah showed his true colors. A team. Supporting each other with love.

The two police officers stepped into the hallway, cuffs out. One hand on their holstered weapons.

Sage shifted. Ready to fight. She would do anything for even the smallest chance she might get away. They'd end up with Victory even more traumatized than she already was and Sage suffering that much more pain.

Pepper prepped the syringe behind her sister's back. "Nugget, Mommy needs to go to sleep now so the police officers can take her to the hospital and the doctors can make her better."

Victory blinked. "Mommy, why do you have to go?"

Pepper's eyes blinked with tears.

"I did something bad. But Auntie Pepper will take care of you." The words grew soft, her voice quiet. She was already halfway there. Sage said, "I love you, baby."

Pepper pressed the plunger and felt when the medicine started to work. A low dose, but enough to knock her sister the rest of the way out. Give her a little peace so she could be helped.

Sage would have to endure the consequences of her actions for years to come. Time would tell how their relationship might work after this. Whether Victory wanted to see her. If Sage would quit hating Pepper.

"Is Mommy sleeping?"

Pepper nodded. "She needs to rest so she can get better. Okay?"

Victory backed up a step. She looked at the cops and blanched. Started to speak. Hesitated.

"Nugg—"

Tennis shoes squeaked on the floor as Victory tore from the room. The cops moved in and blocked her view, more concerned about the criminal than the distraught child Pepper needed to get to.

She peeled off her gloves. "You're calling an ambulance for her, right?"

The younger one—Ramble, according to his name badge—nodded. "We'll make sure your sister is cared for."

Pepper found Allen in the hallway. "Where did she go?"

He didn't look at her, just lifted a finger and pointed the direction of his attention. "She raced for the back door and slammed right into him."

At the end of the hall by the exit, a tall man was on one knee with Victory in his arms. Heavy clothes and a wool cap.

The homeless man from the park.

Victory sobbed. The man didn't look entirely comfortable with the situation, but he held the little girl while she cried.

Pepper turned to Allen. "Who is that?"

"Jim Frees. My father."

36

P epper looked from the man holding Victory, to Allen, then back. *His father.* And when he found out who she was, what would the older man say about that? Pepper's mom had killed the mother of his child.

She took a step back. "I—"

One of the cops came out. "Ambo will be here in a minute." He spotted the homeless man, still comforting Victory. "Hey, Jim. Doing okay?"

Allen's father lifted his chin. Victory shifted out of his arms and turned.

Pepper's focus zeroed in on the child. "Do you want to sit with me in the waiting area?"

Her niece nodded.

Officer Ramble spoke low to Allen. "Saw Jim outside. I didn't know he'd come in though. He usually sticks outside."

Allen nodded. "I'm glad he did."

Pepper started down the hall, Victory's hand in hers. She couldn't have a second of peace to enjoy where her life had landed before something popped up in her way to prevent her from moving forward. Maybe it was the exhaustion talking, but it seemed like she couldn't catch a break. *Lord, will I be able to rest soon?*

Was she going to have to deal with the shame over her mother's choice for the rest of her life?

Behind her, Allen asked his father, "Do you want to sit with us, have a cup of coffee? It's cold out."

She didn't know if his father had accepted the invitation. It seemed like the cop didn't know about their relationship. But not because Allen was ashamed. He accepted how things were. He made the best of what he had.

Her sister was going to jail.

Her mother was already there.

Pepper and Victory could make a life of their own, free to be happy.

They settled onto the couch in the waiting area. Allen moved over to the front-door end of the coffee table. His father took the armchair in the corner, his back to the wall, where he could see every inch of the room.

A defensive move designed for self-preservation.

Pepper reached over and touched the arm of his chair as though she covered his hand with hers. But she didn't touch him. "Thank you."

Victory had needed a safe place to land in that moment, spinning out after seeing her mother.

He grunted. Shifted in the chair and got up. As he passed Allen, the older man reached out and squeezed his shoulder.

Allen watched him exit the front door.

Flashing lights lit up the windows and the glass in the door. The ambulance crew strode through with their gear, and the door swished shut.

"Did my thanking him make him leave?"

Allen shook his head. "He doesn't talk much at all. He goes by the house sometimes and sees my stepmom, but he mostly walks because he doesn't want to be cooped up. He probably saw the ambulance outside and knew this place would get crowded."

"I needed to say thank you." Her cheeks flamed. "Before he finds out who I am."

"You're going to let what your mother did define you for the rest of your life?"

"It's not like I can ask him to walk me down the aisle." Pepper realized right away what she'd said.

Allen grinned.

"That wasn't what you think." She had to fix this. Fast. He hadn't said anything about marriage!

"I accept."

"You accept what?"

"But I'm the one who does the asking."

Pepper rolled her eyes. "I must be more tired than I thought, because I don't recall asking anything."

"I'm saying yes anyway."

"To nothing."

He grinned wider. For some reason, it looked like a challenge. "To *everything*."

"You're never going to let this go, are you?"

"Nope." He wheeled around the table and stopped close to her, almost knee-to-knee. Victory had dropped back to sleep, stretched out on the couch with her head in Pepper's lap. Allen said, "I'm never going to let *you* go."

The Lord knew she'd tried to do the right thing and let him go. Allen didn't want to be released from any obligation toward her. He was intent on sticking by her. Loving her. Taking care of Victory.

How many times had he saved her?

More than she could count.

Pepper bit her lip. "Promise?"

"We're back together now. This is our return."

She stared at him, so grateful she couldn't even form the words.

"Through all the hope and the promise, the trust. All the way to the vows. And every day beyond."

The kind of love that would never expire.

EPILOGUE

THREE WEEKS LATER

Macon James parked his rental car outside the firehouse just before seven in the morning. Adjusting back to this time zone from Australia had him all flipped around, but he wanted to get the lay of the land before he officially came on board as the new chief of Eastside firehouse.

He grabbed his backpack and locked the car.

After being in summer in the southern hemisphere, home proved colder than the reception he'd get from his brother when Houston found out he was back in Last Chance County.

Eastside firehouse was bigger than he'd thought it would be. Bryce had sent pictures of a rooftop cookout they'd had a few days ago to celebrate an adoption. The City Hall liaison who'd hired him had a girlfriend who'd just adopted her niece—or something like that.

No one sat in the chair at reception, but it was still early. He was supposed to meet Bryce here, but not until later.

He heard chatter in the common room. A couple of firefighters in the kitchen were arguing about something, and they weren't holding back their opinions. An older guy in uniform watched the TV like the squabble was entirely normal and he'd learned to tune it out.

Macon spotted an open office door to his left, Allen Frees inside. A woman blocked the doorway, her back to him. A man stood with her, a heavyset, older guy.

On the left side of this hall, the office door said *Chief.* To the right was an empty conference room.

This whole firehouse would be his to command. A thought that caused his steps to falter. Macon needed to earn their respect before he could set them on the right path.

"I'm only trying to help you," the woman said.

"We both are."

"The decision has already been made, Janice." Allen Frees wasn't a man who backed down. That much was clear in his tone. "And you should know this isn't a popularity contest, Mr. Greene."

"Macon James isn't the committee's first choice for chief." Janice balled her fists beside the waist of her calf-length skirt. With gray hair pulled into a bun, she looked like an old school-teacher. "Yet you pushed his name to the top of the stack and gave us no way to refuse you."

Macon pulled up short in the hallway.

"Warrick's recommendation—"

"I'm not hiring the chief of Westside firehouse's fishing buddy."

"James is too young to be in charge. He's too inexperienced in command. Too everything."

"He's a firefighter, Janice. And he's the new chief of this house." Allen's voice rose. "Isn't that right, Macon?"

Both the man and the woman whirled around.

If Macon had to prove himself, that was exactly what he

would do. "I am a firefighter. And once I sign the paperwork, I'll be the new chief."

Allen nodded.

The woman huffed away down the hall.

"My job is to worry about her." Allen held out his hand for Macon to shake.

"And my job is to lead this house."

"It won't be easy."

"Nothing worthwhile ever is."

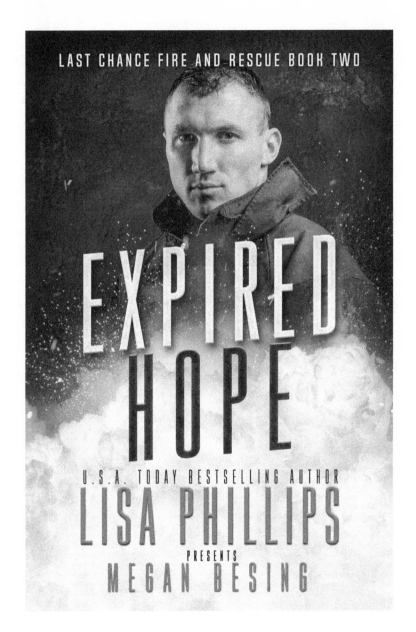

LAST CHANCE FIRE AND RESCUE BOOK TWO

EXPIRED HOPE

U.S.A. TODAY BESTSELLING AUTHOR

LISA PHILLIPS

PRESENTS

MEGAN BESING

Turn the page for a sneak peek of the next Last Chance Fire
and Rescue novel, *Expired Hope*...

EXPIRED HOPE SNEAK PEEK

CHAPTER 1

"Peter, you are not at war. Look for Joey in your backseat. Do you see him?" Natalie Atkinson gripped the steering wheel of her Volkswagen Beetle and put on her hazards. If only counselors had emergency lights.

"Stand down." She spoke loud and clear over the phone connection. "There's no enemy."

Not one they could see.

Trash bags whipped past her window and her mouth fell open. Clearly, the highway department had left sacks on the side of the road all over town. To a veteran who'd served where IEDs were concealed in anything from garbage to ditches to animal carcasses, those discarded bags could have sparked a memory of an explosion—the one that had flipped Peter's Humvee and killed everyone inside except him.

A trigger Natalie should have anticipated. For him, and for herself.

"Peter, I want you to pull over. I'm—"

"I-I'm not at war," Peter rasped. "I'm no longer a soldier."

"That's right." He needed to be grounded by the truth. Being a soldier was only a thing of both their pasts. Not their futures. "Do you see Joey?" His six-year-old had noticed something wasn't right and called her on speaker. "Joey, are you still with us?"

"I'm here, Ms. Natalie." Unlike his father, his voice was steady as a sharpshooter. "We're pulled over."

"Good." The stoplight turned red before her, and Natalie slammed on her brakes. She brushed her bangs back in place, covering her scarred forehead. "Do you know what exit you last passed or what store you're by? I'm heading toward you, but I need your location."

Based on their normal schedule, Peter would have picked up Joey from school and they'd be on their way home. But an errand might have gotten them off the primary route.

"Umm…" A beep echoed over the phone. "Ms. Natalie? The phone's making noises."

"Just stay with me, Joey." Whoever was calling Peter would have to wait. "Can you tell me where—"

"We're by the best french fry place."

That didn't exactly help. "Okay, I'm almost there." Sort of. If it was the mom-and-pop restaurant nearest their house, they were close to home. Almost to safety.

Another beep interrupted the silence.

"Ms. Atkinson?" Peter sounded less dazed.

"Still here, Peter. What are you looking at right now?" Natalie needed to keep Peter talking. Keep him in the present and away from the past. If only she could do the same.

According to the file she had studied when she first got hired at the Ridgeman Center, it had been months since his last episode, and Joey needed him now more than ever. "Do you see any—"

Another beep. Which meant it wasn't someone trying to reach Peter. It was worse.

"Joey, does your dad have a charger for his phone?"

But it wasn't Joey who answered. "I-I can make it home. Have to make it home for my son. I promised to protect him."

She pictured him squeezing the bridge of his nose like he did when a difficult topic arose during their sessions.

"There's no rush, Peter, there's—"

Her earpiece clicked off, and the hum of the tires on the road was anything except comforting. She'd been about to remind Peter there was no rushing the healing process, but now was the exact moment to hurry.

She pressed her accelerator and whipped around the curves.

Peter and Joey's house sat at the end of the cul-de-sac, giving the appearance of a man handling his new full-time, single fatherhood well. Between him and his ex-wife, Angie, Peter had seemed like the most stable to care for Joey. Her boss, Dean Cartwright, and even CPS agreed with Natalie.

But what if she'd misread someone again...

A silver car with a *My student is on the honor roll* bumper sticker was already parked in the driveway. A deep breath in and out slowed her nerves. They had made it home. She hadn't let anyone else down.

Natalie parked and grabbed her briefcase from the seat beside her. The hope of decompressing with a horse trail ride tonight at her cousin's house would have to be postponed, but she was thankful she'd slipped away from the office. Since she had been home, she'd grabbed one of Joey's favorite treats from her pantry. Peter's file had already been in her briefcase in prep for their scheduled meeting at the end of the week.

As she hustled for the front door, her navy pencil skirt restricted her speed and her low-heel pumps pinched her toes.

Peter wasn't pacing or wringing his hands on the porch. Joey wasn't sitting on the steps either. How fast had Peter driven? Only the smell of something buttery being cooked somewhere in the neighborhood welcomed her. Until her foot hit the last step and the door swung open.

"Wel-come ho-ome." Peter's ex-wife stood in the doorframe like she belonged there.

Unlike the first time Natalie had met Angie, the woman didn't have a lick of makeup on, and her hair had fallen out of what, at one point, might have been a bun. Her stained apron was upside down. Apparently, she'd lost even more unnecessary weight since their last meeting.

Natalie squared her shoulders. The day did not need to get any worse for her patient. "Ms. Johnson, does Peter know—"

"Don't you dare call me that," Angie spat.

Right. Well, she was no longer a Mrs., and by court mandate, she wasn't supposed to see Joey outside of set visiting hours. Ones that would be approved *after* her rehab completion.

A slam of a car door had Natalie spinning back toward the street.

Peter ran toward them. Natalie did a quick scan. His face was pale, yet his eyes were focused. First on Natalie, then onto Angie, and finally the open front door. Life wasn't often kind. It had plunged him from one massive problem to another. "How did you get inside?"

Angie narrowed her eyes, not at Peter but at Natalie. "I knew she was the reason we're not together. She's got you believing her lies. I told you, I don't need help. Especially not hers." Angie puffed out her bottom lip. "That's the real reason you both sent me to rehab."

Did Creekside Therapy know she'd left? If only she had agreed to go to the Ridgeman Center where Natalie worked.

Peter extended his palm to his ex. It was steadier than Natalie's heart rate. "Hand over the hidden key."

"Momma?" Joey's freckled face peeked out from behind his father.

"Oh, baby." Angie flung open her arms. "Come here."

Joey looked up at his father. Peter squeezed the bridge of his nose. "Make it quick and then go up to your room."

While Angie hugged and whispered promises to Joey, Natalie stepped closer to the door and set her briefcase inside. She flipped her phone over in her hand. If Angie didn't leave soon, she'd have to call the police.

"Joey. It's time," Peter murmured. "You can play your video game until I come and get you."

Joey wiggled free from his weeping mother and raced inside. His footsteps thundered up the staircase.

"How could you?" Angie brought her hands to her neck. Her face was splotched red and tear-stained, while her gaze filled with what resembled regret.

Natalie fisted her hands and reexamined Peter's expression and body language. Color had returned to his cheeks. His shoulders weren't drooped. The IED trigger had passed. He had gotten himself calmly home and was processing the problem before him in a healthy way. As a father, ready to fight for what was right for his son.

Which meant, patient or not, Peter wasn't the one who required Natalie the most at the moment. She lifted her chin and turned toward Angie. "Why don't I give you a ride back—"

"No." Angie ran her hand through her matted hair. "I'm not the one who must leave."

"Ange, she has to do her job. I need some help or Joey—"

"Don't you dare let her take Joey from you too." Angie pushed her pointer finger against Peter's chest. "You promised me you'd always take care of him. Promised!"

Peter clenched his jaw and rubbed at his chest. "I'm not the one breaking any promises. All you have to do is get sober and stay clean. Then the court said they'd give back your rights."

"They never should have taken him away from me." Angie pressed her lips together. "I'd never hurt my Joey."

Peter's gaze swung to the open door behind Natalie and back. "Our son found you on the floor with a needle still in your arm."

By the flash of rage on Angie's face, Natalie knew there would be no horse riding tonight with her cousin. No moment to decompress after a long day. Not when others' needs were more important.

Natalie stepped in between the stare-off. "Let's take a moment to—"

"I'm tired of your moments." Angie picked up a flowerpot painted with little thumbprint butterflies. "Drugs helped me because you broke my heart. It's your fault I don't have my son. *My* son!" As her voice rose, she thrust the plant at Peter's feet.

Peter jumped out of the way, and the pot shattered on the concrete. The scattered soil and drooped flower served as a recap of how well Natalie was helping. But she could fix this. Had to fix this.

"Get out of my house." Peter's voice was low, and it carried a punch.

Angie moved. But in the wrong direction. She twisted past Natalie and dashed for the staircase. "Joey! Honey!"

As Peter sprinted after Angie, Natalie dialed nine before he reached for his ex-wife and hoisted her up.

She kicked her legs. "Put me down!"

Natalie pressed the one and scanned the stairs. Still no Joey. There had never been a more perfect time for a child to be playing video games.

Angie whimpered and went limp in Peter's arms.

If Natalie finished the call, would it help or hurt Angie's recovery process?

In the driveway, Peter marched her down to the silver car Natalie had thought was his.

Peter planted Angie on her feet. "Don't come back until you complete your therapy. Then we'll talk. Not before. We can't keep our promise to care for Joey if you keep breaking the rules."

Natalie was all for Angie leaving the boys in peace, but did she need to drive? "Angie, when was your last hit? Your last drink?"

Instead of another angry outburst, watery-eyed Angie wilted against her car. "Two days. I promise. I just—I miss Joey. Pete, I'm sorry—"

He shook his head. "If you love Joey, finish the course." Peter gently placed his palm on her shoulder. "If you keep showing up, they might take him from me too. Is that what you want?"

Angie shook her head as a tear rolled off her chin like a last goodbye. "You gotta keep him safe." She hiccupped. "You promised."

At Peter's nod, Angie got into her car. Natalie hung up the phone without completing the call to emergency services.

Peter rubbed his chest again, watching the back of Angie's car as she drove away.

Natalie took in the sweat lining his forehead. His hand rested flat on his chest instead of clenching in rage. Defeat might be written all over his sweat-stained shirt and swimming through his eyes, however, his response in this heated situation showed the hope of growth. He'd thought through the problem instead of reacting. Stayed in the present. He was the right parent to keep Joey in a stable home.

She offered him a smile. "I'm proud of you."

"Yeah, well, I pay you to say those kinds of things."

"You most certainly do not. You pay the Ridgeman Center to help you process life."

He kicked at a rock in his driveway. "I hope you don't plan on raising your rates after seeing how broken I am."

If he only knew who he was speaking to. "Hate to break it to you, but we're all a little broken. Some just hide it better."

Like she had to.

"Maybe." He motioned for the front door and froze.

A cloud of smoke rolled out the door and filled the ceiling of the porch. Peter bolted. Natalie raced on his heels.

Inside, the living room was already hazy. It made her eyes water.

The stove top and cabinets were engulfed in flames. Angie had been wearing an apron. Why hadn't Natalie noticed?

Peter reached into the cabinet under the sink and pulled out a fire extinguisher.

Natalie blinked at the angry flames. She wanted to help. Needed to. Except her arms and legs were heavier than the Kevlar she used to wear.

The heat and the flames...

Instead of being in Peter's kitchen, her mind jumped to her last duty station.

"Clear the area!" the MP yelled.

Natalie jumped the barricade. Something sliced her leg right through her ACUs, but she couldn't stop. She couldn't leave her friend with a bomb strapped to his chair.

"Ms. Atkinson!" Peter held the canister against his chest. His breaths peppered as fast as her own. "Joey..." Sweat oiled his forehead as his gaze danced around the room to each flame. "You—"

Natalie didn't wait for orders. She sprinted for the stairs.

Her shoes disappeared off her feet on the third step. She opened the first upstairs door. A toilet. Sink. No Joey. The next bedroom was empty. She flung open the last door. A twin bed. Dresser and a basketball. Still no Joey.

Had he somehow left the house? A line of lyrics she recognized floated from close by, and she remembered where Joey's favorite place was—his closet.

She hopped over the bed and opened the closet. Shoes. Clothes. A baseball bat. No freckle-faced boy.

"Joey!" She shoved the hangers of jeans and hoodies aside and found a half door at the far left.

Natalie fell to a squat and opened the latch. A lantern and Joey were surrounded by pillows. He held his portable video game, headset on.

"Joey, we've got to go." She gulped as darkness feathered on the outside of her vision. "There's a fire."

"Hold on a sec."

She leaned into the storage compartment that was longer than any normal closet. "No, now. Fire—"

He did a fist pump. "Gold level! Take that, Simon." He stuck the edge of his tongue along his cheek. "Dad usually has a fire when he cooks. He burned nuggets in the microwave once. That's why we order takeout. Is that where we're going? I'd rather have your pretzels."

Natalie didn't wait to explain. She crawled in farther and grabbed his earphones and the gaming device.

"Hey!"

"We've got to get out. There's an actual fire in the kitchen. Your dad needs our help."

Joey blinked at Natalie and then nodded. Natalie had a harder time moving backward in a skirt and the cramped space. She reached the closet door and was hit with another wave of heat.

Joey yanked on his gaming system, and it fell from Natalie's fingers.

She gaped. Joey's curtains were on fire. So was the basketball goal. The posters on his door curled and turned to ash. Flames flickered up from his trashcan.

She threaded her fingers through Joey's. "We need to get out of here." But the door and window were blocked by hot flames. *Please, God, not again.*

Joey gripped her hand. "What do we do?"

CONNECT WITH SUNRISE

Thank you so much for reading Expired Return. We hope you enjoyed the story. If you did, would you be willing to do us a favor and leave a review? It doesn't have to be long- just a few words to help other readers know what they're getting. (But no spoilers! We don't want to wreck the fun!) Thank you again for reading!

We'd love to hear from you- not only about this story, but about any characters or stories you'd like to read in the future. Contact us at www.sunrisepublishing.com/contact.

We also have a monthly update that contains sneak peeks, reviews, upcoming releases, and fun stuff for our reader friends. Sign up at www.sunrisepublishing.com

ABOUT THE AUTHOR

Follow Lisa on social media to find out about new releases and other exciting events!
Visit Lisa's Website to sign up for her mailing list to get FREE books and be the first to learn about new releases and other exciting updates!
https://www.authorlisaphillips.com/sunrise

facebook.com/authorlisaphillips

instagram.com/lisaphillipsbks

bookbub.com/authors/lisa-phillips

goodreads.com/lisaphillipsbks

amazon.com/stores/Lisa-Phillips/author/B00HZSOSOO

CPSIA information can be obtained
at www.ICGtesting.com
Printed in the USA
BVHW040941260323
661154BV00005B/256